Eva sat up.

"It was a dumb kiss," she said. "I don't know why I did it. Just drop it."

Of course she knew why she'd kissed him. She'd dreamed about doing just that for three years, yearning for his body against hers, almost desperate to take one little taste of Jake.

But he didn't have to know that.

"No," he said, wiping his hands on a napkin.

"No? What do you mean, no?"

"See, thing is, that was a crappy kiss. How can I let you walk around thinking that subpar kiss was indicative of what I'm capable of? That would be...a travesty." He reached over and dragged her into his lap, turning her so she tipped à la Scarlett O'Hara into his arms.

"Jake," she said struggling against him even as something way deep down inside her screamed, "hell, yeah."

Dear Reader,

I'm so happy to be back in Magnolia Bend and giving that rascal Jake Beauchamp a bit of a comeuppance with a woman so suited to him. Of course, ol' Jake never thought about how perfectly his best friend fits him. Eva's such a strong woman, fearlessly stepping in to take care of her younger brother and determined to prove to everyone she's tough enough to be the MBFD's newest captain. And Jake has to make amends with a past he's run from for all too long, finding the courage to break out of being the man he created long ago. There is danger, excitement and passion within the pages of this story, and I think you'll like catching up with the rest of the Beauchamp gang.

So come back with me to the sweet Louisiana town where love, life and the good stuff all meet up.

I love hearing from my readers. You can stay in touch with me through liztalleybooks.com or find me on Facebook at liztalleybooks.

Happy reading!

Liz

LIZ TALLEY

—

Sweet Southern Nights

HARLEQUIN® SUPERROMANCE®

Recycling programs
for this product may
not exist in your area.

ISBN-13: 978-0-373-60921-5

Sweet Southern Nights

Copyright © 2015 by Amy R. Talley

Printed in U.S.A.

After being a finalist for RWA's prestigious Golden Heart Award in Regency romance, **Liz Talley** found a home writing sassy contemporary romance. Her first book, *Vegas Two-Step*, starred a spinster librarian and debuted in June 2010. Since that time, Liz has published fourteen more Superromances. Her stories are set in the South where the tea is sweet, the summers are hot and the men are hotter. Liz lives in North Louisiana with her childhood sweetheart, two handsome children, three dogs and a mean kitty. You can visit Liz at liztalleybooks.com to learn more about her upcoming books.

Books by Liz Talley

HARLEQUIN SUPERROMANCE

Home in Magnolia Bend

The Sweetest September
Sweet Talking Man

The Boys of Bayou Bridge

Waters Run Deep
Under the Autumn Sky
The Road to Bayou Bridge
Vegas Two-Step

The Way to Texas
A Little Texas
A Taste of Texas
A Touch of Scarlet
The Spirit of Christmas
His Uptown Girl
His Brown-Eyed Girl
His Forever Girl

Visit the Author Profile page
at Harlequin.com for more titles.

The book is dedicated to the men and women who face deadly fires in order to save lives and property. A special thank-you goes to my childhood neighbor, Captain Guy Mandino, and the Minden Fire Department who so graciously gave me a tour, answered questions and modeled what it is to be an everyday hero.

I would also like to thank Bora Sunseri, who helped me in regards to Child Protective Services.

And finally, the person who gave me a chance to blossom into the writer I am today. I will forever be grateful to Wanda Ottewell for guiding me, teaching me and being my friend.

CHAPTER ONE

EVA MONROE ADJUSTED her helmet as Engine One roared up to the Magnolia Breeze residential complex.

"You ready?" Jake Beauchamp asked her, his blue eyes intense.

"I'm always ready," she said, fitting the Nomex hood over her braided hair and securing the Velcro on her bunker coat. Her heart galloped in her throat. Didn't matter that she'd done this hundreds of times. Preparing to battle a fire always felt the same. Like sex. Didn't know how good or bad it was going to be, but you were going to get hot and sweaty either way.

Captain Sorrento crossed himself as he shifted the engine into Park alongside a curb grown wooly with overgrown crabgrass. A string of tired duplexes squatted next to the one smudging a sky the color of Cozumel Bay with dark smoke. "Check your radios. Everyone safe."

"Everyone safe," she and Jake repeated the department mantra.

Eva fitted her SCBA, strapping the air tank securely before pulling her mask over her mouth. She glanced at Jake, who'd done the same, his eyes crackling with intensity and focus.

Jake was always focused.

"FD2, go to C and give a status. FD5, start initial attack at A." Captain Hank Sorrento already stood at the helm, flipping levers and barking directives at the engines pulling in behind. "Catch me a hydrant, Engine Four."

Eva bailed out after Jake, just the way she liked it. When she first joined the squad, one of the older guys tried to let her out ahead of him saying "Ladies first."

It had pissed Eva off…and Jake must have noticed because he said, "You kidding? She ain't no lady. She's a goddamn fire swallower, ready to put this bitch out."

His words had made Eva laugh…and Dutch Rinaudo frown. Dutch was a home-grown Louisiana boy who still struggled with the fact Eva was his equal on the squad. Jake had grinned at Dutch and then pushed Eva back, bailing out before she could.

Later when she rolled the scene around in her mind, she wondered if his charging in first was because he couldn't wait to face death or because he wanted to protect her.

Probably the first one.

Though she'd been friends with Jake for years, she didn't doubt that embedded deep within his modern brain was the masculine desire to protect the weaker sex.

She snorted at the thought of her being weaker.

Weaker, her ass.

Jake hooked his accountability tag on the large cone designed to help keep track of who had tanks and was active on the scene before jerking back around to face her. "Want me to get the beast so you can break the window?"

Eva gave him the look, and Jake grinned. Ever since she'd nearly broken her hand trying to break a thick plexiglass window with the Halligan tool, Jake had given her grief.

Her heavy gloves prevented her from giving him the finger.

Smoke poured from the upper right corner of the freestanding, single-story apartment building. When Eva reached the backside as the captain instructed her to do, she called in her position and assessment. The captain barked commands, and Eva noted Moon Avery attaching the LDH to feed the pump.

"FD5, get the front door. Start initial through A. Let's push this back. FD2, report to front." Jake would go through and attack, while Eva headed back to the front to assist…or whatever the captain wanted her to do.

Moon set a ladder against the front side of the building and started securing the hose straps. Moon drove Engine Four and had worked for the department for almost twenty-three years. Martin drove the snorkel truck, which idled behind the two pumpers, the aerial bucket dangling like a forgotten toy.

Moon looked at her and jerked his head to an older woman huddled with a young girl, both crying.

Eva's stomach flared aggravation. She shook her head.

Her radio crackled and Captain Sorrento said, "FD2, interview residents."

"Shit." Eva gritted her teeth, pissed that once again she wouldn't be part of the attack and that she'd been relegated to deal with the teary-eyed while Jake and Martin smashed in the front door and knocked down the fire.

But then Eva looked at the older woman standing in a striped housecoat, dampness streaking her cheeks, anguish in her eyes, and softened as she headed toward where the pair held each other. Chief Blume met her there.

Eva pulled off her mask. "Anyone else in the building, ma'am?"

"Just me and Kiki. The people next door are at work. Ollie puts Zeke and Zara on the bus at ten to seven before she leaves for the day," the woman said.

With sad eyes, the woman watched the hoses begin to pump. "They gonna ruin my mama's quilt." The girl she held to her looked about ten or eleven years old, and she watched stoically as the other firefighters scrambled to get into position.

Eva slid off her gloves, hooking them on her bunker coat. "We have tarps, and once we access the apartment we'll do our best to cover your furnishings."

The chief leveled bushy eyebrows at Eva. "I'm not

assuming command, but I'll send Martin next door to clear the apartment."

"I can go," Eva said.

"No, you stay here with Ms.…."

"Glory Mitchell," the woman managed, wiping her eyes with one hand.

"Ms. Mitchell," the chief repeated, glancing back at Eva. "Take care of things here, Eva. Thanks." The chief walked away before Eva could protest. She snapped her mouth shut, tamping down the sour taste of disappointment.

Over her shoulder, she heard Jake burst into Glory's apartment using the battering ram. The older woman sucked in an injured breath before moaning and turned away. Her threadbare cotton robe swished against the tall hitchhiker grass peppering the yard.

"Oh, Jesus, they broke the door," Glory said, her shoulders shaking. "I can't believe this. I just can't believe this."

"It'll be okay, Ms. Mitchell. You're safe, and that's most important. Doors can be fixed."

The older woman nodded, trying to staunch the emotion shaking her.

"So, can you tell me what happened?" Eva asked.

"When I saw those curtains on fire, I grabbed Kiki and we ran out the back door. She had her phone so I called 911."

"Very smart, Ms. Mitchell," Eva said, taking the older woman's elbow and moving her back toward the sprawling mimosa tree on the edge of the yard. Seemed like the only thing that grew on the hard-scrabble lot. Glory shuffled back, but her eyes remained fixed on the apartment building.

Captain Sorrento released the valves, and water started pumping out of the blue hose strapped to the ladder and the red hose Jake had dragged in through the front door.

"Ms. Mitchell, do you have any idea what may have sparked this fire?" Eva asked, placing a gentle hand on Glory's shoulder.

"I don't rightly know. I was cooking breakfast, and Kiki was in the bathroom. You do somethin', Kiki?"

The girl shook her head but her gaze slid away.

"Then I heard Kiki start screaming."

"So you don't know where the fire started?"

Glory shook her head.

"Uh, the bedroom. I think," Kiki said. "I mean, there was this, uh, lighter sittin' on the dresser."

Glory stiffened. "What's a lighter doin' in you and your mama's room?"

"Ms. Quita gave Mama a candle that smells like peaches. She been lighting it at night so our room don't smell like feet," Kiki said, her voice almost a whisper.

Glory grabbed Kiki's shoulder, pulling her toward her. "Girl, did you start this? Did you?"

"No, Ma Glory," Kiki said, whipping her head back and forth. "I didn't do nothin'. Mama lit the candle last night but she blew it out. I think. I don't know. I just saw that lighter. That's all."

"Don't make no sense," Glory said, anger crackling in her voice even as she released the girl. "A lighter don't suddenly light itself."

"I opened the window," the girl said.

"Why you do that?"

Kiki swiped an arm across her nose and stuck out her chin. "I was hot. We ain't had no air-conditioning in a long time and I don't wanna go to school sweaty. That's all I did. I only told this lady the lighter was there 'cause there's fluid in it that catches fire, right?" The girl looked at Eva.

"That's right," Eva said, scanning the area. A few residents of Spring Street had gathered, all in various state of morning dress, some holding coffee cups. Nothing like a fire to bring out lookyloos.

Eva flinched when she saw a Magnolia Bend Police cruiser lurch to a stop behind the snorkel truck. Funny how every time she saw one of the town's finest stepping from a police car, she tensed for a confrontation. Her break up with Officer Chase Grider was recent enough to still make her uncomfortable.

Thankfully, it wasn't Chase but his brother Cole.

Eva excused herself, radioed the point of origin to the captain and went to Engine One to get the prefire plan binder so she could start the on-scene report. Hank was still busy running the fire, which looked to be knocked down, while Moon was at the back of the engine, pulling out the positive pressure fan to clear the smoke and blow some good air inside the still-smoking apartment.

Bobby John Crow, the department's fire investigator, pulled in behind the police cruiser, meeting Cole, who held a coffee from the Short Stop. Bobby John's motto was that every fire was potential arson. Eva had argued with him about it once, to which Bobby John had flipped a beer bottle cap and declared it was his job to prove it wasn't.

Whatever. Wasn't her job.

Jake came trudging out, still on his tank, tugging the red hose. Moon had already cut off the blue one. Acrid smoke hung in the air like a persistent salesman, and the apartment building looked forlorn and lost.

"Morning, fellas," Bobby John said as he approached the engine. Eva grabbed the binder and stood, nearly bumping her head on the top of the engine. Bobby John made a face. "Oh, sorry. Didn't see it was you."

But he had known damn well it was Eva bent over in Engine One.

He was the only guy who took pleasure in needling Eva about being a female firefighter. Yeah, Jake teased, but he respected her. And Dutch was just old-school and found it hard to step outside the social mores he'd been raised with. But Bobby John outright didn't like the fact Eva had been hired—period. She'd overheard him once tell Dutch she was a token, that women didn't belong in the department.

He also hadn't let go of the fact that when he'd hit on her the first night she was in town, she'd shot him down.

Eva turned, shapeless beneath her gear, her dark wavy hair concealed under her helmet. "Easy mistake, since you don't get to see the female form that often."

"Ouch," he said, the smile not quite reaching his cold blue eyes. "What've we got here?"

"I think you'll find your origin in the back bedroom. Ten to one, the curtains blew into a lit candle, but the residents are over there." She pointed toward Glory and Kiki, who were now talking to a few neighbors.

Bobby John's gaze flitted over her face, lingering a bit too long on her lips. For the umpteenth time in her life, Eva wished she was plain.

Yeah. Most girls wanted to be dainty and pretty.

Not Eva. Because being small and attractive wasn't a plus when a gal was fighting for equality in a nontraditional occupation for women. She figured if she'd been born country-strong with a blockier form and a jutting jawline, she'd probably have climbed the ladder of the firefighting profession more quickly. Only a handful of female firefighters had made captain or chief in other Louisiana municipalities.

Eva barely met the required weight for being a firefighter, and her upturned exotic eyes, long dark hair and breasts a bit too big for her body type didn't help when it came to hefting hoses and swinging axes. So she used her smart-assed mouth and brains to gain respect.

It worked, for the most part.

Sometimes the guys even forgot she had boobs.

But most of the time they didn't, cracking jokes about her orchid shampoo or blanching when they found a box of her tampons under the sink at the station.

In some ways it felt like the 1960s in Magnolia Bend.

She probably should have taken the job in Slidell, but the charm of Magnolia Bend and the fact that it was only a short drive to where her mother lived had swayed her.

And then there was Jake.

"Hey, Eva," Jake called, jogging toward her, mask connector dangling, his jacket split open to reveal the softball T-shirt that clung just tight enough to show how trim his stomach was. "Want to work out later?"

"Sure. But I already told Clint I'd meet him there." She worked out with Jake's childhood friend several times a week. Though Clint was in a wheelchair, he was a gym rat.

"That's cool. I can pick him up and head to Ray-Ray's from there."

She and Jake were on C shift and had been since she'd started three years ago. She'd transferred in from Baton Rouge FD with six years under her belt. Jake had the exact same number of years' experience and an easy way about him. Captain Sorrento had put them on the same shift, and they'd pretty much stayed together unless someone was on vacation.

Jake was probably her absolute best friend.

And he had no idea she'd fallen head over heels for him the first time she laid eyes on him.

"Perfect," she said, pulling his tag off the clip on the cone and handing it to him. "I'll be glad to kick your ass again."

"Pfft," Jake scoffed, rolling those pretty eyes before tossing his bunker coat in the back and grabbing the nearest hose. "You kickbox like a girl."

"Damn right."

"Which means she fights dirty," Moon snickered, lifting the ladder back into place.

Jake glanced up, cracking a smile, making Eva's heart skip a beat. Why did the man have to be so gorgeous? Why did his T-shirt have to cling so spectacularly to his torso? Why did—

The radio crackled, distracting her, as Martin relayed that the apartment was clear. Time to clear the scene.

Eva tugged off her helmet and bunker coat and found a pen. Normally, she'd help stow the equipment, but since Hank had pulled her around front and several volunteer firemen had arrived to assist, she filled in the paperwork normally done by the driver. Might as well save Hank some time and earn her some brownie points. With Wendell contemplating retirement in order to run a yard service full-time, Eva wanted to make captain.

Only Jake stood in her way.

And that was a huge problem.

Not because she loved Jake, but because he deserved the promotion as much as she did.

And she might get it over him just because she didn't have a penis—which didn't sit well with her. Not the *not* having a penis part—she really didn't want one—but that she'd get the job not based on merit but rather on her gender. The word *token* flitted through her mind again.

"Hey, miss."

Eva ripped her gaze from the paperwork fluttering on the clipboard to find Kiki standing beside her. "Hey, Kiki. You need me?"

"I'm just worried about Zeke."

Zeke? Who was that? A cat? Eva had forgotten to ask about pets. "Who's Zeke?"

"He lives in 30A. He's only eight."

Eva grabbed her mic. "Did we clear 30A?"

"No occupants detected. All secure," Hank responded.

Eva looked at Kiki. "We didn't find anyone."

"Well, he ain't gonna answer. He ain't supposed to be home. He said he was gonna stay home because Jarvis Bell said he was gonna whip his ass for telling Mrs. Haydell he cheated on his spelling test. His Big Mama will whoop him good if she knows he's home." Kiki looked at the closed door of the apartment housed next door to hers.

"Christ," Eva breathed, grabbing her mask and attaching her accountability tag to the PVC pipe atop the cone. "Stay here, Kiki."

Eva ran toward the closed apartment, calling into her mic. "FD2, reassessing apartment A. Resident indicates possible child on the premises."

"Shit," Hank shouted.

Eva pulled on her gloves and connected the mask to the tank, sucking in the cool oxygen. She hopped onto the porch stoop and tried the front door—it was locked. Behind her she saw Jake and Martin coming toward her with the battering ram in hand.

Eva eyed the flimsy doorknob.

Then she kicked in the door. The wood of the jamb splintered and the door flew back, slamming against the interior wall. The apartment revealed in the morning light showed a place that was definitely lived-in, with breakfast dishes piled in the dated kitchen sink and a tired tweed green couch covered in laundry.

No active smoke.

Eva pulled off her mask, sucking in the acrid smell. "Zeke?"

No answer.

"Jesus, Eva. We had the beast," Jake said behind her. "But nice kick."

She didn't say anything. Just moved toward the dark yawn of the hallway.

"Zeke?" she shouted again.

The heat in the apartment wasn't a result of the fire they'd extinguished next door. The combination of a humid August and the heavy bunker gear she wore made Eva feel as if she'd entered the mouth of hell. She flung open the first door she came to—an empty room with a floral bedspread and lace curtains.

She motioned Jake inside as she stepped toward the other bedroom.

The door stood open, a huge fathead of some basketball player dominating one wall. A small unmade twin bed sat in one corner; pajamas and tennis shoes littered the carpet.

"Zeke?" she called.

From the open closet a head emerged. Two big brown eyes, popped wide, met her gaze.

"Zeke?" she asked, softening her voice.

"Yeah?"

Eva released a pent-up breath of relief. "What are you still doing inside? Don't you know there was a fire next door?"

He crawled out, a small Matchbox car rolling as he emerged from the depths. "I don't wanna get in trouble."

Zeke looked about eight years old with closely shorn hair, gorgeous chocolate skin and—Lord help her—the cutest dimples she may have ever seen. "Trouble smouble. No one stays in a burning house."

"Y'all put it out," he said, shuffling toward her.

His feet were bare, and he wore only a pair of faded athletic shorts that clung to his small hips.

Jake appeared at her shoulder. "Jesus. He was in here the whole time?"

"Yeah." Eva toed the tennis shoes toward Zeke, nodding her head for him to slip them on. "Chief is gonna freak. Who was supposed to clear?"

Martin appeared in the room, looking like a thundercloud. "I did. Front door was unlocked and I came in each room. Even opened the closets. Never saw him. Cleared it and locked the front door, you know, outta courtesy." Martin glowered at the boy, who studied the shoelaces he'd just tied sloppily. "Young man, why didn't you answer me when I called out?"

The little boy didn't look up. "'Cause you're a stranger, and I ain't supposed to talk to strangers."

Eva slid her gaze over to meet Jake's laughing eyes. She tried not to smile, but her lips twitched in spite of herself.

Martin grumped. "So *she's* not a stranger?"

"She knew my name," Zeke said, shrugging thin shoulders. He looked up and tilted his head. "'Sides, I seen her on the field trip. She let us climb on the fire truck."

"Pfft," Martin said, turning around and trudging toward the front of the house, muttering under his breath things no eight-year-old needed to hear.

"Come on, Zeke. We need to call your grandmother," Eva said.

"No. She's gonna whoop me good. I ain't supposed to be here. I faked getting on the bus."

"You'll have to deal with those repercussions. Even without a fire next door, you put yourself in danger. Small boys cannot stay home by themselves." Eva placed a hand on his shoulder and steered him toward the front door.

"I'm gonna get a whoopin' either way, I guess," the boy said, his shoulders slumping.

"Maybe not," Eva said, glancing over her shoulder at Jake, who watched the boy with a grin. She was about to go on about how Zeke could have been injured or even killed, but then when she looked back at the forlorn boy, who wagged his head, looking resigned to dealing with his grandmother, she zipped her lips.

"Oh, I'm gonna get it, all right. Big Mama don't forget. But I'm glad you saved me anyway."

Eva pressed her lips tightly to keep from laughing. Damn, the kid was cute.

Eva turned the child over to Chief Blume, who stood with Glory and Kiki. Glory renewed her waterworks after clutching Zeke tightly and groaning about how stupid the boy had been.

Eva slid the on-scene report into the binder filled with preplans for all the municipal buildings and businesses in the small town and then decided to help the rest of her team put away the gear. She'd just grabbed her accountability tag when Cole sauntered up, grinning like a kid at a fireworks stand.

"Well, looka' here. If it isn't the hottest fireman I've ever laid eyes on."

"You don't get around much. Not surprised, since you're such a mama's boy," Eva returned, lifting her eyebrows, silently inquiring whether her favorite cop wanted to keep going toe-to-toe with her.

Cole laughed. "Call me pretty boy again and I'll file a complaint." He pretended to fluff nonexistent hair. Cole had gone prematurely bald at twenty-five and now shaved his head smooth. But he *was* pretty nonetheless. And absolutely gay. Not that anyone besides her and his brother knew. Cole swore he'd bolted the closet shut the minute he was sworn in as a police officer in Magnolia Bend.

"I said *mama's boy*."

"Oh, well. That's true," he cracked, lifting his foam cup in a mocking toast.

"How they hangin'?" Jake said to Cole as he extended his fist. He handed Eva one of the bottles of water he carried in his other hand.

"What's up, Jake?" Cole asked, popping his knuckles against Jake's.

"Just puttin' out fires," Jake said, jerking his head toward the apartment before sending a devilish grin Eva's way. "Someone's gotta do it."

This time her glove wasn't in the way of the finger she shot Jake.

Cole laughed. "She's gonna kick your ass for that."

"Yeah, she thinks she is, but ol' Jake Beauchamp's

got a little something left in the tank," Jake cracked, wiggling his eyebrows at Eva.

"I'm surrounded by the deluded," Eva said, rolling her eyes.

"Gotta skedaddle. I'm meeting Chase out at Jennings. Someone's been stealing copper out of their units," Cole said, tossing the cup toward the trash cans standing sentry at the end of the driveway.

"Oh? Usually you're investigating the doughnuts over at PattyAnns," Eva called.

Cole mimicked a gun firing with a finger and thumb and staggered back toward his cruiser. "You got me," he said with a flirty wink before sliding back into the car.

She and Jake stood for a minute, sucking down water and watching as Cole pulled away. He issued a wave and then hit the siren once as he rolled away.

"I think he's in love with you," Jake said, turning back toward the duplex.

"I'm pretty sure he isn't," she said.

"Because of Chase?" He made a face just uttering her ex-boyfriend's name. Jake wasn't a fan of Chase's. They'd gone to school together, competing against each other for starting linebacker...*and* for who got to date the prettiest cheerleader. When Eva had broken things off with Chase, Jake had gotten a little easier to be around. She'd like to think it was because deep down underneath his playboy image, he carried a small torch for her. But she knew that wasn't the reason. Jake had just gotten tired of Chase always hedging in on their gym time together, trying to outlift him.

"Yeah. Something like that," she said, emptying the rest of the bottle.

"Hey, Wendell put in his papers. His wife's gonna throw him a retirement party next month. Guess it's official." Jake took her empty bottle and walked it over to the trash can.

"What is?" she said.

Jake smiled against the sun peeking over the top of the trees, his auburn hair glowing like embers. His bright blue eyes, strong jaw and white teeth prominent against his tanned skin. He looked like pure sex. Like the kind of guy who knew right where to place his lips, right where to stroke, right where to tease. He was like a walking fantasy—teenaged heartthrob, rock 'n' roll drummer and dangerous outlaw rolled into one. "That I get to arm wrestle you for the captain's spot."

Eva laughed and chucked him on the chin. "Give it your best shot, Maverick."

CHAPTER TWO

THE SCENE AT Ray-Ray's was the same. It was always the same.

Jake peeled the label from his NOLA beer and watched as his older brother, Matt, threw darts with one of the teachers from the school where Matt was principal. Jake couldn't remember the older guy's name. Only that he was from Oregon and drank Johnnie Walker Black Label.

Across from Jake sat the guy he'd talked into peeing on an electric fence when they were eleven years old, the guy he'd caught his first bass with, the guy who'd stolen his old man's cigarettes and shared them with Jake. Clint Cochran had been his best bud only since forever, and every week Jake picked him up and sat with him at a table while he nursed a gin and tonic.

"What's wrong?" Clint said after several minutes of them listening to Trace Adkins belt out a tune. His friend took a sip of his drink, and Jake noticed how big Clint's biceps had gotten. All his gym work with Eva had paid off...as had the fact that Clint had to heft himself into bed, to the toilet and into the car. It took tremendous strength to move the bulk of his lower half around.

"Nothing's wrong."

"It's this town, isn't it?" Clint asked, his dark eyes searching his for some weakness, hoping Jake would finally crack. It was a game they played sometimes, a guilt-riddled, smoldering resentment of a game.

"Nah. Why would it be the town?"

"'Cause you've been here all your life and you're sick of it. Hell, you've dated every woman within twenty miles and could drive the streets blindfolded. You're done."

Clint wanted Jake to admit he hated Magnolia Bend. He wanted Jake to say he was only here because he felt guilty. That if Clint hadn't been paralyzed ten years ago that Jake would be in LA or Chicago or even Baton Rouge. That he'd be anywhere but at a run-down bar, eating stale pretzels and babysitting a cripple.

But Jake would never say that...even if sometimes it felt true.

"I'm not sick of it. I could be the goddamn mayor if I wanted. Right here is a walking poster for tourism." Jake thumped his chest, trying to summon lightness.

"Hell, yeah, it is. I'd take a tour," Vicky Barrett drawled, twirling a piece of hair over his ear before sinking down on the empty chair to Jake's right. "What you boys got on tap tonight?"

"Well, I'm thinking about doing a couple of shots, dancing the two-step with a sexy lady and then getting laid," Clint said with a wry laugh before looking down at his withered legs. "No, wait. I forgot."

Vicky laughed and the sound grated on Jake's nerves. "You're such a hoot, Clint. And hell, you don't need legs for two of those things."

Jake didn't say anything because Clint's being in a wheelchair—no matter whether he could joke about it or not—would never be funny to him.

Never.

Clint knew that, but his friend danced on the edge tonight. He wanted a fight with Jake, but Jake wasn't picking up what Clint was laying down. Been there, done that, hated himself for it.

The door to the bar opened, and Eva walked in accompanied by her friend Jenny, who worked for the sheriff's department. He raised a hand, noting that Jenny looked pretty damn good in her tight jeans and halter top. He'd actually dated her back in the day. Maybe it was time to get reacquainted with the lithe Jenny, who if he remembered correctly made a good omelet and insisted on brushing her teeth before kissing him good morning.

Eva had her hair up, with hoop earrings that brushed her long neck. She wore a T-shirt that stretched her broad shoulders, framing a nice rack. Her shorts were a bit too short. He didn't like her showing off her long legs any more than he'd like his sister, Abigail, doing so. No need to advertise the goods. He waved an arm and Eva inclined her head, giving Jenny a little push in the right direction.

Vicky noticed and frowned.

"What's up, ladies?" Jake said, scooting his chair back and grabbing an empty one from the table behind him. He smiled at Jenny and patted the chair. "Have a seat."

Eva rolled her eyes, snagged another chair from behind her and sank down next to Clint. "Hey, Clint. How're things?"

Clint shrugged but his eyes lit up at the sight of Eva. "Same ol' same old. Nothing's changed since I saw you three hours ago. Or from yesterday when you stopped by with those brownies for Dad. They were good, by the way."

"You know I didn't bake them, right?"

"Duh," he said, flashing a smile that made Jake's heart ache. He'd seen that smile a million times... just not from the man currently in the state-of-the-art wheelchair. That smile was like a whisper of the past sliding past him.

"What'll you have?" Jake asked Jenny as her leg brushed his, tearing his mind away from the maudlin. She smelled good—like wildflowers or some other crap women liked to slather themselves with. She wore a push-up bra that lifted her small breasts, creating a delicious valley for his perusal. He jerked his gaze away and lifted his eyes, meeting Eva's. She mouthed "pervert" and he grinned. Hell, if Jenny wanted to show them off, he was obligated to look.

"I'll take a glass of white wine," Jenny said, grabbing a napkin to spit her gum in.

A tired waitress trudged toward them. "What'll it be?"

Jake took out two twenties. "White wine for Jenny, a Miller Lite each for Eva and Vicky and another round for me and Clint."

"You don't have to pay for my drink, Jake. I got my own, Bonnie," Eva said.

"Ah, let him," Bonnie growled before trudging back to the bar.

The place was only half-filled because it was Thursday night and just barely eight thirty. Things would pick up closer to ten, but by that time Jake usually had Clint in the car heading back to Duck Blind Bayou and the custom-built, handicap-friendly lake house where his friend lived with his father. These nights with Clint were obligation nights. Not nights to pick up women or forget the clock. He could only lay the groundwork for something more with Jenny later.

If he wanted to go in that direction.

His personal life had felt desolate lately, as if he'd reached a plateau and didn't know what direction to walk in. Up until early summer he'd dated a lethally sexy librarian. Kate had a smoking body beneath her pencil skirts, and she even wore those nerdy black-rimmed glasses and pinned her hair up. But the woman was flippin' wild in the sack. She'd worn him slap out, but eventually it had been sex, sex and more sex, and contrary to what most men said, eventually you have to talk to each other.

Kate tanked when it came to conversation. She couldn't name a single National League team, thought NASCAR was stupid and ate weird food like goji berries and flaxseed. Eventually they stopped calling each other for hookups.

But dating Jenny could get complicated. She and Eva had become good friends. He didn't need the obstacle of having to watch everything he said to Eva or having her run to tell Jenny if he'd flirted with a woman at the grocery store. So maybe he'd forgo laying that groundwork.

"You want to dance?" Jenny asked, leaning toward him, her blue eyes soliciting an invitation.

"Sure," he said, sliding his chair back. "Let's work up a thirst."

Clint's gaze moved over the two of them as they escaped to the dance floor. Jake usually didn't dance when he was with Clint because it felt too shitty to do something his friend could not, but for some reason, he had to get away for a moment. To think.

And to hold an armful of something sweet and warm.

Jenny looped her arms around his neck. "You look good tonight, Jake. I like your shirt."

"This old thing?" He plucked at the fabric with his thumb and forefinger. It was a gingham plaid shirt from some preppy catalog his mother favored. The blue matched his eyes and set off the tan he'd picked up fishing with his brother all summer. His jeans were tight and his boots well-worn. He skipped wearing a cowboy hat, unlike most of the guys in the bar, because he didn't actually ride bulls or drive tractors. "Thank you, darlin'," he said.

And then he proceeded to pull Jenny tight against him and whirl her around the dance floor to a Luke Bryan song that made him long for another day on the lake and a cold beer.

For a few minutes he lost himself in the song, enjoying Jenny snug against him. Felt good to forget about the job, the fact he needed to repaint his garage apartment and the birthday party he had to attend for his cousin Hilda on Sunday. *Let go and feel.*

But the song ended too soon, and he found himself leading Jenny back toward the table. Clint and Vicky sat there, silently nursing their drinks. Eva was gone.

Jake picked up his beer and took a swig. "Where's Eva?"

"Outside. Someone called and she said she had to go out for a sec," Clint said.

Jake crooked an eyebrow. "Who was it?"

"How would we know? But she looked kind of surprised," Vicky said.

He sank back into his chair, glancing toward the swinging glass door that Raylan had covered with inky tint. The name Ray-Ray's was scrawled across the front, and the parking lot light looked like the glowing tip of a cigarette through the darkened glass. "Huh."

Wasn't his business, but still something rose on

the back of his neck. Eva going off to meet someone wasn't his concern. She was a big girl who could handle any man, a roaring fire and a passel of second graders wanting to scale the fire truck. Nevertheless, he was her friend. Hell, he was almost her family.

"I'm gonna check on her," he said, standing.

"I'm sure she's fine," Vicky said with a wave of her long-tipped fingernails. "Eva could handle anyone."

"Let me just take her the beer," he said, grabbing the frosty longneck and a napkin.

As he got up and left he heard Jenny say, "I love a man who looks out for a gal, but Eva hates nosy people."

Jake passed his brother's group, giving Matt a brusque "hey, dude," as he continued toward the door. He pushed out into the dying day, twilight settling around him as he crunched through the gravel, looking for Eva. Cigarette butts and bottle caps littered the long concrete pad in front of the cinder-block bar. No one was in the front lot so he headed to the right, skirting the empty ice machine and weathered benches set out for the smokers. He heard raised voices as he rounded the corner.

Eva stood, arms on her hips, facing off against a pretty massive dude whose back was to Jake.

"Eva?" he called.

She leaned around the dude, her ponytail swinging out. "Oh, hey, Jake. I'll be in in a minute."

The guy turned and took in Jake. He had massive

biceps, both tatted, and a tight T-shirt that stretched across the continent of his chest. He had a shaved head and wore motorcycle boots. *Sons of Anarchy* had nothing on this dude.

"You sure, Eva?"

The dude sneered. "You hard of hearing or something?"

"No. Got a clean bill of health from the doctor last month. Hearing's perfect."

"Then get your ass outta here," the giant growled.

"Did someone piss in your cereal this morning or something?" Jake responded, moving toward Eva and King Kong. He shifted the beer bottles so he held them in one hand.

"It's okay, Jake. Chris is about to leave. No big deal." Eva gave him a determined smile and a look that said "please don't do this."

Jake didn't know what to do. He could tell Eva was upset, but he didn't want to make things worse for her. He also didn't want to back down like a pussy. Jake wasn't chopped liver, but the guy had a good four inches and forty pounds on him—he would likely grind Jake into hamburger meat. But at least his attention on Jake would give Eva a chance to get help.

"I'll just stay here," Jake said, leaning up against the steel siding replete with rust marks.

The giant's thunderous expression told Jake his declaration wasn't appreciated, but the man stayed where he was.

"Chris." Eva placed a hand on the man's arm. "Let's just talk about this later, okay? Nothing has to be decided today."

Chris grunted. "Things have to be settled by Monday. That's the court date. And I leave next Wednesday." With that remark, he picked up the motorcycle helmet sitting on the hood of Eva's Jeep and tucked it under his arm before turning toward Jake. "This guy need his ass whipped before I go?"

Eva managed a smile. "Nah, that's just Jake."

"If he bothers you, let me know. I could use some fertilizer for my roses."

Jake had no idea what was going on, but he was tired of the subterfuge. Looking at Eva, he said, "Who *is* this asshole?"

Chris growled and took a menacing step toward Jake.

Eva jumped in front of Chris, punching the beast on his arm. "This is Chris, my older half brother."

"*This* is Chris?"

Eva nodded. Chris bared his teeth. Jake started laughing.

"This is the guy who developed the prize-winning hybrid teacup roses? The horticulture guy?" Jake asked, relaxing a little.

Chris crossed his arms. "You know, I get tired of this shit. What did you expect? Some skinny dude slumped over in a lab coat, looking at you through Coke-bottle glasses. What? A botanist can't have tats?"

"No, you just surprised me. The way Eva talks about you, I just expected—"

"A pansy?" Chris said, a slight twinkle in his eye even though he still looked annoyed.

Jake pulled himself from the wall and walked toward Chris. He handed Eva her beer and extended his hand. "I'm Jake Beauchamp. I stand shoulder to shoulder with Eva every day."

"Not really," Eva said, her tone slightly peevish, but Jake knew what she meant. It was rare the captain sent Eva into an assault first. It was a hard thing, being a female firefighter. Most of the men in their unit had been brought up with the notion of carrying packages or opening doors for the fairer sex. Times were a-changing, but the very nature of the men in Magnolia Bend had a lot of catching up to do. Most still said *yes, ma'am*, and some thought a woman's place was either in the home or in traditional female-dominated jobs like being a teacher or nurse.

"But we do work together."

Chris took his hand and delivered a bone-crushing handshake. "I'd say it was good to meet you, but you've already pissed me off."

"Oh, come on." Eva punched him in the biceps again. "Be a sport. No one expects a guy like you to dote on dahlias."

Chris managed a grin that nearly cracked his face. Like the Tin Man, he probably needed some oil. "Dahlias are my weakness. Okay, what the hell. Bygones and all that."

Jake pulled his hand back and tried not to wince at the throbbing pain that the man's handshake had induced. "I'm glad to finally meet you."

Chris jerked his head toward the bike. "Gotta run. Guys are waiting."

"I'll talk to you later, okay?" Eva said, lifting on her tiptoes. Chris bent down so she could buss his granite jaw with a kiss.

Then with a slap on her ass, Chris straddled his hog and fired it up. "Later."

Both Jake and Eva turned and watched him roll out.

"What was that all about?" Jake asked, turning toward his friend.

"Just stuff," Eva said with a shrug of her shoulders, shoving her hands into the back pockets of her shorts. She used her fake happy voice. Something was wrong, but she wasn't the type to lay her cards on the table. He'd find out…eventually.

"Worried me for a moment. Looked intense."

Eva made a face. "Jeez, Jake, you think you have to save the world, don't you? I'm not some weak female who needs the tough Jake Beauchamp rescuing her."

"I know. And I don't treat you that way. You know that. But you'd do the same for me."

She tilted her head and it made her look cute. Like a teenager. He liked when she did that. "I don't interfere with you and what you do in a parking lot anymore. Remember?"

Jake laughed. "It was a bucket list thing."

"Twins?"

He wasn't going to admit they'd just been goofing off and not really having a three-way. He'd become legendary after Eva and Monk Lewis had caught him with the Bertrand twins messing around in the back of his pickup truck. Okay, so the twins had stripped down to their underwear and they'd all been a little drunk. The whole thing had ended there, and he'd never even scored with either one of them that night...but Eva didn't know that. "It's every guy's fantasy."

"You're sick, you know that?"

"But you love me anyway," he said, slinging an arm around her neck and tugging her into a noogie.

"Stop, Jake, you're messing up my hair," she shrieked, elbowing him in the ribs, trying to keep hold of her beer.

He let her go, grinning at her. Her slick-backed hair stuck up in big mounds. "Looks better."

She tugged the rubber band from her hair, and thick brown locks tumbled around her shoulders. "Now look what you did. I don't have a brush with me."

Her hair had honey highlights that caught in the parking lot lights. She looked pretty with her hair down, softer and more like a woman. "I like it like that. You should wear it down more often."

Eva's lips turned down. "Gets in the way."

"But it makes you look pretty. Keep it down.

You'll have a better chance of getting lucky tonight." Even as he said the words, he wanted to reach out and snatch them back. Eva was his friend, but even so, he didn't like the idea of her with another guy. Which was stupid.

She snorted. "With who? Do you ever look past the bimbos in Ray-Ray's? It ain't exactly brimming with available guys…who have all their teeth."

"Then why are you here?"

Eva started toward the entrance. "Because I'm tired of watching reruns. Nothing on TV and Jenny wanted to get out. She's on the rebound. The banker broke up with her."

Jake rubbed his hands together. "Perfect."

Eva turned around and pressed a hand into his chest. "Don't."

"Why?"

"Because you *can* be a nice guy, right? Dance with her. Buy her drinks. But don't prey on her, Jake."

Something in her tone punched him in the solar plexus. "That's what you think of me? Jesus, Eva, I don't screw everything in a skirt."

"No, you screw everything in a skirt, pants and shorts. I've been around you for a few years. I know you." That tone again. Eva thought he was nothing more than a gigolo, spreading himself around town. But he wasn't. Well, not really. He'd never sleep with someone who couldn't go toe-to-toe with him.

For the first time in forever, he felt embarrassed

about the way he lived his life. At the hands of Eva. She never made him feel lacking. Eva was always on his side.

Her censure surprised him.

"Maybe you don't really know me," he said, his words soft as the night descending around them. Eva's face glowed in the light cast from above them. She looked so different with her hair down that he wanted to touch her.

Which freaked him the hell out.

This was Eva, his best bud. The person who complained about him using all the toothpaste and eating all the yogurt. The woman who left a nest of hair in the drain and beat him at Scrabble every single time they played at the station. This was the one woman he'd never let himself have the slightest attraction for.

So, yeah, freaked out.

Eva bit her bottom lip, and Jake found himself really looking at her lips for the first time. They were perfectly proportioned—not too big, but not thin. Pretty lips covered in a creamy lipstick the color of plums.

Weird.

"I'm not trying to be mean, Jake. You know I love ya, dude, but just give Jenny some space. She'd go home with you tonight, but she doesn't need that right now. You know?"

"I wasn't planning on taking her home. I was joking when I rubbed my hands together. You know what a joke is, right?" He sounded petulant. Like a kid who'd asked for dessert and got a big fat no.

Eva smiled then. A strained smile but a smile. "Sure, Jake. I'm acquainted with jokes. Just last week there was that snake in my bed. Ha-ha."

"That snake was cute. Admit it," he said.

"Only you would think a snake was cute." She opened the door and slid inside Ray-Ray's, leaving him outside contemplating the odd dynamics that had just occurred between them. Or maybe it wasn't between *them*. Maybe it was him.

Something he couldn't explain had ricocheted out of nowhere and popped him right in the face.

And he didn't like it.

He wanted a take-back because he didn't want to see Eva as anything other than what he'd always seen her as—his bud. Sure, he knew she was attractive. He hadn't missed that. Pretty obvious. But from day one, he had shifted her into a sort of "family" slot.

But something had happened just a minute ago.

No. It was just a trick of the light or something—it had to be. Nothing had changed. Eva was Eva. And he was the same as he'd always been.

Mostly.

So he felt itchy in his skin and maybe dissatisfied with his life. That wasn't new. He went through periods of melancholy…of dwelling on *what if*.

What if he'd gone to law school?

What if he hadn't tried to avoid that deer?

What if Clint hadn't ended up in a wheelchair?

What if Angela hadn't died?

What if he didn't live in this godforsaken town anymore?

Yeah, his life was a pile of what-ifs.

CHAPTER THREE

Eva HANDED THE stack of trendy jeans to Fancy Beauchamp. "Here, Mrs. Beauchamp. These go on that table up front."

Frances "Fancy" Beauchamp was the chairman of the Ladies Auxiliary Annual Rummage Sale to benefit the local women's shelter. She had hair the color of rhubarb, a smile as wide as her son Jake's and plenty of pluck to temper her image as the perfect pastor's wife. "Thank you, darlin'," she said, taking the jeans. "And if you keep calling me Mrs. Beauchamp, I'm going to go lookin' for my mother-in-law. We don't need that battle-ax around today."

Eva reached deeper into the last black garbage bag councilwoman Hilda Brunet had dropped off at the church and pulled out a pair of heels she was certain cost the same as her new flat-screen TV. "Don't let Jake hear you call his MeeMaw a battle-ax."

"Ooooh," Fancy said, forgetting about MeeMaw Mollie and snatching the shoes from Eva's hand. She snuck a peek inside the shoe. "Manolo. I might buy these myself."

"They look like they'd hurt your feet."

Fancy laughed. "Well, honey, sometimes we must

suffer to look a little taller and thinner. I'm willing to make that sacrifice."

"You're a preacher's wife. Aren't you supposed to be above lust?"

"I'm pretty sure Paul didn't know the relationship between women and shoes when he talked about the sins of the flesh," Fancy joked. Then she twisted her lips. "I'm teasing, you know. I don't have to have Manolo shoes. I'm content with what I have. But they *would* look great with my black skirt and the sequined sweater I bought *on sale* at Chico's."

"Well, if they match, you should go for it. It is, after all, for charity."

"Right!" Fancy snapped her fingers before giggling. "I knew you'd validate me, Eva."

Eva smiled at Jake's mom. Like her son, she kept things light and fun. Always joking, cajoling, fattening people up with her "special" recipes, which was code for "a lot of butter." Fancy was the mother Eva never had.

"That's me. Validator."

Fancy motioned toward her daughter, Abigail. "Hey, Abi. Eva wants to be called Eva the Validator."

Abigail pushed back dark hair with the cool swoosh of silver. Eva always thought Abigail looked dramatic…and a little like Cruella de Vil. "Why? Is she in charge of validating parking or something? I thought it was free."

Fancy giggled at her joke. "No, she just validated my purchase of your cousin's shoes. Look."

She held them aloft and Abigail rolled her eyes. "Mom, you'll break an ankle in those. I'm not ready to change your diaper yet."

Fancy frowned. "As if I'd let you change my diaper. Jakey will take care of me, won't you, honey?"

Jake had been walking by, carrying a large box filled with kitchen items. "Whatever you need, Mama."

"See?" Fancy said to Abigail, propping a hand on her hip.

"She wants you to change her diaper," Abigail called after him.

"I'm out," Jake said.

"Wait a minute, I changed your diaper until you were nearly three. You owe me, buster."

Jake set the box down and grinned, "I'll get married and put that in the prenup. My wife will have to give me foot massages and learn how to make good cornbread, throw a baitcast reel and change my mother's diaper."

Abigail snorted. "Good luck with that, Neanderthal."

Eva chuckled, happy to be with Jake's family. They were so normal, and they loved each other so much that the goodness spilled over and splashed onto those around them. Eva had never had that sort of family life, and ever since she'd moved to Magnolia Bend it was something she'd lusted after. Should have made her pathetic—her accepting any opportunity to be part of their family—but she couldn't help herself. The Beauchamps were just plain fun.

"Can you believe this, Eva? My own children pawning me off on some poor unseen, unknown woman. God help the girl who marries Jake. He's always been difficult. You know, when he was a baby, he refused to crawl because he didn't like the way the carpet felt on his knees. And he spit out his peas...and squash. Still won't touch green peas. And—"

"Mom, stop giving her ammunition," Jake said, pulling a pot and toaster out of the box and setting them on the table. Abigail immediately sped over and started helping him, pointing to this table and that, brooking no argument. Abigail was the general of the family.

"She doesn't need ammunition. She knows you," Fancy said, setting the shoes aside.

Eva didn't validate that particular observation because lately she wondered how well she really knew Jake. After Thursday night's soft-spoken rebuke of her assessment of him, she had a feeling something had changed.

Or maybe deep down under the facade she presented to him—his bud, his comrade, the person who helped him pick out what to wear on dates—she wanted something to change.

But regardless, on a personal level for her, everything had changed. Mostly because she was about to become a mother.

To her six-year-old stepbrother.

That was why her half brother, Chris, had stopped by at Ray-Ray's. Their stepmonster, the surviving widow of Eva's father, had been arrested Wednesday night for possession, solicitation and child endangerment. The dumb-ass had left Charlie home alone overnight while she went out, got high and then got busted for prostitution. After Claren sobered up enough to remember she had a kid, the police went to her apartment and found Charlie with a neighbor, crying and wearing dirty clothes. CPS stepped in, placing him in a temporary foster home, after contacting Claren's elderly parents in Ohio. Finally, a foster care worker called Chris, but because he was scheduled to spend a month in France doing research on some cross-pollination genetics thing with roses, he couldn't step up to take Charlie. So that left…

Yeah.

She had to be in court at nine o'clock Monday morning when Claren appeared before the judge. But before that, the CPS agent would be coming to her house for an inspection and background check on Sunday so she could take temporary custody of Charlie.

Eva had no experience in taking care of a child, but what option did she have? She couldn't leave her own flesh and blood with strangers, especially since poor Charlie had been saddled with a crazy-assed mother. Plenty of challenges lay ahead, including a schedule that wasn't ideal for playing at being a substitute mother.

She felt totally lost.

She wanted to talk about it with someone other than Chris. Normally, she'd confide in Jake, but he didn't know anything about being a parent, either. He bought his nephews and nieces totally inappropriate gifts like fireworks and giant chocolate candy bars. Fancy would be perfect to talk to, but Eva felt embarrassed about how craptastically screwed up her family was—she had two half brothers from two different mothers, not to mention her own mother had been married three times, too.

Monroes weren't the luckiest when it came to love.

"I need to find my sweet husband and ask him a few questions about the schedule for tomorrow," Fancy said, wadding up the black garbage bag and tossing it toward the trash barrel sitting on the perimeter of Burnside Hall. "Can you finish with this table?"

"Sure," Eva said.

"Jake, come help Eva. I have to find Dan," Fancy ordered, already heading toward the large double doors that led to the offices of the First Presbyterian Church of Magnolia Bend. Jake had been slumped against the wall, tapping on the phone. He looked up, his forehead crinkling.

"She said to go help Eva," Abigail told him,

returning her attention to tagging the kitchen items she'd commandeered from Jake.

Jake pocketed his phone and started toward Eva. He wore an old workout shirt that had a tear in one sleeve and a pair of athletic shorts that showed off his toned thighs, still tanned from summer days on the lake. He looked absolutely yummy…as usual.

"I don't need help, so if you want you can go out and see if Matt needs some?" Eva said, rearranging the shoes on the rack below the table.

"Nah, it's hot out there." Jake grinned, picking up a pair of sensible flats. "Hey, Abi, I found you some new shoes. Think Mrs. Crofton donated these because they were too nerdy. Right up your alley."

Abigail looked up and rolled her eyes. "I'm oblivious to your taunts. Plus Leif likes me barefoot."

"I bet," Jake drawled, making Abigail shoot daggers at him with her pretty green eyes. He turned back to Eva. "What do you want me to do?"

"Start putting these out," Eva said, toeing a box of shoes his way.

Jake obeyed for a few seconds before reaching up to tug her ponytail. "So you're back to wearing your hair up."

"I told you, gets in the way otherwise," she said, smacking his hand back.

"I like it down," he said.

"You don't get a say-so."

He frowned. "I know what looks good."

Eva laughed. "I'm aware of that particular talent,

but I'm more interested in keeping it out of my eyes. And why do you care? You've never cared before."

"I don't," he said, picking up some espadrilles and eyeing the ribbon ties. "These look uncomfortable."

"Women don't mind uncomfortable as long as it makes their legs look long and lifts their butt. You, of all men, ought to understand this."

"They'd look incredible on you. You already have great legs," he said matter-of-factly.

"What's wrong with you?" Eva said, her stomach feeling hoppy at his words. He sounded almost flirty in the way Marshall Mitchell had flirted with her in the seventh grade. *Your binder is girly. Can I touch your hair? Let's just try kissing and see what it feels like.*

"Nothing. Why? What's wrong with you?"

Everything.

"Nothing. You're just acting weird. Like flirting with me. You outta practice or something?" She snorted so he'd know she knew the idea was ludicrous.

"Why wouldn't I flirt with you? According to you, I sleep with every woman who has a pair of tits and no ring on her finger. You fit the criteria. Especially the tits part." His eyes slid to her boobs, making something hot slither down her spine.

What the hell?

Jake had never—

She put the kibosh on that notion. Jake wasn't into her. He'd never commented on her being a woman, beyond a little teasing here or there. As usual he was being outrageous, totally irreverent. Just Jake.

But his comment made her realize she'd hurt his feelings last night when she'd told him to lay off Jenny. "And here I was thinking the ring thing didn't matter."

His head jerked up, outrage in his eyes. "You know I don't mess with married women."

"I'm joking. You know what a joke is, right?" she said with a smart-ass smile, repeating the same phrase he'd used last night. "I've heard of honor among thieves. Is there honor among man whores, too?"

Jake threw a wadded-up nylon knee-high at her.

"Gross," Eva shrieked, pushing away the object he'd pulled out of the espadrille.

"You know I'm sensitive about being a man whore," he cracked, his blue eyes dancing, white teeth flashing.

Her heart squeezed at the sight of a laughing, sexy Jake. God Almighty, the man was gorgeous with that brown hair that glinted red in the sunlight, strong jaw and hands she'd fork over her next paycheck just to have run over her naked shoulders and down her back. Eva swallowed, blocking out the irrational desire for a man who was her friend.

Friend.

"Well, you don't have to throw someone's nasty old knee-high at me. I'll try to remember you're sensitive about spreading yourself around."

"Spreading myself around?" Jake parroted, withdrawing the other wadded-up hosiery from the toe of the other shoe. "Do you want to rephrase that?"

Eva took a few steps back. "Don't you dare."

Jake flashed an evil grin that was also sexy as hell. "Oh, I dare."

Eva scrambled backward, nearly tripping over a stroller. "Don't you do it. Jake!"

Jake lunged for her, and Eva sidestepped, scrambling behind another table displaying candle holders and ashtrays. He dangled the stocking that was stained black at the toes. "I think this would look nice on you, Eva."

"You two cut it out," Abigail yelled. "We've got lots to do."

"You heard your sister," Eva warned, shifting left and right as Jake swung the offending thing her way.

"Since when do I listen to her?" he said, lurching around.

Squealing, Eva ran toward the emergency exit door. "Stop, Jake!"

He ran behind her, laughing like a lunatic.

Eva slammed out the door and tried to push it closed on him. The metal door was hot from the sun beating down on it, scorching Eva's hands. She jerked back and Jake barreled out, catching her around the waist, pushing the hosiery toward her face.

Eva wiggled against him, pulling at his arm locked around her. "Don't you dare, Jake Beauchamp."

He laughed against her, his breath warm near her cheek. She sank down, trying to wriggle away, which caused Jake's arm to move up and his hand to cradle her left breast.

They both froze.

A second ticked by. Then another.

He let go, and Eva stumbled away, feeling the heat scorch her cheeks while at the same time acknowledging how good his touch had felt.

If only…

She spun around, her eyes meeting his. He'd lowered the stupid stocking, laughter gone, an odd look on his face.

Her gaze met his, and she saw in those fiery blue eyes something she'd never seen before.

Swallowing, she shrugged. Because she couldn't think of anything better to do in an awkward moment such as this. Painfully awkward.

So Jake had grabbed her boob. It was an accident, a by-product of him acting like a silly little boy. No big deal.

Jake gave a small chuckle. "Oops."

"Yeah," she said, dropping her gaze. "My fault."

"No, it wasn't. I was the one who grabbed you."

Eva wanted to forget it. Pretend it hadn't happened, so she looked at the forgotten knee-high in his hand. "If I slide by you, do you promise not to put that on me?"

He looked down at the stocking and then back

up with a twinkle in his eye. "Why don't you try and see?"

Eva gave him a flat look. "Please. Like I trust you."

He merely smiled, his gaze actually dropping to her lips. She resisted the urge to lick them. And then this weird thing happened.

She'd been in some dangerous situations, heated situations that caused frissons of alarm to raise the hair on her neck.

This was how she felt now. Crazy electrical.

Eva moved forward slowly, placing her hand on the door handle, her eyes on Jake as she inched very, very slowly past him. He didn't move, but his gaze held hers, mischievousness fading as something hot took over.

Something Eva had wanted for a long time...ever since Jake had come out of the shower at the station, towel looped around his lean hips, droplets of water dotting his chest, the first week she'd worked for the Magnolia Bend FD.

Carefully, she started inching the door open. She'd put about five inches between the metal door and frame when Jake leaned back on the door, slamming it shut.

"Don't," she said, narrowing her eyes as he turned his right shoulder in, blocking her escape, lifting the hosiery.

He grinned and then tossed the stocking over his shoulder.

She gave a nervous laugh.

And then he moved, slamming into her. Not hard. But emphatic.

Her brain received the signals, processing the sexual energy slaking off Jake. He reached up, his hand brushing her ear. He was going to kiss her. Finally.

So Eva made it easy for him. She raised onto her toes, closed her eyes and met him halfway.

Her first thought was he tasted like spearmint gum. Her second thought was to wonder why he tugged at her hair. Her third thought was *oh, shit*.

Because Jake hadn't been about to kiss her…he'd been about to give her a trademark noogie.

But being Jake, he didn't gasp in outrage, ripping her from him.

No.

Jake Beauchamp would never embarrass a lady like that. He dropped his hand and made his lips soft.

Eva dropped down and wiped her mouth with the back of her hand, half of her reveling in the small taste of the man she loved. The other half of her praying the earth would open beneath her feet and swallow her whole.

Surely that could happen, right?

Surely God would have pity on a fool who'd mistakenly kissed the devil out of a man against the wall of the First Presbyterian Church of Magnolia Bend… when he'd only been about to give her a noogie.

CHAPTER FOUR

JAKE ENTERED THE Tenth Annual Rummage Sale to benefit the Magnolia Bend Women's Home like a man hunted. Not because he didn't want to be there supporting his mama and her pet project early on a Saturday morning, but because after yesterday afternoon's incident with Eva, he didn't want to face the discomfort he knew would be between them.

Eva had kissed him.

And though at first he'd been shocked to the toes of his Brooks running shoes, he'd settled into it and enjoyed all one point seven seconds of the kiss.

But then Eva had stopped kissing him, wiping her mouth and looking horrified.

As though she'd walked into junior high naked.

Plain appalled.

He'd stepped back and arched an eyebrow and simply said, "Wow."

She'd looked as if she might choke, her face flooding with color, her eyes bulging, hands fluttering at her side. She'd managed an "excuse me" before bolting through the door he'd shut, leaving him behind not knowing how to handle what had just happened.

"Hey, Jake," his brother Matt called, waving from behind the tables set up with cash registers donated by Maggio's Office Supply store, according to the sign that said as much. "I need more of this paper tape. Can you grab Ma and see where she put the supplies?"

Jake waved a hand in affirmation, scanning the crowded hall filled with racks of coats, tables of folded jeans and shelves holding knickknacks. He saw his sister and her fiancé, Leif, his niece Birdie, who was walking around selling raffle tickets for a quilt stitched by his aunt Opal, and his brother John's wife, Shelby, who was hand-selling some strappy shoes to Merlene Dibbles, who had no business wearing anything strappy. His father swilled coffee at the refreshment table with several other men, shooting the breeze, no doubt discussing the likelihood of St. George's football team making the playoffs again. But he didn't see his mother.

And he didn't see Eva.

Maybe she hadn't come. She hadn't answered any texts or phone calls he made from Ray-Ray's last night. Which meant she was avoiding him. Which meant the ball was in his court. And he didn't know how to handle this situation other than to get it out in the open and talk about it. Wasn't going to go away. And since their shift started Monday at five o'clock in the evening, they couldn't continue avoiding it.

He looked at Matt, who'd just finished checking out several ladies carrying totes provided by First Magnolia Bank. "Hey, where's Mom?"

Matt didn't look up. "Dunno. If I did, I wouldn't need you to get me the paper."

"Right." Jake made his way down the housewares aisle, smiling at people he'd known forever plus a day, almost colliding with a cute three-year-old escapee who was making for the toy section with the harried mother following behind. He finally made it to his dad.

"And that's why we'll struggle on offense. Gary's got to get that o-line beefed up. Feed those boys," Dan Beauchamp said before slapping him on the back. "Right, son?"

"Uh, right. Hey, where's Mom?"

His dad shrugged. "Saw her head to the kitchen with Eva."

Dread pinged inside Jake. He knew what he had to do, but he liked talking about emotions just as much as every other man liked talking about emotions... which meant not at all.

Thing was he'd liked kissing Eva, and that was bad news. From the very beginning, when he'd found out that the chief had hired a woman in order to diversify the department, he'd vowed to leave her the hell alone. Every man knew you didn't shit where you ate. Or whatever that saying was. So before he'd even met Eva, he'd vowed to not go there. When all the other guys hemmed and hawed about sharing a shift with her, he'd stepped up. Hell, he liked the idea of having someone different to shoot the shit with. Moon wore him out with talk of hunting everything that moved, and Martin wanted to play dominos non-stop. He figured having a woman around would be interesting. And Jake liked interesting.

But then Eva had walked into the station with her dark hair braided, face free of makeup, a confident smile in place, and he'd felt shell-shocked. This wasn't the way a firefighter should look, so…so pretty. Wasn't as if she was delicate or girly, either. Quite the contrary, Eva was athletic, fit, full of vitality. Her squared jaw gave her a sexiness he wasn't supposed to notice, and she looked mighty fine in the uniform that had been tucked in at a trim waist with the baggy pants failing to hide the rounded hips and tight ass. He'd been hit with full-on attraction.

So he'd shaken her hand, excused himself while the chief gave her the tour of the main station, went to the bathroom, sat on the toilet and had a little talk with himself. When he'd finally come out, to Moon joking about the burrito he'd eaten the night before, Jake had determined he'd treat Eva just like he treated Abigail. Treat her like a sister. Respect her, protect her and bug the hell out of her. And never, ever see her as anything but a friend. No ifs, ands or buts. Eva Monroe was off-limits.

But yesterday had changed everything.

Last night he'd been haunted by the way she'd felt against him, breasts to chest, pelvis to pelvis, lips to lips. It had felt so damn good it had shaken him to his core…and that was probably why he dreaded seeing Eva today. If it had really been nothing, it would be one thing, but she'd knocked down that careful wall of friendship he'd built years ago, and he could no longer pretend the attraction didn't exist. Like the flip of a light switch, he'd gotten turned on to what kissing Eva was like. And that was very dangerous. He felt off-kilter, as if he might do something crazy. Like kiss her again.

He pushed through the swinging door into the huge stainless-steel kitchen, where they prepared the monthly Feed Our Neighbors dinner. His mother and Eva were deep in conversation.

Fancy's head jerked up. "Jake, glad you're here. Take this receipt tape to Matt."

Eva didn't look at him. Instead, she fiddled with her fingernails, picking at her cuticles. Probably meant she was avoiding him or uncomfortable.

Duh.

"Sure. That's actually what I came for," he said, deftly catching the roll of paper his mother tossed to him. "Morning, Eva."

"Morning," she said, not lifting her gaze.

He stood there for a minute, and his mom gave him a puzzled look.

"Hey, E, when you have a sec, I wanted to talk to you," he said. They couldn't go on like this. They'd have to talk about it. Put it behind them so they could go back to the way they were before. Just f-r-i-e-n-d-s.

He had no clue why he'd spelled it out in his

thoughts, but then again, he had no idea how he was going to see Eva as his sister ever again.

"Sure," she said, still not meeting his gaze.

And that's when Fancy caught on to the discomfort. She looked from him back to Eva and then back to him, lifting an eyebrow. Jake tried to warn her with his eyes, but she plunged in anyway. "What's going on?"

"Nothing," they both said in unison.

"Huh," Fancy said, her eyes narrowing. "Well, none of my business anyway."

Which was code for "I'll rake you over the coals later, Jakey." His mother didn't like being out of the loop. Her job was to manage the lives of her children, leaning heavily at times, backing off at others. She danced the Mom dance rather well.

"That's right," Jake said, giving her the nod. The one that said, "Don't bother. I won't give up my secrets."

Fancy just smiled. "I'll see you later, Jakey."

Jake sighed and melted out the door, back into the chaos of the rummage sale. The buzz of conversation had elevated to a dull roar in the acoustically challenged community hall. Jake ducked around a gaggle of women arguing over which purse would be the right size for the LSU home opener that weekend and ran right into his brother John.

"Here, hold her," his brother said, shoving Jake's five-month-old niece into his arms. Lindsay cooed and gave him a toothless, drooly grin. "I gotta pi... uh, go to the bathroom."

"Wait—" Jake said, tucking the receipt tape under his arm and shifting the baby to his left arm.

Lindsay smacked him in the face with a wet hand, and John disappeared behind the women, heading toward the lobby and the restrooms located there. The baby hit him again.

"Hey, Linds. Don't go abusing your ol' uncle Jake," he said, smiling at the baby who had blond wisps sticking out all over her head and blue-green eyes that crinkled when she laughed at him. "Oh, you think that's funny?"

He tickled her little round belly, making her squeal.

"Well, if that don't melt an old woman's heart," someone said to his right. He turned to find Carla Stanton standing there.

"Mrs. Stanton. How you doin' this fine morning?" he asked, trying to avoid Lindsay's fingers creeping into his mouth.

"Pretty good. Still getting over a headache. My blood pressure was out of whack," she said, her eyes not on him but instead riveted to the baby he held. "That's John's baby, isn't it?"

"Yes, ma'am," Jake said, juggling the baby, who stared at Carla with wide eyes before squealing again as if she had something to say to the older woman.

Carla was John's late wife's mother, who had given John and Shelby a lot of grief when they'd first gotten together last fall. Bitter with pain over the death of her only child, she'd held on tight to the idea John couldn't...wouldn't be happy if her daughter couldn't be happy. Hadn't mattered that Rebecca was dead. But Shelby, Jake's vivacious, generous new sister-in-law, had taken the high road, insisting they name their daughter in remembrance of the woman who John had loved and lost. Lindsay Rebecca Beauchamp was radiantly untouched by the pettiness of adults and turned all her adorableness on the older woman who'd nearly ruined her mother's life.

Carla watched the baby, a small smile on her lips. "She's a pretty baby."

"Yeah, she is. Takes after her uncle Jake, of course," Jake said, making a face at Lindsay. "Don't you?"

The baby smacked him again and laughed. Carla's smile grew.

"Here, you want to hold her?" he asked, shoving Lindsay at the woman. Her hands came up to hold the little girl, likely out of self-preservation.

"Oh, no, I shouldn't—" she started just as he withdrew his hands from around his niece.

The baby stared at Carla for a few seconds before babbling something.

"Oh, really?" the older woman said to the baby, smiling and nodding her head. "I didn't know."

Jake scanned the room and saw Shelby watching

them. She caught his eye and smiled, a sort of secret knowing in her eyes.

"I'm gonna hand off this tape to Matt and I'll be right back. You got her?" he asked.

"Of course I have Lindsay Rebecca. We're already old friends, and I certainly know how to take care of a sweet baby girl," Carla said, catching the hand the baby lifted to smack her and giving it a kiss.

So she knew the baby's name? Huh.

Jake hustled over to his brother, who had started beckoning him frantically. A line had formed and he looked harried. Jake tossed him the roll of tape, which he deftly caught. Matt was the athlete of the family. Though both Jake and John had been fairly proficient, Matt had been the star, netting a scholarship to play at Tulane. He might have gone pro as a tight end if he hadn't blown out one of his knees.

"Thanks," Matt called.

"No problem," Jake said, turning back so he could take his niece from Carla. But John had already arrived and stood in conversation with his former mother-in-law. So Jake turned, intending to hunt Eva down, but Fancy appeared at his side like a specter from long ago.

Woo woo woo woooo. Woo, woo, woo, woooo. The *Twilight Zone* theme song played in his mind.

"So what's going on with you and Eva? That was weird back there," his mother said.

"Jesus, Mom, you couldn't wait until—" he glanced down at the watch that wasn't on his arm, since he didn't like to wear a watch like most guys "—seven minutes had passed? They should use you down at the police department. I'll talk to Uncle Sam about putting you on the force."

She pinched him under the arm, the way she used to years ago in the second pew to the right of the pulpit.

"Ow." He twisted away.

"Don't forget I'm your mother. And that when you call on Jesus it better be for something important and not in vain, Jacob Edward."

"Yes, ma'am," he drawled with only 10 percent sarcasm. "But I'm pretty sure Jesus understands. He had a mother, too."

That made Fancy smile. His mother could be awfully bloodthirsty for a preacher's wife. "Even so, you know that your behavior—"

"Doesn't reflect on you or Dad. I'm my own person," he said, knowing he probably sounded like a petulant child. What was it about mothers that did that to a guy?

He knew what people around town said about him—that rascal Jake's the family rebel. He drinks, whores and avoids church. Real degenerate. He didn't mind that version of himself. No, because that version prevented people seeing through him to the pitiful coward beneath the bullshit.

He couldn't pretend to be the tortured hero, because he hadn't been a hero on that lonely stretch of highway, in the twisted wreckage beneath that huge harvest moon. He'd lain in his friends' blood, crying like a baby. He hadn't been able to help Clint… hadn't been able to save Angela. In fact, his weak attempts to tug Clint from where he lay had done more damage than good.

Jake Beauchamp…coward.

So he covered it up with being a degenerate. He knew he was the perfect head case for a shrink, but he didn't care enough to change. Because changing meant he'd have to remember, have to dig the knife beneath the skin to clear all the gunk. Change meant hurting again.

"I know who you are, honey, and neither your father nor I have tried to change you. Your behavior, however, is never off the table."

He nodded because she was right. Neither of his parents rode his case like they could.

His mother patted him. "Just remember you're in your father's house."

"God?"

"No, Dan's. Well, you know what I mean. Now, what's going on between you and Eva? Because I gotta tell you, Jake, I think she's really going to need some support in these upcoming months."

A thread of alarm cinched his heart. "Why? What's wrong with Eva? Is she sick?"

"Of course not. She's healthy as a horse, but that's exactly my point—you don't know what's going on in her life, and that's abnormal."

"Wait, what's going on in—" Jake left off the rest

because the good town doctor, Jamison French, had stopped right in front of them.

"Morning, Jake. Mrs. Beauchamp," Jamison said, giving them both his best bedside smile.

"What's up, James?" Jake asked, extending a hand and giving the man a good firm Beauchamp hand-shake.

"Good morning, Jamison, and it's just Fancy," his mother said.

"Of course. Well, looks like a good turnout," Jamison said, making polite conversation the way any decent human being would.

So it wasn't that Jake didn't like Jamison. He liked him fine. It was just that Jamison was the Cary Grant to Jake's James Dean. They were both single, good-looking guys in their thirties with all their teeth. No baggage, from good families with a decent income. And the target on their backs in Magnolia Bend had been fixed. The thing that made him twitch was the fact that Jamison was the better of the two, with his perfectly combed blond hair and artsy-fartsy hipster glasses framing sparkling blue eyes brimming with wit and goodness. In contrast, Jake crushed beer cans, peed in the woods and wore old frat T-shirts.

"It *is* a good turnout." Fancy nodded, a pleased smile curving her lips.

"By chance have either of you seen Eva?" Jamison asked.

"Eva? What the hell do you want with her?" Jake

snarled, puffing up his chest, hands curling into fists. He spit at Jamison's feet and bared his teeth.

Okay, so he didn't actually do either of those things…but he thought about it. After all, Jamison Fancy Pants had no business asking after his Eva.

Correction. Just Eva.

"She *was* in the kitchen," Fancy said, pointing over her shoulder, her eyes holding a question.

"Great. I'm picking her up for the Zydeco Festival over in Garden City. Buckskin Nash is performing at noon, so…" Jamison looked at his watch. He actually had one. Nice Swiss Army stainless steel, with all those gauges divers needed. Figured.

"Here I am, Jamison," Eva said, from behind Jake. They all turned toward her, and Jake noticed for the first time how pretty Eva looked. She'd worn her hair in a ponytail and had put on makeup…or at least shiny lip gloss that made her lips kissable. She wore a strapless short romper thing, which looked too sexy to be wasted on Jamison. "You ready?"

"I thought you wanted to talk," Jake said.

Eva finally met his gaze. Her eyes looked defiant, almost angry. "You were the one who wanted to talk. I have a date, so you'll have to wait until later."

Jake frowned…something he rarely did. "Fine."

Eva lifted a bronzed shoulder that also looked kissable. Wasn't as shiny as her lips. Just luminous. "Ready?"

Jamison smiled and damn him, his eyes moved

down Eva's body. If the man had had a mustache, he might have twirled it. "Absolutely."

Jake clenched his fist and turned away. What the hell did he care who Eva dated? She'd dated at least three dudes since she'd moved to Magnolia Bend, and he'd not blinked one eye. Of course, that had been before she'd kissed him, chiseling a brick out of the wall of indifference he'd built between him and her obvious charms.

"See you around, Jake," Jamison said, using his manners.

Jake grunted.

"Bye, honey, have fun," Fancy said, giving Eva a motherly smile. "We'll talk later. Don't worry. Everything will be fine."

Eva looked at his mother with a grateful smile and followed Jamison out of the hall. She hadn't even told him goodbye. Had treated him as if he didn't matter, as if he hadn't even been worth the kiss she'd given him yesterday.

"Where are you going, Jake?" Fancy called as he stalked off.

"To the bathroom," Jake said, not needing to go to the bathroom but wanting to find a place where no one would talk to him or meet his eyes. He didn't want the confusion to show, and the urinal worked as well as any place.

CHAPTER FIVE

EVA TAPPED HER toe to the music and sipped the ice-cold beer Jamison had bought for her. The band on stage was decent, and the sun had finally retreated behind a cloud, giving them all some relief. Listening to zydeco was fun…when it wasn't ninety-two degrees and you were sitting beneath a shady tree. Garden City hadn't planned for the heat, which was stupid because they were holding a festival in September. That equaled scorcher on the scale of Louisiana weather.

"You okay?" Jamison asked for the third time in an hour. He looked crisp and cool. She had no idea how, because he wore linen pants.

"Fine," she said, taking another sip and fanning herself. "I'm having a good time.

"Good," he said with a smile, raising his arms and clapping along as Beebo Nash cranked up a solo on the accordion. The ocean-blue polo Jamison wore rode up on his toned biceps and revealed a trim stomach peeking out above his pants. "I've been dying to take you out for a while. I'm so glad you said yes this time, Eva."

"Yeah, well, I'm stubborn that way. Wanted to

wait a couple of months to date after I ended my last relationship."

Jamison slid his gaze toward her and grinned. "You have rules about dating, too?"

"No, not really. Just felt right to wait. Do you have rules for dating?" she asked, acknowledging with a wince the sun once again coming out from behind the clouds. Felt as if it was beating them down with the heat.

"Sort of. Having dating rules makes things easier for me," he said with a smile, looking way too handsome.

Strange. Eva didn't have real rules, just gut feelings. She sorta thought rules for dating were a bit too anal. "Like for first kisses, sex, what?"

"More like gifts, family, house keys. That sort of stuff," he said, curving an arm around her waist, jerking her forward as a drunk guy stumbled their way. The weight of his hand felt good on her hip. Deep down even the most vehement feminist had to innately appreciate the protective instincts of a man. Or maybe it was just Eva who felt that way. She spent much of her time as one of the guys, subject to discussion on bodily functions and field-dressing a deer. Being treated like a woman felt nice every now and then.

"You okay?" Jamison asked yet again, concern etched on his handsome face.

"I think you've asked me that four times within

the hour. Must be the whole doctor thing spilling over," she said, pressing her hands against his chest.

His forehead crinkled, but he didn't move his arm from around her waist. Instead, he grinned at her, his blue eyes growing almost smoky. "You know, you're right. I say that a lot, but then again, I have to. Most women aren't too comfortable with me. Hazard of the profession, and another reason I'm really glad you haven't scurried away from me."

"Maybe if I wore a paper gown?"

He snorted.

"Besides, you're the pot of honey," she teased.

He stared at her lips, and Eva prepared herself to be kissed, but Jamison must have decided against it. He dropped his hand and stepped back. "Honey?"

Eva tamped down the disappointment mixed with relief. She didn't know if she wanted him to kiss her or not—or if she was insulted or not.

"Yeah, you're a honey pot. Women swarm like bees around you." She raised her voice into falsetto. "Dr. French, you're so wonderful. Buzz, buzz, buzz."

That made him laugh, and the man looked good laughing. His eyes crinkled behind the lens of his glasses, and his bright teeth flashed against his tan skin.

He said nothing more, merely turned his attention to the stage where a slim woman with dark hair, a lithe body and a helluva voice worked the microphone. The crowd cheered as the band shifted into a new song that showcased the singer's raspy voice.

"She's good," Eva said.

"Yeah, that's Morgan Cost."

"No kidding! She was married to Jake's sister's ex-husband."

"I didn't know she married Cal," Jamison said, clapping along to the song. "I mean I knew he ran off to California with her a few years back. Anyway, Morgan released a record last month, and it's getting good airplay on country music stations. There was even an article in the *Baton Rouge Advocate* last week."

"Huh," Eva said, impressed by the woman's voice but little else. Morgan had run off with Abigail Orgeron's husband in the middle of a party they'd been throwing. Jake's sister had been left with a daughter, a huge mortgage on a bed-and-breakfast and a scandal. In Eva's eyes, Morgan would always have that black mark against her, no matter how talented she was.

She hadn't known Jake back then, but he still got steamed when someone brought up the topic of Calhoun Orgeron. Eva didn't like the man much, either, especially since he'd already hit on her at church earlier that year when he'd dragged his butt back to Magnolia Bend after Morgan had dumped him.

"Well, she's definitely a good singer. I'll give her that, I guess," Eva said, joining Jamison on the clapping.

Hours later, after eating jambalaya, drinking another cold Abita beer and sharing a sno-ball with

Jamison, who obviously didn't mind swapping spit in that manner, Eva stepped onto the porch of the cute bungalow she'd bought in the Laurel Creek subdivision. Jamison trailed behind her, still giving off the breezy yacht-club vibe. The man's pants weren't even creased, and no sweat ringed the undersides of his shirtsleeves.

Eva pulled at the filmy material of her romper. The silly thing, bought in a moment of insanity, was plastered against her chest, advertising the wares a little too well. She found her house key and stuck it in the door. "Thanks for inviting me, Jamison. It was fun."

"It was. I'm glad you went with me."

"Would you like to come inside for a drink? Or to use the bathroom?"

Why had she asked that? Just because the beer had done a number on her didn't mean he had to go to the bathroom, too. Jeez, she sucked at dating.

Jamison grinned. "You're asking me in to pee?"

Eva never blushed, but she felt close to it in that moment. "Sorry, I know you have a bit of a drive home. That was stupid."

"Nah, it was cute," he said with another blinding smile. "I really should go, but I hope we can do this again."

With Charlie about to come live with her, things felt uncertain in her life. But taking in her brother didn't mean she had to quit being who she was. "Yeah, I'd like that."

"Good. So maybe… Tuesday night? They're showing *Bringing Up Baby* at the Grand. Want to share some popcorn with me?"

Eva shook her head. "I have some things going on early in the week, but maybe by Friday I can get away."

"Well, that movie won't be showing, but I bet we can find something to do," he said. Any other guy would have made the last statement sound sexual, but not Jamison. He sincerely meant they'd find something to do. That thought almost made Eva giggle.

"That sounds great," she said, twisting the key.

"It's a date, then," Jamison said, moving toward her.

Okay, so now he'd kiss her. She turned toward him, but he merely gave her a quick squeeze of her shoulders. "See ya then. Thanks."

Then he was gone, moving quickly down the steps toward the new Mercedes he'd parked in her driveway.

Eva watched him before giving him a quick wave as he climbed inside the car.

Maybe Jamison was gay, but she didn't think so. But what man turned away from a kiss—twice? She didn't know many who would, but perhaps it was one of those rules for dating that he professed to have. Maybe kisses on the first date weren't allowed no matter what. Or maybe he wasn't into her. Maybe he was—

"Hey."

Eva jumped, dropping her keys. "Jake, you scared me to death."

Jake grinned like the devil he was. "You look alive to me…and I must say, damn nice in that short thing you're wearing."

Eva bent over to grab the keys she'd dropped, holding a hand to her bodice so the fabric didn't gape and show her boobs to the man she'd always wanted to show her boobs to. "Um, thank you."

"Guess ol' Jamie didn't appreciate it, huh? No good-night kiss."

"It's not night," Eva said, twisting the doorknob and pushing into the blessed coolness of her house. She didn't bother asking Jake to come in—she knew he'd do so anyway. The only thing she cared about was going to the bathroom.

He closed the door. "But it *was* a date, right?"

"I guess," she said, dumping her cross-body purse onto the piano bench, setting her keys atop the instrument. "You want a beer?"

"I always want a beer," he said, checking out the picture of Eva's mother, which she'd hung above the flowery club chair in the living space. It had been taken when her mother had graduated high school and was the way Eva liked to remember her mother—as a laughing girl. Not as the emotional wreck she was now.

Eva pulled off her sandals and padded barefoot through her small kitchen and into the bathroom, which she made quick use of. She then pulled two beers from the fridge, popped the tops and walked back to the living room, sinking onto the couch. "How was the sale?"

"What?"

"The rummage sale. Did they raise a lot of money?"

"I don't know. I didn't ask." He walked over and grabbed the beer she held out before dropping onto the couch beside her.

Eva didn't want him to sit next to her. Any other time it would have been fine, but at the moment a kiss sat between them. She'd spent all of last night and half of this morning berating herself for being a damn idiot.

She'd kissed a man who'd been trying to give her a noogie. Who did that? Especially when she'd been so successful in holding back her feelings for him for the past three years. But, like a valve bursting on a pipe, she'd gone and spewed forth the desire she had for him. It was another problem piled onto a plate that felt suspiciously full at present.

"So we gonna talk about what happened yesterday?" he asked.

"No. We're not."

He studied her for a few minutes as she pretended to be impassive. Finally, he reached out and picked up the TV remote control. "So you want to watch Ohio State and Notre Dame?"

"Do what?"

"Play football." His voice was incredulous.

"Not really, but sure."

Jake put the game on. A couple of announcers were discussing the OSU quarterback's injury and how with one turn of an ankle, his college career was over.

Yeah, tell her about it. One innocent little misread and things could turn upside down fast.

About mid-beer, Jake looked over at her. "So you wanna talk about why you had to talk to my mom?"

"No."

"Eva, this is ridiculous."

"It's not ridiculous. It's none of your business."

He actually looked miffed. Turning his attention back to the TV, he finished his beer and sat the empty bottle on the coffee table littered with health magazines and one copy of *Parenting*, which she'd snagged at the grocery store yesterday.

Charlie coming to live with her scared Eva silly. She knew nothing about living with a boy. Her half brother, Chris, had already been eight years old when she emerged on the scene, and since he lived with his mom, her father's first wife, in Belle Chase, Eva rarely saw him. And by the time she could actually interact with Chris during his visits on random weekends, he was too busy for a snot-nosed girl. Not that Eva dealt with sinus issues or anything.

As a teen, she'd rarely babysat. And when her father had married his third wife, Claren, Eva had been in her twenties. The odd time they'd brought Charlie over to visit, she'd been at a loss for how to change a diaper or even how to entertain him. The only time her career put her into contact with kids was when she conducted a field trip tour of the fire station.

Mother material she was not.

She tucked her feet under her, careful not to touch any part of Jake's naked leg. Unlike Jamison's very put-together style, Jake wore athletic shorts, a T-shirt he'd cut the sleeves off, and his thick hair looked as if he'd raked his hands through it a million times that day. A five o'clock shadow finished off the gruff, sexy image. Polished wasn't Jake's vibe. Rumpled sex god was more like it.

"I guess I should go," he said. Jake looked uncomfortable, something he never seemed to be. And it was her fault. She'd screwed up, and now she was acting as if things were different. If she wanted to erase the kiss and its repercussions, she had to go back to being herself.

"You don't have to. The game's nearly over, and I think Georgia plays South Carolina next. I could order pizza from Gumbeaux's."

See? Everything was normal. Just like always. They'd watch TV, share a pizza and never, ever talk about the kiss.

Ever.

"Sounds good but I don't like this vibe between us. You're acting weird after the ki—"

"Uh-uh. Don't say it. Please. It never happened."

But it did. She knew it. He knew it. But maybe—

"Fine. It didn't happen. Erased."

She breathed a sigh of relief. "Good. So pizza?"

"Yeah. Get extra olives on my half," he said, toe-ing off his sneakers and propping his socked feet on her coffee table. As if he was her brother. As if he'd already forgotten.

Gotta love the single-mindedness of a dude.

Perfect.

"I know what you like." Eva uncurled and padded toward the kitchen to grab her phone and the number for Gumbeaux's. After ordering Jake's extra ham-burger, extra olives pizza, she slipped off to her room to change into a T-shirt and some shorts she'd made from an old pair of sweatpants. She even took out her contacts, washed her face and put on her glasses.

She returned to the living room and held out her hand.

Jake moved his head around to catch a play.

"Money."

He looked up. "For…"

"Pizza. No freeloading."

Jake reached for his wallet, pulling the pocket in-side out and leaving it that way. Yeah, Jake wasn't anything near Jamison French…other than being good-looking as the devil himself. He handed her a couple bills. "That's too much," she said, shoving a ten back at him.

"Keep it."

"No, this isn't a date. We go halfsies."

"I'm drinking your beer. Keep it."

Eva shrugged and tucked the money into her wallet, plopping onto the wing-backed chair far away from Jake. He watched the game until a commercial came on, and then he turned to her. He wrinkled his nose. "Why'd you change?"

"Because it's just you."

"What's that supposed to mean?"

"It means I don't have to stay gussied up."

"But you did for Jamison?"

He sounded almost jealous. Weird. "Of course. It was a date. Don't you take a shower, brush your teeth and douse yourself in cologne when you go on a date?"

"I don't douse myself."

Eva laughed. "Well, I guess it's better than smelling like gym socks."

Jake faked outrage. "I hope you know my gym socks smell like a summer's day."

"Exactly. Ripe."

A short while later the doorbell rang and Eva answered, taking the piping-hot pizzas and inhaling the deliciousness. Seconds later she grabbed paper plates and set the boxes on the coffee table, lifting the lids. Jake dug in, pulling out several pieces, dangling the stringy cheese into his mouth before taking the first bite.

"Ah, now that's some good pizza," he said, chewing and making an orgasmic face. Or at least that's how she envisioned his orgasmic face. Yeah. She'd fantasized, in the small darkness of her room, snug beneath her down comforter, her mind going where she normally wouldn't let it in the brightness of the day. "Come sit by me, Eva."

He'd patted the couch next to him, offering her a nonwolfish smile.

"Why?" she asked, pulling out a slice of the classic pepperoni with extra cheese pizza that was her favorite.

"Because it's stupid for you to sit in that uncomfortable chair over there. Your couch is squishy and comfy, and I won't bite you…even after the event that shall not be named."

Eva realized she was being silly. This was Jake. And even though he said he'd forgotten the kiss they'd shared…and even if he'd already brought it up as a *shall not be named* happening, she couldn't see the TV all that well from the scratchy chair she'd inherited from her grandmother.

She got up and slumped down on the cushion next to him, chewing her pizza thoughtfully as the Notre Dame quarterback ran the ball into the end zone for a touchdown. "I don't want to refer to that thing yesterday as anything. You said you'd forget it."

For a few seconds Jake chewed. Finally, he said, "What if I don't want to forget it?"

Eva's belly flopped and it had nothing to do with the pizza. "Why wouldn't you?"

He shrugged. "I didn't expect it, but it was interesting."

She sat her half-eaten pizza on the plate, rubbing her fingers against the paper towel she'd placed in her lap. "Interesting? No, it was insane. I don't know why…ugh, you know, this is why I didn't want to discuss it. Why I wanted to forget about it. Makes everything so weird between us."

Jake tossed his empty plate on top of the pizza box. "Yes, it does, but still, I have questions that need answering."

Eva sat up. "It was a dumb kiss. I don't know why I did it. Just drop it." Of course she knew why she'd kissed him. She'd dreamed about it for three years, yearning for his body against her, almost desperate to take one little taste of Jake.

But he didn't have to know that.

"No," he said, wiping his hands on a napkin.

"No?"

"See, thing is, that was a crappy kiss. How can I let you walk around thinking that subpar kiss was indicative of what I'm capable of? That would be…a travesty." He reached over and dragged her into his lap, turning her so she tipped à la Scarlett O'Hara into his arms.

"Jake," she said, struggling against him even as something way deep down inside her screamed "hell, yeah."

His eyes held devilment, humor and something deeper. Almost tender. He lowered his head, rubbing his soft lips against hers. She immediately stilled at the sweetness, the hand she pushed at his chest turning to knot his T-shirt.

He lifted his head and crooked an eyebrow. "That comparable?"

Eva didn't have words so she nodded.

"Not good enough," he said, dipping his head again, settling his lips against hers with gentle but insistent pressure.

Open to me.

His tongue traced the top of her bottom lip as his free hand slid up to her face, thumb tracing her jaw. Eva let go of his T-shirt and moved her hand to wrap around his neck. She opened her mouth and Jake delivered, his tongue sliding against hers.

He tasted like pizza—warm, yeasty and so damn good. Desire unwound in her belly like a hose slipping from the fire engine, spiraling low in her pelvis. That sweet, achy throb pulsed as he shifted her in his arms, his kiss softening before becoming demanding. Finally, after several seconds of kissing the daylights out of her, he used his teeth to nip at her lower lip, tugging it before lifting his head.

Their eyes met, their breaths mingled.

Jake gave her a triumphant smile.

Then he tipped her up, setting her in her original spot. He grabbed his beer and took a swig, throwing an arm over the back of the couch. "There."

Eva knew her eyes were as wide as the pepperoni pieces on the pizza slice she'd abandoned. "What the hell was that?"

Jake opened the box and set another two slices on his plate. "That was correcting what happened yesterday."

Eva pulled the plate from his hands.

"Hey," he said.

"You can't just kiss me like that and then pretend it wasn't anything more than blowing your nose."

"It was way better than blowing my nose, babe."

"Don't call me babe. I'm not one of your bimbos. I'm not the sort of girl you can casually tip into your lap and maul, you arrogant, self-centered…ass."

"Eva," he said, holding up his hands in surrender. "Now, don't go getting mad. It was merely payback. You kissed me. I kissed you. Now we're even."

"Even?" she repeated, her hands still shaking even as the desire shriveled up like the fern his sister had given her as a housewarming gift. "You are insane."

Jake laughed. "Maybe so, but at least you won't walk around town thinking I'm bad at kissing. I mean, if we're gonna kiss, we might as well do it right. That's all I was thinking."

She pressed her hand against her lips and then slugged him.

"Ouch," he said, ducking her next swing.

"Get out," she said, feeling overly dramatic, but not caring enough to stop or calm herself.

Jake thought the kiss was no big deal. Of course he did. He went around having sex if the wind blew right—a kiss might as well be a handshake to him.

But it wasn't to her. That kiss hadn't been anything like the chaste, embarrassing thing she'd given him yesterday. No, that kiss had been toe-curling, panty-dropping, pure ecstasy, and it had awoken a hunger that hadn't even poked its head out of its cage yesterday.

Full-on, body-quaking desire.

Absolute, bone-jarring lust.

Something she couldn't hide with a man like Jake.

"I'm sorry," he said, leaning away from her. "Stop making it something it's not."

"You stupid, big-headed idiot," she said, pushing off the couch, standing over him.

"Come on, Eva. Calm down."

"Don't tell me to calm down," she growled.

"God, you're acting like a normal woman."

"I am a normal woman, you creep. You can't do what you just did."

"Why?" he asked, his eyes focused on her hands.

"Because."

"Because?"

Eva backed away from him. "You and I both know why I'm pissed. Because you turned that into something. You…" She couldn't say it.

A few seconds ticked by.

"I made you want me," he finished, the teasing gone from his voice.

"Yes. Why did you do that? God, Jake." Eva backed away, shoving her glasses up her nose, feeling as if she wanted to run to her room, slam the door and lock him out. Physically she could do that, but that would be childish…and he'd still be in her head anyway. She'd still taste him on her lips.

"I'm sorry. I wasn't trying… I don't know why I did that. I've been feeling strange when I'm around you lately."

"Why?"

"I don't know. You're Eva. I shouldn't feel uncomfortable around you. I shouldn't notice your lips, the way your boobs look in a tight T-shirt. I shouldn't think about…" He stopped, his face registering that he hadn't meant to be so honest.

"What are you saying?"

"Nothing. I shouldn't have done that. I'm sorry," he said, shoving his hands in his pockets and getting off the couch. "I'll go."

She watched him, not knowing what to do. Things had gotten out of control.

Jake set his hand on the doorknob, turning back to her. "I'll see you Monday, right?"

Eva shook her head. "Dutch is covering for me. I have to go to New Orleans for family business."

"Then tomorrow? Hilda's birthday party?"

"Maybe." She wasn't sure if she was going. She had to go to Baton Rouge and get some things for Charlie so she could turn her girly guest bedroom into something a little boy would feel comfy in. Plus, the lady from CPS was coming over to do an inspection and meet her.

So much in her life was about to change, and to top it off, so had her relationship with Jake.

And that scared her because now he knew…somewhere deep down he had to know how she felt. It had been in her kiss.

"Don't be mad at me, Eva. I didn't know it would turn into that."

And then Jake slipped out the door into the fading day.

Leaving her wanting…leaving her knowing that she could never be the same woman she'd been just days ago.

CHAPTER SIX

JAKE WALKED INTO his cousin Hilda's house and nearly stepped on his sister, who looked to be hiding in the foyer's coat closet.

"What the hell?" he whispered, righting himself against the door frame of the closet.

"Shh!" Abigail said, putting a finger to her lips. "Cal's mother is in there—" she jabbed a finger toward the formal dining room Hilda rarely used "—telling Violet I was the one who made Cal leave in the first place."

"What?"

"Shh!"

"But—" he started before Abigail cupped a hand over his mouth.

"I know, but I still want to hear the conversation since it's about me." Abigail cocked her left ear toward the dining room. Jake grew still and listened, too.

"Well, after working on the Laurel Woods Art Fest committee with her, my opinion has certainly changed," someone said. Jake was almost certain it was Violet Joyner, the Magnolia Bend First Baptist Church's pastor's wife. Sounded like someone with a stick up her ass, and Violet *always* fit that description.

"What do you mean?" Minnie Orgeron, Abigail's former mother-in-law, asked.

"Well, you'll never believe how crassly Abigail behaved, running around with that hippie guy, acting positively like a heathen. Never would have thought it of the daughter of a minister, but you never know with people. Of course they *are* Presbyterian."

Abigail's eyes widened and she stifled a laugh.

Minnie sighed. "I agree, Violet. What a person sees on the surface is one thing, but the inside is quite another."

Jake whispered, "Jeez, don't they know heathens have more fun?"

"I thought that was blondes?" Abigail whispered back.

"Yeah—blond heathens have double the fun."

"I know," Abigail said, wiggling her eyebrows obviously because her new fiancé was very blond and quite possibly a heathen.

"Why are you letting those old hussies get away with talking bad about you?" he whispered, trying to peer out behind the door.

"Because I don't give a rat's ass," Abigail said with a giggle. Then she stepped out of the closet and shut the door loudly before sashaying into the dining room.

"Oh, hello, ladies," Abigail trilled. "Have either

of you seen Hilda? My mama wants to cut the cake soon."

Jake could almost feel the two old gossips' guilt slink past him. Five seconds later the ladies themselves slunk past him, giving him a quick hello, before trotting off toward the back patio, where Hilda's seventieth birthday party was in full swing. Of course, no one would mention that they'd been celebrating her seventieth birthday for the past three years.

Abigail sauntered by, slapping him on the butt and giving him a knowing grin. Jake laughed.

To think his once socially conscious, uptight sister got a thrill about being gossiped about made his heart warm. Yeah, Leif Lively and love had made Abigail a lot more pleasurable to be around.

"Hey, there, Jakey," his father said, coming around the corner, holding a glass of fizzing, fussy punch. "Your mama's been looking for you. She said something about Eva."

His stomach fluttered. "Is Eva here?"

"No, she sent her apologies and a gift for Hilda. She already opened it. One of those kinky firefighter calendars. Eva sure has a strange sense of humor."

And beautiful eyes. And soft lips. And breasts that would… Jake stopped right there. Because that's where his thoughts had kept tripping for the past twenty hours. Okay, seven of those he'd been sleeping, but still. He was in trouble.

'Cause he'd upset the apple cart.

He'd lifted the rock and looked beneath to find the creepy crawlies.

He'd spun the chamber and pulled the trigger.

Too late now because every shade of gray muddled his thoughts. Yeah, no more black-and-white with him and Eva. And it was his own damn fault.

Or at least most of it was.

"Son?"

"Oh, sorry. My mind went somewhere it shouldn't."

His father frowned. "Everything okay? You haven't been yourself these past couple of months."

"Nah, I'm fine. Did Mom say where Eva is?"

"I think she had to go to Baton Rouge. No, maybe it was New Orleans."

Jake didn't know whether he was sorry Eva wasn't there or relieved. He had to get his feelings under control, and as of 3:11 p.m., which was the current time reflected on Hilda's antique clock, he'd failed to get a grasp on that damn kiss.

He had thought it would be funny to kiss Eva like he'd kissed almost half of the eligible female population in Magnolia Bend, but it had backfired and blew up in his face.

Because it hadn't been amusing in the least.

On the contrary—the kiss had been hot.

And it had rocked him to his core, even though afterward he'd pretended it hadn't.

Three years ago when Eva had strolled into the station with her no-nonsense braid and her chin jutted in determination, he'd drawn the line. Black-and-white. But now everything was gray. Like concrete. Slam-his-head-against-concrete gray. That should be a new Sherwin Williams paint color.

Hilda appeared at his elbow. "Hello, Jake, dear. Something to drink?"

Jake dutifully kissed her cheek. She smelled like Paris…the expensive part with the fancy perfumeries. "Happy seventieth, cuz."

Hilda blinked and then smiled. "Yes, I can't believe that many years have already passed. I feel positively twenty years younger."

Dan barked out a laugh. "I hear seventy-five is the new twenty-five, right?"

Hilda sniffed. "As if I'd know."

Jake looked over Hilda's shoulder for his mother. He had no idea why Eva would be in either New Orleans or Baton Rouge. She was a homebody and hated the traffic that plagued both cities. Must have something to do with her brother Chris. Or maybe something else in her past? Worry wriggled into his gut. She'd been secretive over the past few days. Could have to do with her mother. Eva's mom was in a constant state of fragile health paired with financial ruin. But why would Chris be involved? They shared a father, not a mother.

Maybe it was something to do with their father's estate.

Or not.

"Now, Jake, since your brothers and sister have

found love and marriage, it's time to work on you," Hilda said with a gleam in her eye.

"No, thank you," Jake said, stepping away from Hilda's long fingers as they grazed his forearm.

"Oh, don't be silly. You've played around long enough. I'm very happy to help you out. After all, I practically gave your sister that delicious man on a silver platter." She nodded toward Leif, who stood next to Abigail, absentmindedly rubbing the small of his sister's back.

Dan could hardly hold in his laughter. He slapped Jake on the back and choked out "good luck" before slinking off toward the kitchen and the no doubt elegant cake bought at Swiss Confectionary in New Orleans. Jake's father was known for his enormous sweet tooth. In fact, his mother always told people she'd landed the handsome new Presbyterian preacher after he'd tasted her caramel cake she'd baked for the Ladies' Auxiliary fund-raiser.

"Now, let's start with your clothing. You canter about town wearing sloppy T-shirts and gym shorts that should have seen the bottom of the rubbish pile years ago. I have some lovely catalogs I will loan you. Don't worry, I'll mark up the selections I think will suit you best. You're a handsome man beneath all that scruffiness."

Jake bristled. "I'm not scruffy." He rubbed his recently shaved face.

"Darling, it's not just about your hygiene, it's the whole look."

"I like my look. I don't want to come across like—"

"Jamison French," Hilda said, pointing toward the dapper man chatting with Shelby and John. Jamison wore a pair of pressed trousers and a long-sleeved shirt with a blue sweater vest. He looked like a rich prissy pants. "Now, that's a man who knows how to play up his best assets."

"He looks like a guy who waxes his brows." Jake wrinkled his nose. "He probably gets manicures and moisturizes."

"And what is wrong with that?" Hilda asked, taking in Jake's jeans, boots and short-sleeved polo shirt that may or may not have been clean. Hell, he was a dude. He bathed, put on deodorant and smelled his shirts before he pulled them on.

"I'm not moisturizing."

Hilda laughed. "I see. You like all that maleness, huh?"

"Uh, yeah."

"Okay, so sexy lumberjack." Hilda tapped her chin and stared out into space. She seemed to be serious about the new makeover project. He needed to get away from her. Fast.

"I see my mother. Better say hi." Jake didn't exactly run from Hilda, but he did frighten his mother when he rolled up on her as she was cutting cake in the kitchen.

"Oh, Jake," she said, clutching her chest, nearly dropping the cake she'd been about to place on a plate.

He kissed her cheek. "Hey, Mama."

"Missed you in church this morning," she said. Like she always said. Jake rarely went to church unless it was Christmas or Easter. He was a charter member of the C and E crowd.

"Thanks. Uh, why's Eva in Baton Rouge?"

Fancy shrugged one shoulder. "Well, she had to get some things. Charlie will be here tomorrow."

Charlie? Who the hell was he? Jake racked his brain, trying to remember her mentioning a Charlie. Sounded familiar. Maybe it was an ex-boyfriend? Or a friend who needed a place to crash? "Who's Charlie?"

His mother frowned. "You still don't know about Charlie?"

"Is this some guy she's been seeing? Someone I don't know about?" Jake didn't want the jealousy stealing up his spine to seize him, but it did anyway.

"If you don't know what's going on with Eva, there's a reason. And it's not mine to tell, Jake. Talk to Eva," Fancy said, handing him a plate with cake on it before patting him on the shoulder and walking toward Matt, who sat with his boys at the kitchen table. She put down the cake and pulled out a chair, effectively dismissing her youngest child.

Jake made a grumpy face and stared at the piece of cake she'd handed him before turning and nearly tripping over Clint, who'd rolled up, holding his own piece of cake.

"Who pooped in your punch?" Clint cracked sarcastically.

Jake actually looked down at the glass of punch he held in his other hand. "Nobody. Just trying to figure out what's going on with Eva."

"Eva? Thought you were her biggest confidant," Clint said, his voice holding a trace of...something. Clint and Eva had been spending more time together since she broke up with the cop. She said Clint needed her help to train for an upcoming parasport race, but Jake wondered if there was something more to it.

"Guess not. My mom said a *Charlie* is coming to stay with her."

Clint made a face. "Charlie? Huh. The name sounds familiar. Maybe an old boyfriend?" He didn't look any happier than Jake. Which made Jake wonder again what was going on in that department.

Which was strange, because Eva hanging around his best bud wasn't something new. She'd been dropping by to visit the Cochrans ever since Clint's mother, Ruthie, had passed. Clint's father, Murphy, owned a manufacturing company specializing in tires for construction equipment. At one point Bayou Bengal Tires had supplied most of the Southeast US, but production had fallen off with Clint's health crises and Ruthie's death. Both Murphy and Clint were lonely in the rambling lake house, either sniping at each other or silently resenting each other. Eva's weekly visits to bring muffins or a pie had always been a godsend to Clint. Or at least that's what he said.

Just another reason why kissing Eva had been a bad idea.

"Wanna go out back? It's freezing in here," Clint said, jerking his head toward the back patio, where only a few stragglers sat, one smoking a cigarette, one tapping on his phone. Clint had to reverse his chair a few times to clear the door's threshold, but they eventually made it out into the Louisiana sunshine. Jake felt the sweat break out on his lip after only a few seconds outside.

"So how are things?" Jake asked out of habit.

"Fine." Always Clint's response. Even when things weren't fine. Jake knew this week would be tough. Anniversary of the wreck, anniversary of Angela's death and anniversary of the day everything changed in both their lives. Every year this awkward thing sat between them until eventually they both silently tucked the memories away and soldiered on yet again.

"Good," Jake said, sipping the punch, watching his friend take a few bites of the cake. Clint had added a lot of upper-body bulk, and his movements were more fluid now—a relief, since for a while he'd been unable to use his left arm after the accident. A deep gash had severed a number of nerves in the arm and atrophy had set in, necessitating intensive therapy. Jake looked away. "You watch the LSU game last night?"

"Yeah."

"Looks like we finally got a quarterback."

"He looks good. Uses his legs," Clint said before adding a faux-cheerful, "I remember what that was like."

Wasn't funny. Jake knew it. Clint knew it. The first time Clint had tried to make light of his disability, Jake had nearly choked on his beer before rushing from the table at Ray-Ray's. He'd said he needed a smoke.

Jake rarely smoked anymore, but that night he'd needed something. Something to help him forget that he'd been responsible for all that had happened on that parish back road. Something to make him forget how badly he'd failed his friends. How badly he'd failed himself. The nicotine had soothed him, made his hands steadier. He'd returned to the table where Clint nursed his beer and said, "Don't ever do that again."

And Clint rarely did. But here lately he used jokes about being disabled to needle Jake, to get the opening he needed.

"Don't," Jake said.

Clint set his half-eaten cake on the concrete balustrade of Hilda's elegant patio. "Why not? Shit, I'm tired of tiptoeing around you. Tired of pretending I'm not a damn cripple."

Jake looked down at his friend, his heart aching,

his gut clenched with guilt. Ever-present guilt that never flipping went away. "I know what you are, Clint."

"So you want to carry me around, huh? Just won't effing let it go."

"I don't want to talk about it."

"Ten years, man, and you still can't face the truth. You pretend it away. I know what you do, Jake. I know the reason you pick me up and carry me to Ray-Ray's. It's not so I can drink, man. It's 'cause you like the guilt. But it's a shitty thing, brother. So stop. Okay? Stop making me your albatross."

"I don't," Jake said, even as part of him knew he was lying. He loved Clint. The dude had been his best friend for as long as he remembered, but too often their "guys' night out" approached with a sense of dread these days. For the first few years after the accident, it had been easier, but here lately, Jake couldn't wait to drop Clint back off at his house. Their conversations were stagnant, almost rehearsed, and when he finally lifted Clint from the passenger seat, settling him into his chair in front of the ramp to his house, Jake felt he could finally take a deep breath. Wasn't fair to Clint, but Jake didn't know how to stop it.

"Bullshit. I'm tired of being your burden, and I'm tired of this crappy town." Clint picked up his plate and tossed his half-eaten cake over the rail. Hilda's dog would eat it and probably throw up on her expensive carpet. Jake would have to pick it up after Clint left.

"Yeah, that I get." Jake sighed because that made sense. He felt the same way. Trapped by his decisions from long ago. Like a string stretched tight, he'd begun to fray. Obviously, Clint felt the same way. "So what are you going to do?"

Clint's dark eyes blazed, and for the first time in a while, Jake really looked at his friend. Clint's dark hair was peppered with silver, and his eyes were haunted. His friend looked faded, like an old tattoo. At one time Clint had been a tall, gangly jokester. His full smile, dark wavy hair and pretty brown eyes had driven the girls crazy and had allowed Clint to get away with anything at St. George's Episcopal, where he'd graduated salutatorian to Jake's valedictorian. They'd been partners in crime with devilish charm and extravagant youth on their side.

Until that goddamn night.

"I don't know, but I can't keep pretending things are good anymore. I'm shriveling up." Clint looked down at his useless legs. "Not my body. My soul. I gotta move toward something more. I wish things were…uh." Clint closed his mouth and sat there. Seemingly no words could define what he felt.

Jake wanted to say something profound. He wanted to say that things between them were the same as they'd always been, but he knew that elephant in the room grew bigger. The accident, all that he'd taken from Clint, would always be between them. Jake didn't know how to change that.

So he didn't have words, either. Hell, he didn't have the emotions. He felt an empty shell.

Maybe that's what this whole Eva thing was about—wanting to feel. He was grasping at a way to do that, and Eva was the closest person to grab on to.

Clint looked up at him. Jake met his eyes, trying like hell to communicate something. Anything.

His friend shook his head and then maneuvered his chair, rolling back on the stone patio, heading toward the French doors and the sanctity of a silly birthday party.

Jake stared out at the shadows falling over the still green manicured yard and thought about bumming a cigarette from the produce guy at Maggio's, who stood hidden behind a statue of David. The reproduction sported one notable alteration, and if anyone knew Hilda and her sense of humor, they'd know why she'd added a few inches. The produce guy didn't seem to care. He looked as lonely as Jake felt, so Jake decided not to bother him. Maybe the patio was the perfect spot for lonely losers.

And maybe Jake needed to fix that about himself.

If he needed distraction, if he needed to get his mind off Eva, he needed to be proactive.

One sure way to distract himself was to call Kate. The sexy librarian knew just where to scratch an itch…and she loved to have sex in the stacks after the Magnolia Bend Library closed for the night.

Maybe it was time for Jake to return the last book he'd checked out at the library. And since it was late, he'd have to pay a penalty—a kinky, toe-curling penalty.

He pulled out his cell phone.

Yeah. That would fix things.

Or not.

He looked at his phone, at Kate's number in his contacts, and then tucked the phone back into his pocket. Kate wasn't an answer. She couldn't drive this thing with Eva out of his head.

CHAPTER SEVEN

EVA TOOK CHARLIE'S hand and led him carefully down the steps of the government office building. The Superdome threw its shadow on them as people hurried to and fro on the busy street in the Central Business District of New Orleans.

Chris had just said his goodbyes after Eva signed papers granting her temporary custody of her brother. But Charlie had yet to say a single word to her.

That morning Eva had attended Claren's hearing before the judge. She'd met the foster care worker who'd be monitoring Charlie's case, and she got to thank the temporary foster parents for taking care of her brother. After the judge heard the recommendation of CPS, she was granted physical custody of Charlie. Claren had cried the entire time.

Hadn't been the easiest hour Eva had ever spent.

"It's been a long time since breakfast. Let's grab something to eat. What sounds good to you, Charlie?" she asked, turning toward the large parking garage sitting beside the Civil District Court Building.

Charlie didn't say anything. Just stared straight ahead, his Captain America backpack over one small shoulder.

"Oh, I know," Eva said, forcing cheerfulness into her voice. "How about pizza?"

He gave a noncommittal shrug.

"Okay, pizza it is." Eva tried not to panic at the thought she was now responsible for Charlie...at least until Chris returned from England. But even so, she may not be able to just hand him over to her older brother. And that wouldn't necessarily be fair to Charlie.

His mother would be in court-ordered rehab for eight months since she was a repeat offender...and that was *if* the nutcase stopped fighting against being an addict and started making a true attempt to kick her addiction to the curb. At present Claren was too busy making excuses for her actions.

Eva hated moving Charlie to Magnolia Bend when he'd already started his first grade year at St. Matthew's, but she had no alternative since Chris would be out of the country. And even if he weren't in England, her brother's life was too untethered to give stability to a small child. Claren's parents lived in Ohio and were currently in a senior care facility. They definitely weren't capable of taking care of a six-year-old. So it was either take Charlie in and do the best she could or surrender him to the foster care system. And though the two people she'd met earlier seemed perfectly nice, she thought she could do better than placing him with strangers.

But she wasn't sure.

The foster care worker assigned to Charlie's

case hadn't been keen on Eva taking Charlie so far away from his normal setting, but Eva had been adamant—she'd take care of her brother, but she wasn't moving back to New Orleans. At least in Magnolia Bend she had a support system. Fancy Beauchamp had volunteered to care for Charlie when Eva was on duty and Jake's brother Matt, the principal of St. George's Episcopal, had found a place for Charlie in Mrs. Snyder's first-grade classroom.

When they reached her car, she opened the back door. "I got you a booster seat. Um, I think you're supposed to use one, right?"

Charlie dropped her hand and climbed inside, settling into the booster seat, clicking the seat belt into place. He didn't say a word.

"Okay, then," Eva breathed as she closed the door, making her way around the car, sending up a prayer that she could do this.

Please help me do this. Please help me not screw him up. Please help his dumb-ass mother to get better so she can be the one he goes to therapy to complain about.

Therapy.

The social worker said she'd push through the paperwork necessary to acquire a therapist, but since Magnolia Bend had only one mental health professional, Eva would have to call Macy Hebert at the local women's shelter and see if she could provide what Charlie needed. Obviously, her brother had some issues. The poor thing had been left by himself for almost twenty-four hours while his mother partied, got high and then tried to charge a NOPD undercover vice cop a cool hundred for a blow job.

Her brother had survived on dry cereal, soured milk and the Disney Channel. According to the foster care worker, Charlie had been plagued with nightmares, had wet the bed every night and hadn't talked beyond muttering directives.

Yeah, Eva wasn't equipped to handle a normal kid, much less a kid with emotional trauma.

"Okay, off we go," she said, cranking the engine and eyeing her brother in the rearview mirror. He stared stoically out the window, his sandy-blond hair falling into a perfect bowl cut, his brown eyes so emphatically sad. She knew Charlie had always been a shy child, but he'd always had a smile for his older sister when she came to take him to the zoo or to a movie. They hadn't been close to one another since Claren divorced her father a few months before he'd passed away, but they'd always known they were family and thus fell into an easy way with one another. Not so this go-around. "Why don't we go to a pizza place that has a cool arcade? I like playing skee ball, do you?"

Charlie shrugged but didn't verbally respond.

An hour and a half later, after spending thirty bucks on tokens, watching Charlie pick at his pizza and failing to establish any kind of bond with the six-year-old, Eva drove them to Magnolia Bend. She had a panicky feeling deep inside. It didn't help that she'd spent all of Sunday not just worried about bringing Charlie home, but also anxious over how things between her and Jake had changed so quickly.

She wanted to call him and talk to him about Charlie, and yet she didn't, because she was scared of the feelings unleashed at just the touch of his lips.

Jake had texted her earlier. He had wanted to know who Charlie was. The tinge of jealously in his breezy question might have made her smile if she'd not been so twisted into knots over all the turmoil in her life.

But she'd deal. She always did.

"When is my mom coming to get me?" Charlie asked.

At his sudden question, Eva jerked the steering wheel to keep from going off the highway. "Oh, um, I'm not sure, honey. She's at a place that's helping her get better."

"But she's not sick."

Eva turned her head to look back, not trusting the rearview mirror. Charlie glared at her, anger in his eyes, his mouth pressed into a mulish line. "In a way, she is."

"I don't want to stay with you. I want my mom."

"I know, Charlie."

"I can stay with Chris. I'd rather stay with Chris. He has a dog and lets me eat doughnuts for breakfast."

"Chris is leaving for England next week," Eva

said, trying not to be hurt that Charlie would rather stay with a man than with her. Weren't little kids supposed to gravitate toward women? Maybe her maternal gene was nonexistent. Maybe Charlie had hated every outing they'd taken. Maybe he didn't love her, didn't like her and wouldn't even piss on her if she caught fire.

"Where's England?"

"It's really far away. Look, Charlie, we have to do things this way. You don't want to stay with strangers, do you? And where I live is nice. Remember the fire station and the pancakes we had at PattyAnn's?"

"Yeah, but I don't want to go to a new school. I want to go to St. Matthew's. All my friends are there, and I was going to be on the basketball team."

"You can play basketball in Magnolia Bend if you're still here when it starts. Let's just look at this as an adventure. Like a summer camp…just not in summer."

He shrugged and went back to staring out the window. The exit for Magnolia Bend loomed ahead, and Eva tried not to allow the tears welling in her eyes to slip down her cheeks. She felt overwhelmed, sad and scared for Charlie, and she wished she'd made a stronger effort to get to know her younger brother better.

Her father's final wife, Claren, had not been the easiest person to deal with. Eva would call to make a date to see Charlie, and the woman would drum up some excuse as to why Charlie couldn't go. Eva should have pushed harder to spend time with the boy; she should have paid more attention to Claren and what was going on in her life. She knew she'd had a problem with prescriptive drugs when she'd been with her father. She knew how screwed up Claren was, so she should have realized the woman was using again. God, she'd been buying Oxycontin like it was a grocery item. And the fact that she had been prostituting herself to score the drug was mind-boggling.

Charlie had needed Eva, and she'd been too busy trying to climb the ladder toward captain of the MBFD to notice. She'd been too involved in herself, and now Charlie had to pay for the adults in his life ignoring his needs.

Eva would work to fix it. She'd make sure of that—

"What about my birthday?" Charlie asked.

Oh, snap.

Charlie's birthday was…next week.

"We'll have a party, uh, if you want one. You want one, right?"

The boy shrugged. "Mom said I could have a campout, like with a tent."

"Uh, no problem. We can have a campout in the backyard. We can even roast marshmallows and tell ghost stories."

"But who's gonna come?"

Good question. "I don't know. Yet. But we'll have fun. I promise." God help that to be true.

He fell silent as they wound around through the thick woods surrounding her subdivision. Laurel Creek contained small patio homes built in the Creole cottage style. The development sat behind the grand Laurel Woods, a stately historic house turned into a bed-and-breakfast by Abigail Orgeron. Thick trees and the wildlife that accompanied the woods surrounded her house. Hopefully, Charlie would like the backyard with the squirrel feeder and the room she'd spent all day Sunday decorating with a nautical theme. She'd gone with bright sailboats instead of the predictable fire truck.

"Here we are," she said, pulling into the driveway. Newly purchased ferns swung on the shady porch, and someone had left a bag with a gingham bow on her doorstep.

Charlie unbuckled himself and climbed from the car, his little face grave as he looked over the yard. "I never seen this house before."

"That's because I lived in an apartment the last time you came to Magnolia Bend. I just moved here in the spring. Do you like it?" she asked, proud of the tended flower beds and pretty stacked-stone columns.

"It's fine," he muttered.

She ignored his less than enthusiastic response. "And someone left us…oh, dinner." She lifted the bag filled with storage containers that were still warm. Looked like spaghetti, French bread and salad. Had to be Fancy's handiwork.

"I'm not hungry."

"Yet," she said, giving him a cheery smile while she unlocked the door. Charlie carried a backpack with his underwear, socks and a change of clothes. Thankfully, the social worker had emailed her the sizes she'd found in Charlie's closet, so Eva had picked up some new jeans, shirts and a spare pair of sneakers for her brother. Fancy had already put in an order for the St. George's uniforms, borrowing a few items that had grown too small for Matt's two boys.

Eva pushed open the door and looked back at Charlie, who moved at a snail's pace up the walk. Just as he finally stepped onto the porch, Jake pulled into the drive.

He drove a red Chevrolet Silverado, sports package with flashy chrome and a fresh wax job. Firemen had a thing about polished chrome and shiny trucks. Jake hopped out, jogging around the side, only to come to a halt when he saw Charlie standing next to Eva.

"Hey," Jake said cautiously, still eye-balling Charlie.

"Hi," Eva said, not knowing whether to be aggravated Jake had poked his nose into her business or relieved to have someone else there to serve as a distraction. Either way, Jake looked especially gorgeous in the dying light of day, so that was something.

"Who's this?"

"I'm Charlie. Who are you?" her brother said, looking interested in the man standing at the foot of the step, trim and hunky in his uniform.

"This is Charlie?" Jake asked, lifting his gaze to hers.

"My younger brother," Eva said, placing a hand on her brother's shoulder. Charlie stepped away, his eyes still on Jake.

"Oh, the third wife's kid. That's right. I didn't remember his name."

"Who are *you*?" Charlie asked again.

"This is Jake. We work together," Eva said.

"You're a firefighter?" Charlie asked.

Jake nodded and gave Charlie a smile. Sticking out his hand, he made a fist. Charlie responded with a fist bump—a male ritual even a six-year-old obviously understood.

"What are you doing here?" Eva asked Jake.

"I'm on my way to work. Just thought I'd check on you," he said.

Eva made a face. Jake never checked on her. She had a sneaking suspicion it had to do with the previously unknown Charlie. Just why Jake was so intrigued baffled her, even as something deep down inside lifted its head at the thought Jake might be interested in her life because she was more to him than a mere friend.

Maybe she wasn't the only one affected by the kiss. Maybe…

No.

She didn't have the luxury to entertain anything different than what was. She and Jake were coworkers. They were friends. Nothing more. So she had to stop reading into every action Jake took.

"Well, do you want to come in? Looks like your mama left us dinner. Spaghetti."

"Nah, I had some at her house earlier. I need to get to the station and now that I can see you're okay..." He trailed off.

"Why wouldn't I be?"

"I don't know. You know. Just things."

Yeah, she knew. He thought she was still mad about the kiss. He wanted her to forgive him. "I'm fine."

His blue eyes met hers and something passed between them, reminding her she was a liar. She wasn't fine. Things weren't the same.

Two kisses had changed everything.

"Okay, then. I'll miss you tonight."

That should have sounded the way it sounded anytime Eva switched a shift and Jake bitched and moaned about having to put up with Dutch's snoring and blistering farts. *Don't leave me with Dutch. I'll miss you.*

But this time it sounded intimate.

So weird.

"Don't worry, Dutch will keep you warm. His wife always cooks red beans and rice on the second Sunday of the month," Eva joked, trying to regain their easy camaraderie. Trying to go backward had become a habit. But she had to try.

Jake made a face. "I'm letting him sleep in your room."

"Don't you dare," Eva said.

"Wait, is he your boyfriend?" Charlie asked, pointing to Jake.

"No!" they both said in unison.

Charlie looked from her to Jake and then back to her. "Can I go watch TV?"

"Sure, the remote's on the coffee table," Eva said, nudging the door open with her foot. Charlie slipped inside.

"I gotta run," Jake said, his eyes sliding away, something in his expression bordering on embarrassment. It was a characteristic rarely seen in the overconfident man.

"Okay."

Jake started toward his truck but then turned. "Hey, E."

She lifted her eyebrows.

"I want to help you. Uh, be there for you. I don't know what's going on in your life, with Charlie and all, but you're my friend."

"I know I am."

"You'll always be my friend, even when you're pissed at me or things are weird. Okay?"

"Okay."

"So what can I do?"

Eva hadn't a clue. At this point with a damaged

Charlie under her care and the whole attraction thing for Jake busted wide open, she wasn't sure she needed Jake around. "I don't know."

"Just give me something, anything I can do to make up for the jackass I've been."

"You don't have to do anything. All that…strange stuff between us was just temporary insanity. We're good. You don't owe me anything."

He crossed his arms.

"Okay. Fine. How about you come over Friday night? Charlie could use a guy around. He's been a little light on male influence in his life…unless Claren had someone around I didn't know about. Which could have happened and scares me to death."

Jake crooked his eyebrow questioningly.

She just shook her head. *You don't want to know.*

"I can do that," he said. "What time?"

"Around six thirty okay?"

Jake nodded.

Eva watched him climb into his truck, offering a wave as he backed out. She'd planned to tell Jamison she couldn't go out with him Friday night, but since Jake had volunteered to help, he could stay with Charlie.

But then again, maybe she should cancel with Jamison.

But if she did, then the doctor would think she wasn't interested. To be honest, she wasn't sure if she was. Jamison was nice, but almost too nice. Still, he kept her focused on something else besides Jake and the Texas-sized torch she carried for him. Dating Jamison made her look less interested, less desperate for the warmth of a certain hot-as-hell firefighter.

"Eva!" Charlie called.

She jerked her thoughts off the men in her life… well, sorta in her life…and went in to the male who'd be the center of her world for at least the next few months.

Charlie sat on the couch, frowning at the TV. Eva glanced at the screen and nearly screamed. Two naked people rolled around in bed.

"I can't get this to work. I wanna watch Nickelodeon."

Eva jerked the control out of his hand, fumbling for the button that would turn the channel.

Where was the damn guide button?

"What are those two people doing with their clothes off?"

"Nothing," she moaned, jabbing at the off button but missing and hitting the menu button. The screen shrank, but the two actors were still moaning and saying really, really inappropriate things.

"Is he hurting her?" Charlie asked, scooting forward and squinting at the left corner where some actress was pretending to have an orgasm. "She sure is screaming."

Eva ignored his question, finally hitting the correct button. The TV went dark. "There."

"You turned it off," he said, looking at her as if she'd stomped on a baby bird or something.

"Yes, because I wanted to show you around. I fixed up your room and bought you some new jeans and stuff. Don't you want to come see?"

He made a face. "All you bought was clothes?"

"And some books," she offered.

"Books?" he repeated, wrinkling his nose.

Eva sighed and set the remote on the table. In the span of an hour Charlie had gone from the walking wounded to an irritable kid...who had questions about sex.

And she was *so* not going there.

"You know what?" Eva asked. "Why don't you...ah...go wash your hands and check out your room while I heat up dinner and fix the TV?"

Charlie shrugged, grabbed his backpack and started for the hallway. Eva clicked the TV back on only to see the two actors kicked back in bed, twisted in the sheets, looking sweaty and satisfied. She found the parental controls on the menu and quickly set them so Charlie didn't have to see people getting their heads blown off or some random actress *getting* off with—Eva squinted her eyes to identify the actor—Richard Gere.

"Yep, until Charlie leaves, no one is getting any," she told the actress snuggling into Richard Gere and looking up at him with a dopey smile. "Especially me."

CHAPTER EIGHT

JAKE FLIPPED DOWN the mirror in the truck and ran a hand through his hair, checking his teeth for any pieces of lettuce left over from his lunch with his sister. Abigail ate like a damn rabbit and had only prepared a large chef salad for them to share. He'd had to eat three servings, but still it was nice to see his sister and visit with Birdie, who had just started eighth grade at St. George's. He could hardly believe how fast his niece had grown into a full-fledged teenager.

He popped a breath mint and then shook his head. Hell, why was he acting as if this was a date?

Eva was Eva.

Besides, he was just coming by to hang out with her and Charlie. After several days cooped up with her brother, he suspected his good friend needed a break. Their one conversation a few days ago had indicated she had her hands full. So far she'd taken Charlie to the doctor for his immunizations, which required a trip for ice cream afterward, to the dentist for a cleaning, which meant a small filling... and tears, and had visited St. George's Episcopal, which was declared a dumb school. Eva had also said

Charlie wet the bed every night, which necessitated lots of laundry and resulted in a lack of sleep.

So Jake was there to help out, provide distraction, change lightbulbs… Whatever she needed.

'Cause that was what good friends did for one another.

They were not, however, supposed to trim their toenails, pop breath mints or take care to wear a shirt that complemented their eyes. That was what a date did. And this was not a date.

Jake set the roll of mints back in the ashtray and climbed out. The days were growing shorter and cooler as October rolled in, which was a relief for the summer-weary residents. Jake was tired of working up a sweat by just getting out of his vehicle.

Jogging up the steps, he pressed the doorbell.

Charlie answered. "Oh, it's you."

Jake smiled. "Who were you expecting?"

"The doctor guy." Charlie stepped back and let Jake inside. The normally neat living room looked as if a storm had hit, tossing blankets, toys and empty soda cans around the room.

"The doctor guy?" Jake said, picking up a blanket and lifting a diet soda can off the coffee table. "Are you drinking this?"

Charlie looked guiltily at the can. "Well, I found them in the back of the fridge. They aren't as good as orange soda, but I'm sick of water and milk."

"Where's Eva?"

"She's in her room getting ready. She takes really long showers."

"What are all these blankets doing out?" Jake asked, folding the one in his hand.

"I'm building a tent. My birthday's next weekend, and Eva said we'd have a campout in her backyard. I'm practicing. See? I used these chairs and put the blankets on top of them. It doesn't make a good tent, though." The little boy shook his head at the chair with the blanket hanging from its back.

Jake set the folded blanket on the couch just as Eva emerged from her bedroom, wearing a dress and pulling a shoe on her right foot. She stood, her eyes growing wide at the disaster of her living room. "What did you do, Charlie?"

"I built the tent. You said I could."

"Well, you need to pick all this up," she said, taking an earring from her palm and threading it into her earlobe. Her gaze rose and she finally saw him. "Oh, Jake, you're here. Good."

Good?

Jake stared at Eva, who was way overdressed for hanging out. The dress she wore hugged her generous curves, and her hair fell in soft waves onto her shoulders. She secured the other earring before running fingers through her pretty curls.

"You look nice," Jake said, still feeling totally confused.

"Thank you," she said, moving into the kitchen,

peeking through the open area over the bar. "Now, I've left some dinner in the oven."

"Yuck!" Charlie screeched.

Eva shot him a withering look. "I didn't make it. Jake's mom did. Wait, did you drink soda, Charlie?"

Charlie plopped down on the hardwood floor and started moving his trucks around, making *vroom* noises, shutting Eva out.

"Oh, my gosh, how many did he drink?" she asked Jake, pulling a notepad from beside the cordless phone.

Jake looked around. "Uh, two? No. Three?"

"Jeez." Eva sighed, scratching something on the pad with a pen. "Now, you have my number. I'm just setting his medication right here beside the coffeemaker. He needs one antibiotic with his dinner."

"Wait, are you leaving?"

She looked up at him. "Yeah. I have a date."

A date? Jake shook his head like a cartoon character. What the... "A date?"

"With Jamison. You volunteered to come tonight to babysit Charlie. Remember?"

Something hot and almost viscous blanketed him. Eva was going out with Mr. Stuffy Pants and leaving him here with Charlie?

Bull to the shit.

"I didn't volunteer to *babysit*," he said, glancing over at Charlie. "I thought you wanted to hang out."

She tilted her head in an adorable way. Well, it would have been adorable, if he hadn't been so absolutely pissed at the moment. Then she twisted those delectable lips. "Oh, well, I suppose I didn't actually mention babysitting. I didn't realize. Sorry. But I have a date and you were so kind to correct being a jackass…"

Jake folded his arms. "I don't know what to do with a kid, and should you be leaving him like this? I mean, it's sorta selfish to go out on a date when your brother is still trying to adjust."

Eva's eyes crackled. "Selfish? Are you joking?"

Jake lifted a shoulder. "I'm just saying."

Eva stalked around, entering the living room, coming to a halt, putting her hands on her hips. She looked pissed, and Jake wondered if he shouldn't have kept his mouth shut.

"What's selfish about it, jackass?" Eva asked.

"Oooh, you used a bad word, Eva," Charlie said.

"Oh, so now you can hear me?" Eva drawled at Charlie, tempering her look at him with a slight smile. The kid turned back to his trucks, and Eva zipped her gaze back to Jake, making him feel squirmy.

"Maybe I shouldn't have said selfish per se," Jake said, putting the coffee table between them. "I just wondered if it was good for you to leave since he's having some difficulty adjusting."

"Charlie, is it okay if I leave you for a few hours to go to dinner while you play trucks and watch *Finding Nemo* with Jake?"

"Sure," Charlie said, making the dump truck climb the side of the TV cabinet.

"See? He's fine. If you want me to pay you, I will," Eva said, turning and grabbing her purse off the top of the piano.

"No," Jake said, realizing that he was good and stuck.

The doorbell rang.

"That should be Jamison."

Jake wanted to answer the door, punch the too-good-looking doctor in the mug and close the door, locking Eva inside with him. But that would be crazy. That would mean he felt something more than friendship for Eva. And he didn't.

Or at least he didn't want to.

Eva opened the door and pasted on a smile he'd never seen before. He assumed it was her "date" smile. He fisted his hands and stared at the coffee table littered with parenting magazines.

"Hey, you," Eva said to Jamison.

"You look incredible, Eva," Jamison said.

Jake clenched his teeth.

"Thank you. And you clean up pretty nicely, too," she said before turning to Jake. "So dinner is warming in the oven. Don't let Charlie have anything else to drink tonight. Please."

Jake nodded but didn't look at her. He didn't want to notice how damn beautiful she looked for Jamison French, MD, resident prissy-pants dork.

"And Charlie," Eva said, waiting on her brother to

look up at her. "You mind Jake…and get this mess picked up before bedtime, which is nine thirty."

"Nine thirty?" Charlie squealed, bobbing up and down in excitement.

"Well, it *is* Friday night," Eva said.

"You'll be home by then, right?" Jake asked.

Eva cast a flirty look at Jamison and then smiled. "Maybe."

Jake frowned, knowing he looked like a spoiled little boy but unable to stop himself.

"Bye, boys," Eva called, stepping out the door.

The sound of the door shutting felt like a sucker punch.

"Damn it," Jake said under his breath.

Charlie looked up. "That's a really bad word."

"There are worse, trust me," Jake said, sinking onto the couch, pulling a superhero figurine from under his left butt cheek. "So what do you want to do?"

"Dunno. I guess you can play trucks with me. I'll let you be the Marsh Monster."

"Negative."

"What's that mean?" Charlie asked.

"It means try again."

"You can help me build a tent."

Jake considered that. He had a tent at his place, but he didn't want to take Charlie across town for a tent. He reached for his phone and dialed his brother Matt.

"What's up?" Matt said.

"Your boys with you this weekend?"

"Yeah."

"What are y'all doing?"

"We're about to head to the St. George's football game."

"Perfect."

"For what?" Matt asked.

"For me to come with you. I'm watching Charlie for Eva and since he'll be going to school with your boys, maybe it would be cool to hang out."

"Sure, the Dragons are playing the Acadiana Tigers. Should be a good game."

"See you in half an hour at the stadium."

He hung up and looked at Charlie, who'd been watching him with a puzzled expression. "So do you like football?"

"Like the Saints?"

"Not the same level, but yeah."

Charlie smiled and nodded his entire body. Jake hadn't realized such a thing was possible, but the excitement in the child's eyes tempered his anger at Eva. And he wasn't sure if the anger was over being suckered into babysitting or that she was going out with another guy…an accomplished, rich guy with the nickname around town of "Hot Doc."

"Then let's get this living room picked up, eat a quick bite and go watch some football like real dudes do," Jake said, extending his fist.

Charlie scrambled to his feet, gave him some dap and said, "Hell, yeah."

Jake laughed but then said, "Don't say that again. Eva will kill me."

"No, she won't," Charlie said gravely. "I heard her saying bad words all week. She burned my waffles and said a really, really bad word."

"Yeah, but still. Let's keep the naughty words to ourselves."

"Okay. I gotta go pee."

"Have at it," Jake said, rising and tidying up the coffee table and folding the remaining blankets before heading to the kitchen. He looked over at the note Eva had left along with the medicine and tried not to be mad at his friend.

Yes, *friend.*

Even if he wanted to punch Jamison, yank Eva toward him and drag her off to his cave. That was a primitive, natural instinct. He'd probably feel a little that way about his sister. Okay. No. He didn't feel that way about Abigail at all. Maybe it was because he cherished Eva's friendship so much, and everyone knew that Jamison French was a womanizer. Okay. So he wasn't a womanizer, but the man didn't stick with any particular woman. He could hurt Eva, fooling her with his slick manners and witty intellect, making her think he had forever on his mind when all he wanted…

Okay, Jake had to stop thinking about Eva.

"Come on, Charlie," he called.

The kid slid on his socks into the kitchen. "What?"

"Let's eat."

Jake dished up the chicken and rice casserole his mother had fixed. It was obvious Fancy was in "helpful mom" mode with Eva. When he'd dropped by yesterday, she'd been making the casserole for today and said she'd already sent spaghetti and a chicken enchilada casserole. Nothing like a friend in need to get his mother cooking…and he'd gladly clean up the leftovers.

After a quick meal and even quicker cleanup, he wiped Charlie's face, proud of himself for thinking of it, and they loaded up to head to the game. Jake had never actually babysat before, but he even remembered to grab the booster seat. Maybe he should make Eva pay him for babysitting. He had mad child-care skills.

They made it to the game three minutes into the first quarter. Matt, his boys and Jake's father occupied their normal seats, and thankfully it didn't take Charlie long to bond with Matt's son Wyatt. Wyatt would be only a grade ahead of Charlie, and they both seemed to like something called Minecraft.

By the end of the game, Charlie had gone from reserved to bouncing off the walls. It might have had something to do with the candy and soda Jake's dad had bought all the boys. But the upside was the Dragons had pulled out a win in the last few seconds of the game, nailing a field goal from forty-four yards. The home side of the stadium had erupted into cheers, and the band had cranked up an old MC

Hammer tune that had the three boys writhing, hopping and jumping off the bleachers.

"Whoa," Jake said, catching Charlie in midair. "I have to take you home all in one piece."

"I don't wanna go back to Eva's yet. This was fun," Charlie said, twisting away and running behind Wyatt, who was jumping up and down the stadium steps.

"Jeez, it's nearly eleven o'clock," Matt said, ruffling his older son, William's, hair.

"Oh, crap," Jake said, digging into his pocket for his cell phone.

Yep.

Eva had called eight times and sent several texts.

Where are you?

Answer the phone, damn it!

I'm freaking out!

So maybe he wouldn't win awards for his babysitting skills.

Jake dialed Eva's number, sending up a prayer that she hadn't called the po-po yet.

"Where in the hell are you? Where's Charlie?" were her first words.

"Calm down," Jake said, belatedly realizing those weren't good words to ever say to a woman. "He's fine. We went to the high school football game with Matt and his boys."

"And you didn't think to text me and let me know? Or ask me? You should have asked. Jesus, Jake, I should have known not to leave him with you. You're irresponsible and thoughtless."

"I can't believe you just said that. I gave up my Friday night to babysit your brother."

"You volunteered."

"Not for that."

"Look, the point is you should have let me know you were going somewhere. I got here and found the lights on and y'all gone. It scared me to death."

"So I forgot to switch off the light and text you. Doesn't give you the right to paint me into some loser who can't take care of a kid. He's fine. He's having fun."

Silence.

Jake had never gotten mad at Eva before. No reason to. But she was acting like his mother, bossing him around, not even appreciative that he'd stayed with Charlie while she went on a date with a total tool. "Oh, and guess what else. He had a Coke and some Skittles. Good luck with that." He pressed End feeling a little childish, a little angry and a lot confused over what he felt for his gorgeous friend.

He'd never felt so ruffled, so lacking, so totally turned around before.

And it was all Eva's fault.

She'd kissed him and changed everything.

CHAPTER NINE

Eva GLANCED UP from her position sprawled on the couch as headlights swept across the living room.

Jake had returned with her brother.

She took a last swig of the wine she'd poured herself to calm her trembling nerves.

Her date with Jamison had been a much-needed break after a trying week. He had put the top down on his sleek convertible as they headed up I-10 toward Baton Rouge. The stars had twinkled appropriately, and the bright moon had hung low in the sky, a spotlight on the busy city. They'd gone to an Asian restaurant, drank saki and ate fabulous sushi. After dinner Jamison had pulled off at the University Lakes and they'd taken a walk. The night had been intimate and beautiful. Jamison had held her hand and even pulled her in for a soft kiss.

She should have been glowing, but she wasn't.

The whole *no Jake, no Charlie* thing when she'd come in from the almost obligatory good-night kiss and promise to call had thrown her into a tailspin.

She'd panicked, plain and simple.

A million different scenarios had streaked through her mind, starting with the notion Jake and Charlie had walked the path to visit Abigail at Laurel

Woods, progressing rapidly to kidnapping and possible murder. Of course, she knew she was being ridiculous jumping to that conclusion. After all, Jake's
truck was absent from the drive, and even though
she watched a lot of *CSI*, she wasn't a moron. Still,
she'd never had to worry about anyone else but herself before. Even though it had been a rough week
with Charlie, she knew the bonds between them had
strengthened. Nightmares and tears at two o'clock in
the morning tended to do things like that.

The door burst open and Charlie bounced in.
"Hey, Eva, guess what? We went to the football
game and our team won!"

"Did you now?" she said, pushing off from the
couch and standing. She felt a bit woozy. Maybe the
two glasses of wine she'd had with dinner paired
with the big glass she'd poured to still her nerves had
given her a buzz. But she'd needed that last glass.

She'd been so scared.

Somehow her once easy life had gotten cluttered
with feelings she'd previously ignored or never knew
existed. She'd never felt protective of anyone before…and she'd never felt so vulnerable around Jake,
either.

"Yeah, it was so much fun. Jake let me sit with
the big boys, and his daddy bought me some candy.
Oh, and there was an army tank there. Can you believe that? A tank!" Charlie prattled as he toed off
his sneakers and left them in the middle of her soft
shag rug.

Jake pushed in, and instead of looking sheepish and apologetic, he looked fierce. On one hand it was sexy as hell; on the other, it gave her reservations about her earlier bitchiness.

"Hey," she said to Jake, watching Charlie as he pulled off his T-shirt. The kid didn't like being dressed, preferring to wear only the Transformer boxers she'd bought him—reminding her just how little she knew about little boys.

"Hey," Jake replied, parking his fists on his hips, broadening his shoulders.

"Charlie seems to have had fun tonight."

"Yeah, he did," Jake said.

"I shouldn't have yelled at you," she said, wishing instantly she'd kept quiet. Better to have ignored her whole outburst. Panicking was so not like her. Eva was even-keeled, dependable, emotionless.

"No, but I should have remembered to text you," Jake conceded.

Charlie looked up from the floor. He'd plopped down and was in the process of pulling off his jeans. "You were mad, Eva? Why?"

"I'm not mad, but I will be if you don't pick up your clothes and place them in the laundry hamper in the bathroom. Remember what we talked about?"

"Yeah, yeah." Charlie sighed. He sounded much beleaguered for a six-year-old. "I'll feed the hamper."

"Oh, and your toothbrush is waiting. No running water over it."

"I know, I know," her brother said, his shoulders slumping. "You sure know how to turn fun upside down."

Eva tried not to smile, but her lips tugged themselves upward. Dang, Charlie was cute. Not so much at two o'clock in the morning when he was covered in urine and crying for Claren, but at that moment her heart played patty-cake.

"What do you say to Jake?" she called.

Charlie turned. "Thank you, Jake."

"No problem, buddy. It was a great night."

"It sure was," Charlie said, giving Jake a wave and heading into the recesses of the hallway.

Eva turned back to Jake. "Thank you."

"Why were you so scared? You're never scared."

"Sometimes I am. I'm just good at hiding it." Uncharted territory again. She didn't talk to Jake about feelings. They talked about baseball, the sales at Maggio's Market and the funny things Hilda did in her new job as Chamber of Commerce president. They never talked about being scared...being lonely...being vulnerable.

Jake dropped his defensive stance, moving closer to her. "I'm not an imbecile. I can take care of a kid for a few hours. Surely you trust me to do that?"

"Of course. I wouldn't have left him with you otherwise."

"So why were you so pissed?"

Eva didn't want to analyze her rampaging feelings. PMS had to be playing footsie with her or something. She'd nearly cried on Monday, and now she felt as if she was drowning in emotion. Her life was unraveling at an alarming rate. She needed to get traction. She had to stop thinking about Jake and the way his lips felt on hers, the way his hard chest brushed her breasts, inflaming her. "I don't know why."

"Look, Eva, I don't like the way things have been between us. It's just not cool."

"I know."

They studied each other, a few seconds ticking by.

"How do we fix this?" he asked finally.

"I don't know. Maybe stop thinking so much about...you know."

Jake lifted a shoulder. "Maybe so."

She nodded, as if it was that simple. As *if* she could stop thinking about Jake. She'd tried that for the past three years to no avail. He was like the plague, sticking to her, surrounding her with his damn masculinity, with the adorable way he scratched his head when he stood in front of the fridge at the firehouse, trying to decide between diet soda or iced tea, with the way he fed the little sparrows crumbs of his sandwich on the doorstep of the firehouse. Sure, she'd stop thinking about how she loved Jake. Easy peasy.

"I should probably go," he said.

"Do you want me to pay you?"

"No." He looked insulted.

"At least reimburse the price of the football ticket?"

"I'm not rolling in the dough, but I can swing a

ticket to a high school football game." He opened the door, stepping out onto the moonlit porch. Eva followed like a good hostess, like a parent sending off the babysitter…like a woman who enjoyed the backside of a certain sexy firefighter.

"Well, good night," she said, lowering her voice in the intimacy of the inky night. The darkness was soft, the way Southern nights often were. Crickets chirped a lullaby.

"Good night, Eva," he said, setting a hand high on the stacked-stone column, staring out at the lawn coated in moonlight.

She waited a few seconds. "Jake?"

"Thing is, it isn't so easy to stop thinking about it."

"It?" she asked, feigning ignorance.

"The kiss."

"Which one?"

He gave a small laugh. "The last one."

The one that had pooled hot, wet desire in her stomach, the one that had smacked through her thinly built wall of immunity to his charms like a toddler knocking down a block castle. His kiss had opened the floodgates of all that she felt for him.

"We said…" She trailed off because they'd already beaten a dead horse with what they should do. *Doing* it was the problem. Staying away from each other, trying to go back to normal, pretending the kiss hadn't happened, wasn't working.

He studied her. "Why can't I stop seeing you in a different light? You're killing me, Eva. You really, really are."

And then he walked back to her, sliding a hand to her face. "You're so beautiful. You've always been pretty. I knew that from day one, but now…now you're like something that needs to be touched." His fingers brushed back her hair, turning so his knuckles bussed her cheek.

"Jake."

"Yeah, and my name on your lips sounds so different now. Like sex. My name on your lips sounds like sex."

Eva inhaled sharply, sucking in the smell of this man she wanted so damn badly. Her pulse skidded out of control, and that age-old need to be claimed flooded her, wiping away intentions. "Jake."

"Exactly," he said, lowering his head.

She rose on her toes, and their lips met.

And this time it wasn't about her kissing him or him kissing her.

This time they kissed each other.

JAKE HADN'T MEANT to kiss Eva.

But once his lips touched hers, he was lost. He'd never imagined she could taste so good, that she could feel so right pressed against him. But now that she was there, he couldn't stop himself from touching her, kissing her, wanting her.

Eva sighed, her arms brushing his waist, fluttering against his biceps as he slid his tongue into the warmth of her mouth. She tasted of wine and warm Eva. Totally addictive.

He nudged her backward so that she pressed into the side of her house, grunting in satisfaction when his body connected with her softness.

And she was so soft.

Tough Eva with her swaggering, trash-talking fearlessness was satin to his steel. Like a song. Like a woman should be.

Lifting a hand, he brushed her cheek, cupping her jaw, angling her head so he could deepen the kiss. At the same time he ran his other hand down the silky material of her dress, savoring the curves. The hemline was short, and the warm thigh beneath firm.

He raised his hand slightly, cupping the back of her leg, sliding up until he touched the lace of her panties.

"Mmm," Eva said, her hands plunging into his hair, holding him fast to her. She writhed against him, and he loved how responsive she was.

Of course she'd meet him toe to toe.

This was Eva.

This…was…oh, shit.

He broke the kiss, dropping the hand he'd been about to slide beneath the leg of her postage-stamp-sized panties.

This was his friend…not a hookup.

His breath came fast and beneath the weathered denim, he was hard as a poker. Ready to go.

"Shit, I'm sorry. I didn't mean to do that. I just… shit."

Eva looked up, eyes dilated, flushed. "You're sorry?"

"Yeah, I shouldn't have—"

"Why in the hell would *you* be sorry?" she interrupted, her frown resembling a child whose lollipop had been taken. "You think *you* were responsible for that? Like you're the only one who wanted something more? Screw that."

She jerked him by the belt back to her, grabbed his head and tugged it down, her lips meeting his once again.

Eva kissed like she did everything—well. His body, still amped from the first kiss, hummed with the rightness.

This couldn't be wrong.

Not when it felt so right.

"Oh, sweet…mmm," he groaned into her mouth, gathering her to him once again. He pulled his lips from hers, moving his mouth down the column of her throat, inhaling the sweet spiciness that was Eva. His hand curved against her ass, lifting her against him, increasing the friction between his hardness and her soft places.

"What're you doing?"

The words slammed against them, making Eva rigid.

Jake looked up to find Charlie standing at the door, clad in his pajamas, watching them intensely.

Eva pushed against his chest and he stepped back.

"Charlie," Eva said, tucking a piece of hair behind her ear. "What are you doing out here?"

"Looking for you." He said it with an unstated "duh."

"Oh," Eva said lamely.

"You and Jake looked like those people on TV. Remember?"

"Uh, yeah. No. We're not like those people."

Charlie nodded. "They were wrestling and kissing in bed."

If it hadn't been so tense, Jake might have laughed. Jeez. Kids.

"Uh, look, go back inside and get in bed. We'll read about the dump trucks and cranes again."

Charlie looked at Jake. "You just kissed Eva. Does that mean you're gonna get married or something?"

"You don't have to marry someone to kiss them," Jake said.

Eva started coughing…or maybe she was choking.

"Uh-huh, people kiss when they're married," Charlie said.

"In my observation they stop kissing when they get married," Jake cracked, trying to bring some humor to the situation. He wanted Eva to look at him, to not seem so horrified to have made out with him on her front porch.

"Nuh-uh," Charlie said, shaking his head. "You have to kiss girls when you marry them. I seen it on TV. And my daddy kissed my mom when they got married. I got a picture of them doing that."

Jake realized he was losing this conversation.

"Charlie," Eva said, clapping her hands. "Bed. Now."

"Okay," he said, slipping back into the house, the door closing with a snick.

"Jesus," Eva breathed, lifting a shaking hand to her face.

"He's funny."

"That wasn't funny. It was horrifying. What person loses her head that way?"

"Someone who's turned on," Jake said, moving toward her. He put a hand on her shoulder.

"Don't," she said, shrugging away his touch. "You can't. It's too much. We can't do this. Jesus, what's wrong with us?"

He shrugged. He didn't know. Why was Eva suddenly on his radar…in a way she didn't need to be?

Could be dissatisfaction with his life. Could be he was horny. Could be he was crazy as a… He couldn't think of something crazy enough to justify nearly sliding his hand into Eva's panties.

And, damn it, he'd really wanted to slide his hand beneath those tiny lace panties.

"We can't ever do that again," she said, crossing

her arms as if she could protect herself from him. As if that would work. "We work together. We're friends."

"Yeah. Of course," he said. What else could he say? She was right. He didn't even know if there were restrictions on dating within the department. Never had to worry about that with an all-male team. And even if it didn't violate policy, was it a good idea? Couldn't be. He couldn't fathom working beside the person he'd slept with the night before.

He swallowed at the thought of sleeping with Eva.

God help him, but he wanted her. All of her. Beneath him, around him, on top of him. On the bed. In the shower. Bent over the kitchen counter. All of her.

But he wouldn't, couldn't, shouldn't let it happen. Bad, bad idea.

"So we're making a...pact? No more kisses," Eva said.

He nodded. "Yeah. I mean no. No more kissing."

"Good."

"I should go."

"Yeah," she said, looking out at his truck parked in the drive and then back at the door she'd closed. "I'll see you on Tuesday."

"You'll be in?"

"Yeah. Your mother's letting Charlie stay with her when I'm on. She's a lifesaver."

"She is," Jake agreed, moving down the steps, his ardor cooling in the night, cloaking him. "See you."

"See you," she said with a wave.

He climbed into his truck as she slipped back into the house, turning on the porch light.

Jake set his head against the steering wheel and took a deep breath, closing his eyes. Every fiber in his body demanded he climb his ass out of the truck, trot up those steps and make Eva let him back inside.

Had to be the frustration he'd been feeling lately. He'd lived with his decision to stay in Magnolia Bend and be Jake the Firefighter for ten long years. So what had changed? Why did he hate his life? Why did the town he loved feel so oppressive now?

Some of it was Clint and the past that kept rearing its ugly head. His friend had pulled himself out of the deep depression he'd fallen into after the death of his mother, who, unlike his father, had always given him confidence that he could achieve a normal life. Clint had started working out and participating in local parasport races. His friend had even mentioned working on his MBA and started the process of applying for grad school. Instead of bellyaching or resigning himself to fate, Clint made it clear he was getting out. His friend had made the leap over his disabled state. And though it had taken a lot of time, therapy and work, Clint was managing to do what Jake could not—give himself a spot to land on the other side.

Jake was still mired in guilt, caked in complacency.

And he hated himself for not knowing what to do about it.

Christ, he felt like a pansy-ass, scared to move beyond what he'd decided long ago. Was it so hard to tell Clint and everyone in his life that he was done with the sentence he'd given himself? That he'd done his time, atoning for all he had taken away from Clint. From Angela's family. Christ, even Angela's parents had left Magnolia Bend. They'd done what Jake couldn't seem to do—move on.

So Jake was near to certain that's why this crazy attraction for Eva had appeared. She was a distraction from what he really needed to do—make a move in some direction. He couldn't keep treading water, pretending happiness when he despised where he was, who he was. And he couldn't use Eva to fill the emptiness, to counter the failure of his life with the comfort she could no doubt give him. But attributing a reason for his desire for Eva didn't make him stop wanting her.

But she was right. They couldn't let themselves fold to desire. That was how perfectly good friendships failed.

So where did that leave him?

How would he fight against this crazy desire to be with her?

He started the truck and backed out, pointing it in the opposite direction of his house. Usually a cold beer and a hot woman could do a lot to distract him. That was how he'd made it through the past ten years of his life—being the great pretender. But he didn't want either tonight.

Just like always, Jakey. Do the things you've always done. Don the man you've always been. Life's a helluva a lot easier when you don't have to show the tears and fears...or the fact you want to bone your best friend. Pack a bag and find a new life.

CHAPTER TEN

Eva HAD DREADED coming into the fire station for three days, but surprisingly the first few hours back at work were pleasant...mostly because Jake wasn't there. He'd volunteered to make a run to the grocery for supplies, not meeting her eyes, causing Dutch to lift his brows with an unstated question. It was fairly obvious that Jake, who hated going to Maggio's, was avoiding her.

And when he came back laden with grocery bags, she returned the favor by burying her head in the fridge, cleaning out spoiled foods and expired salad dressings. After sponging down all the shelves and restocking, she stepped over Dutch's long outstretched legs and headed to the office to file the stack of papers the chief had left sitting on the messy desk.

Idle hands are the devil's playthings.

And she needed to stay away from the devil.

Her father used to say that, sending her out the back door into the jungle of their Metairie home to play. Eva had always loved her backyard, with the wooden playset her father had built her and the high wood fence covered with morning glory. Fat trees provided shade and pretend houses for the imaginative girl who had chestnut curls, dimples and loved fluffy costume dresses. Eva had been the quintessential girly-girl, with a streak of tomboy. Her daddy had doted on her...until he left.

Charles Evan Monroe hadn't been the easiest of men to live with. Being the chief of a New Orleans fire district meant he worked long hours. He missed family meals, birthday parties and the fact that the women in his life didn't appreciate being ignored. By the time Eva had reached middle school, her mother's cold shoulder had become a permanent fixture, and when Eva was in the seventh grade, her father packed his bags and left. Six months later Eva said goodbye to their modest dogtrot with the magical backyard and hello to a cramped duplex on the West Bank. She saw her father every other weekend, but even then, he was often called away. Being a firefighter was his addiction. Charles stayed married to the job until he met a young reporter at an arson scene seven years ago. Then Claren, her father's third and final wife, had been sucked in by Eva's father's dedication, bravery and mature good looks. Unfortunately, not even her gravity-defiant boobs could keep him from the job. The job had always been number one.

But Eva had adored her father, and so when it came time for her to graduate from high school and head off to college, she let her father in on the secret she'd kept buried for so long. It had been a Sunday afternoon and she'd just given her old man a hug for the new laptop he'd given her for graduation.

"So you know I'm thinking about getting my associates degree and going to firefighter school," she'd said as she walked out to the car she'd parked on the street outside her dad's condo.

"What?" he'd said with a laugh. As if it was a joke.

"I'm serious, Dad."

He father had stopped and set his hands on his thickening hips. "Aw, you ain't cut out for that, *ma chère.*"

"Why not?"

Her father shook his head, his dark eyes incredulous. "Baby, girls don't make good firefighters. Just ain't right."

"Dad, how can you say that? You know there are women firefighters out there. I want to do what you do. I want to save lives, save property."

Her dad had laughed and plucked one of her arms from where it hung beside her slight body. "Eva Marie, look at these arms. You can hardly do a chin-up. Firemen have to carry big hoses. They have to lift people out of burning buildings. That ain't for you, sugar. Why not become a nurse or something? Or a doctor? Save lives *that* way."

Eva had wrenched her arm away, shocked her father thought her so incapable of doing what he did. What an egotistical, ridiculous position to take. Hadn't he always told her she could do anything? Hadn't he always bemoaned the fact Chris had gone into botany, refusing to follow in his bootsteps? So what was wrong with his daughter putting her feet in the prints he'd trod?

"I can do whatever I want to do," she said.

"Eva, be sensible. Women aren't cut out for fighting fires. It's a physical thing, honey, and maybe even a mental thing. It's like being a soldier, the mind-set is different. Stick to what you can do."

"I can't believe you just said that."

Charles had set his arm around her shoulders. "Come on, don't be mad, Queen E."

"I am mad," she said, shrugging from beneath his arm. She didn't say anything more on the subject, but in her mind she'd made a vow to herself—she'd go to fire school and prove him wrong. The next day she'd started on her quest, going to GNC and buying protein powder, joining a gym and ordering *Essentials of Firefighting*.

No one told Eva she couldn't do something.

Except herself.

Which is why she wouldn't kiss Jake Beauchamp again. She'd told herself no, and she meant it.

"Hey, you want some cobbler? Mama sent some over." Jake stood in the door, his blue eyes searching, almost pleading, for things to be normal.

She straightened and dusted her hands, jarred from the memory of the day her father had set her path for her...by telling her she couldn't be a firefighter. "No, thanks. I've been eating some of Charlie's snacks and don't want to outgrow my clothes."

Jake's gaze lowered, brushing her body. "That would be a shame. You're perfect the way you are."

She snapped her finger at him. "Don't. Remember what we said. No flirting. No looking at my…ah…"

"Assets?"

"Yeah, that." She closed the filing cabinet drawer.

"Right," Jake said. "I don't know why I said that."

Eva summoned a smile. Just be normal. "Because it's in your nature. You're a nice guy, Jake. You like people to be happy."

Jake's eyes narrowed, his bullshit meter obviously going off. "I'm not nice."

Eva laughed. "You're a Beauchamp. Being a good guy is part of your genetic makeup."

"Why are you being so nice to me? Is this how you're getting past wanting to rip my clothes off with your teeth?"

Eva laughed because he didn't say it as if he meant it. He said it the way he'd always said outrageous things. As if she was one of the guys. Not that he'd ever joke that way with one of the guys. She was certain there wasn't anyone in the fire house that would want to rip Jake's clothes off…but her. "If that's what you want to think, bud."

"So no cobbler? It's peach. Last of the ones Mom froze this summer."

"The answer's still no. Taking care of a kid means facing the temptation of mac and cheese and frosted cereals on a daily basis."

"I thought you were supposed to feed them organic

crap and carrot sticks," Jake said, leaning against the doorjamb, his hair sticking out in eight different directions, his blue eyes bright against his tan. His casual sexiness was off the chart. She looked down at the folder she held and tried to remember what they were talking about.

Food and Charlie.

"Well, I gave him a break this past week. The carrot sticks and whole grain bread are waiting. Figured it was hard enough moving to a new place and starting a new school without taking away his fruity loops."

"How was yesterday, anyway?"

"As expected. He didn't want to go to school, he didn't eat his lunch, he didn't talk to anyone in class and he thinks the mascot is dumb."

"What? Dragons are cool."

"You'd think a six-year-old would think so."

Jake stood there a minute. "Anything I can do to help? Besides babysitting?"

Eva snorted. "Well, I would love some ideas of what to do for his birthday next week. He wants a campout."

"Now *that* I can help with. I have a tent that will sleep six. How many kids? Wait. Who are you inviting?"

"I'm hoping your nephews might come. Otherwise, I haven't a clue."

Jake shrugged. "I can come and bring the nephews as long as they aren't with Mary Jane that weekend. They go to New Orleans some weekends, but I can ask Matt."

"Charlie really liked Wyatt and said they ate lunch together yesterday. Or, in Charlie's case, didn't eat lunch. I'd appreciate your help with the birthday party. Fancy said she would help, but I hate to ask any more of your mother. She's been such a blessing."

"I think selflessness was in the contract for being a pastor's wife," Jake joked, pulling himself upright. "She likes managing everyone else's lives. You and Charlie are fresh blood."

Just as Eva was about to fuss at Jake for making light of having a caring mother, meddlesome or not, the alarm sounded.

Jake disappeared faster than a chocolate bar at a PMS convention. Eva dumped the folder on the desk as the adrenaline shot through her.

Two calls within ten days.

Rare.

She hurried out the door to the bay where the engines and her bunker gear stood waiting. She and the guys spent the first half hour of every shift making sure they could get in their equipment and out of the station in mere minutes, so it took her less than two minutes to slide into her protective gear.

"Grass fire," Captain Hank Sorrento called as he slid into the driver's seat of Engine Five, which meant there was likely no hydrant to catch. Engine

Five had a larger water reservoir and was used for areas without water support.

Eva hoisted herself up, sliding onto the seat opposite Jake. Dutch climbed in, grumbling about the Velcro on his bunker coat. Jake rolled his eyes because Dutch had been grumping about his Velcro for the past year. Then he winked at Eva.

Just a regular run to put out a grass fire.

No sexual tension. No desire. No hippety-hop of her heart.

Easy-peasy normal.

"Dutchtown got the call. We got a call for mutual aid," Hank called as he hit the lights and siren and maneuvered through Magnolia Bend.

Grass fires happened this time of year because Louisiana was often drier than normal in the fall. Burning the sugarcane fields before harvest started in late August, and the slightest mismanagement of ashes could cause small pop-up fires around the parish. Most farmers were very conscious about the controlled burns, but fire is unpredictable and can run away, causing unintentional damage. Just a few years ago the crossties of the railroad going through town had been burned when a fire jumped the tracks and burned a field not slated for burning.

By the time Engine Five arrived on the side of the rural parish road, the unit out of Dutchtown had already started knocking down the stringy fire that stretched along the highway. Their team provided support, making sure the smoldering, blackened areas were completely out. Seemed obvious this fire wasn't a result of an uncontrolled sugarcane fire but rather a lit cigarette landing in dry scrub lining the sides of the road. Eva worked the hose, something she normally didn't do, but since it was a small fire and they were only providing backup at this point, the captain didn't say boo.

She suppressed the usual aggravation that welled in her gut at her being treated as subpar. She'd approached Chief Rinaudo before, relaying Hank's propensity to assign her less-demanding jobs. The chief had looked at her as if she were bat-shit crazy, making her feel paranoid. So she kept her mouth shut, because though she hated feeling as though she was given special treatment for being a woman, she didn't want to make her working environment needlessly difficult. Maybe she *should* kick up a fuss, but she'd rather work it differently, proving herself steadfastly through her efforts. Rome wasn't built in a day…and female firefighters couldn't expect automatic respect without proving themselves.

Just as she finished helping the guys load up the engine for the short ride back to Magnolia Bend, her phone rang.

"Hey, Fancy," she said, recognizing the number, worried since Fancy had said she'd only call if it were an emergency.

"It's me," Charlie said.

"Oh, hey, Charlie. Sorry I haven't had a chance

to call you. But we're on a run now, so I'll have to call you later."

"No. I want to go home," he said. He sounded whiny.

"Hey, we talked about this. Your mom is getting better but you'll have to stay with me until she's fully recovered."

"No, not my house. I want to go to your house. I don't want to stay here."

Eva glanced over to Hank, who had sent her a frown. Their captain didn't prohibit personal calls but it was understood they didn't engage on a scene. "I can't talk now, Charlie. You have to stay with Fancy. She's sweet. You'll be fine."

"Please, Eva. Come get me. I'm scared."

Her heart twisted. "Charlie, I really can't talk, sweetie. I'm at work. We talked about this."

Charlie didn't say anything. Instead, he cried.

She put her hand over the mouthpiece and muttered, "Shit."

Walking away from the engine, she stared out at the pasture dotted with cattle. Small clouds scudded across the horizon ridged by the Mississippi River levee. "Look, Charlie, I know things are scary right now, but you are being taken care of by a sweet lady who will spoil you rotten. You're fine and I can't come home. I have a job and it's how I afford hamburgers at PattyAnn's and getting an Icee at the Short Stop."

He didn't stop crying.

"I have to go. Everything will be okay." Then she hung up.

And felt like the cow patty sitting next to the fence line.

Sweet Jesus, she'd never known how crappy a person could feel by disappointing a kid.

"What's wrong?" Dutch asked, passing by her as he lugged the blue hose they'd used.

"Nothing," she lied.

"Doesn't look like nothing. You never take calls."

"Well, I had to take this one, and everything's fine." She turned, pocketing the phone, pushing her shoulders back. Not as if she could do anything about Charlie being scared, even if she wanted to flag down a car, hop in and force the driver to take her to Reverend Beauchamp's house so she could scoop her brother into a hug and tell him it was okay.

Thing was she wasn't certain Charlie would ever be okay. Losing your father and having a drug addict mother and an uncertain future weren't things that were easily overcome. Sure, he was only six and she was trying to help him, but having such an unstable environment wasn't good for a kid.

She knew firsthand.

She'd been dragged in and out of living situations by her mother. At one time her mother had been the quintessential suburban mom, making crustless sandwiches and organizing carpools, but once she fell out of love with Eva's father, she fell out of love with being a mother. At one point she'd asked Eva to start calling her by her first name. But Eva had refused to say, "What's up, Helene?" when she came home from school to find her mother entertaining the bass player for a local rock band, or a weird artist—whoever it happened to be that day. Eva had to draw the line somewhere.

Jake eyed her but didn't make a remark as they loaded up.

As Hank pulled away, Eva set her helmet in her lap and looked out at the rushing scenery, her emotions a tight tangle. She'd never felt this way, so helpless. She didn't know what to do. Charlie had gone through so much, and like a thoughtless brute, she'd dumped him on the first stranger who'd offered to help.

Okay, Fancy wasn't a stranger, but still, she was responsible for her brother and now he was crying and wanting her.

"Eva," Jake said softly.

She jerked her head around.

Concern etched his face. "Everything okay?"

Same question Dutch asked, but somehow when Jake asked it, she didn't feel so prickly. "Sure."

"Eva," he said again. His voice felt like the sun coming up in the morning, softly probing the world it brightened.

This time she looked at him. "Charlie's crying."

"Why?"

Dutch looked up from where he tapped on his phone. "Is that your brother?"

"Yeah," Eva said, accepting the fact that everyone in town likely knew she was taking care of Charlie. That was the negative of living in Magnolia Bend. Once one person knows, everyone knows. "He's six and Jake's mom is watching him while I'm on duty. He called crying. I don't know what to do."

Dutch smiled—a rare occurrence. "Now, this is where I can help you. See, kids know how to yank your chain. They know exactly what to say to make you feel guilty, especially when it comes to things like day care."

"He's not in day care. He's at Fancy's. That's like being at Disney World, but with better cooking and no weird characters."

"Well, if my uncle Carlton shows up, you can strike the weird character thing off that list," Jake joked.

"So you think he's just manipulating me?" she asked Dutch.

"I know he is. Don't you remember how shredded my nerves were a few years back when I had to drop Maisie off at day care? She stood in the window with her hand pressed against the glass crying "Daddy" over and over again. It was brutal. But Mrs. Sandifer said as soon as my truck disappeared she'd skipped over to play with her friends as if nothing was wrong."

Jake pulled his cell phone out of his bunker coat pocket and tapped. "Hey, Dad."

Both she and Dutch stopped talking and listened in on the conversation. Jake hit the speaker button.

"So how's Charlie doing?"

"Oh, he's great," Dan Beauchamp said, sounding slightly out of breath. "We just got through playing a little basketball. Now he's doing his homework with your mother. Just a worksheet or something."

"What about emotionally? Like, is he upset?" Jake asked.

"Naw, he's been eating oatmeal cookies, helping your mother make dinner and playing ball. He didn't look happy about homework, but once your mother told him Wyatt and Will were coming over for dinner, he ran for his backpack. He's doing great."

Eva clasped a hand against her chest as relief flowed through her. "Thank God."

Dutch gave her the "told you so" look and went back to tapping on his phone, playing one of those addictive-as-crack games on Facebook.

Jake pocketed his phone. "Feel better?"

"Yeah." She sighed. The engine swung into the station a few minutes later and they scrambled out, peeling off their gear before doing routine maintenance on the engine. Later Jake and Dutch would wash the truck down, and Eva would inventory the equipment, making sure everything was in place and functional. Being a good department with high ratings meant being prepared and efficient. By the time Eva completed her tasks, it was nearly Charlie's bedtime.

She called to check on him and Fancy answered on the first ring. "Hey, Eva."

"Hi. Is Charlie doing okay?"

"Of course. He completed all his homework, ate most of his dinner and brushed his teeth without my asking. He's a delight and I'm so glad you're letting him visit."

"Fancy, I can't thank you enough."

"Oh, pish posh. I love having Charlie here. He's an awesome kid."

Eva could tell that her brother likely stood right beside Jake's mother, and no doubt the kid grinned ear to ear to hear himself described in such glowing terms. Charlie needed that. He needed to hear people thought he was awesome…that he was worthy. "Can I talk to him?"

"Here, Charlie, it's your sister."

"Hey, Eva. Guess what?"

Eva smiled and propped her socked feet on the ottoman. Jake and Dutch were still messing with the truck, which meant she got the primo spot on the comfy couch and control of the clicker. She pressed the power button. "You ate all your peas."

"Gross. We didn't eat peas. I get to sleep in Jake's room."

"Oh, cool. Better watch out for his dirty socks. He leaves them all over the station."

"No, he doesn't," Charlie said, his tone reproachful. So here it was, the utter hero worship of Jake.

She could relate, though the dirty sock thing *was* a deterrent.

"He has some cool trophies and stuff. He played basketball, too. His dad said he was a point guard. Do you know what that is?"

"Not really, but I bet you want to try that position, too."

"Yeah. You have to be a good shooter. I've been practicing with the rev."

The rev?

Jake walked in, plopped down on the couch beside her and reached over to grab the clicker out of her hand.

"Well, that's good, Charlie. Keep practicing with the rev and you'll be the best on your team this year." She shook her head at Jake and held fast to the remote control.

"Please?" he mouthed.

She knew he wanted to watch football, but she was set on watching *Dancing with the Stars*. It was their normal Monday night struggle, though it was usually solved by whoever got the remote first.

"No," she said.

"No what?" Charlie asked.

Jake started rubbing her leg, making puppy dog faces. She smacked his hand and shot him a look. Normally, she wouldn't think twice about him touching her, but that was before she'd stuck her tongue down his throat.

Okay, she hadn't actually played tonsil hockey with him, but it had gotten close. Dangerously close.

"Never mind, Charlie. I was talking to someone else, who should mind his manners."

Jake grinned and walked his fingers over her bare thigh toward the remote.

"Are you kidding me?" she squeaked, pushing his hand back.

Jake sobered as he realized what he was doing.

"What's wrong, Eva?" Charlie asked, sounding concerned.

"Nothing. Jake's just being a pest." She glared at Jake but held firm to the remote. She hit a few buttons and the reality dance show popped onto the screen. Jake slapped a hand over his face and flopped back onto the couch. Eva smiled and turned up the volume. "I'll let you go, little brother. Say your prayers and have a good night."

"Okay. Mr. Beauchamp—that's our principal—is going to pick me up in the morning. I get to sit in the backseat with Wyatt. Cool, huh?"

"Very cool. Night, Charlie."

"Night, Eva."

She clicked the end button, setting her phone on the table. Then she looked at Jake, who had lifted one part of his hand, peeking out at her. "Don't even pretend you didn't try to use your sexual powers to get control of the remote."

"I didn't. I swear."

"Liar," she said, redirecting her gaze back at the

TV, where some nubile starlet pranced with one of the bare-chested dancers.

"Did they work?"

"Not even a little," she said, tucking a pillow behind her lower back. "I'm watching *DWTS*. You can see the end of the Cowboys game when I'm done."

"Are you saying there's nothing I can do to change your mind about watching this stupid show?"

"Nope."

"Not even the dishes?"

"Uh-uh."

"I could write up all your reports for the next week," he offered, sitting up and focusing his attention on her.

"Not a chance. I live for the fox-trot."

He snorted. "I could paint your toenails? Pull weeds from your flower bed? Scrub your toilets?"

Eva smiled. "Let's see. No, no, and still no."

"Fine," he grumbled, throwing a toss pillow onto the recliner Dutch usually sat in.

"Where is Dutch, anyway?"

"He and Hank went to check a hydrant."

"We're here alone?" Eva asked, sudden pricklies dancing in her tummy.

At that Jake's mouth twitched. "Yeah, so maybe I should rephrase some of those things I can do for you."

"Don't," she said, inching away from him. She didn't trust herself to be on the couch with a flirty, determined Jake. They'd vowed to forget about the kisses, but she knew that tossing out the vow would be as easy as snapping her fingers.

"I'm not doing anything," he said, feigning innocence but leering at her like a horny frat boy.

"Yes, you are. Just yesterday we said we wouldn't do this."

"I'm not doing anything. I'm *suggesting* doing things."

"You're horrible," she said.

"And you're sexy," he said. "So what are we going to do about that?"

CHAPTER ELEVEN

JAKE KNEW HE was playing with fire, sitting beside Eva, teasing her about what they'd vowed never to mention again, but he couldn't help himself.

She looked so damn adorable in her gym shorts, tennis socks and navy department T-shirt stretched tight over her no doubt magnificent breasts. Shit fire, he wanted to see those breasts. Cradle them, taste them, roll her nipples between his teeth.

Yeah, he'd been thinking about what he'd do to her ever since she'd lifted herself onto her toes and kissed him outside the church just over a week ago.

He'd promised he wouldn't, but he couldn't stop himself.

"We're not doing anything about anything," Eva said, holding up a finger. "You promised, and you're a man of your word. Remember the complications? Think about that. We work together."

"But what about the pleasure?" he countered. "Pleasure has a way of making complications small. Almost the size of a BB."

Jake traced a finger along the length of her thigh. Her skin was gorgeous. Not a flaw on her. And she was soft as angel's wings, or something equally downy.

He heard her intake of breath, felt the triumph surge in his blood. Eva wanted him. No doubt about that. But could he use her desire against her?

What would that make him?

A creep? A man whose word meant nothing?

He curled his fist. Then he scooted across the couch, putting distance between them.

Eva glanced at him. "What?"

"Nothing."

"No, what?"

He pushed a hand through his hair. "You're right. We said—I said—that we wouldn't play with fire, so I won't."

"Play with fire? Is that a joke?"

"Oh, because we're firefighters? Or because you don't understand how much I want to drag you into my lap, kiss you until you lose any concept of reason and then find out just how close I came to guessing your bra size. 34D?"

Eva's mouth gaped a bit and then she swallowed. "Uh, 36DD."

"Hell," he breathed, looking away…at the fridge. At the flyer one of the guys from another shift had taped to it, advertising a band playing at the Rocking J Saloon in Gonzales. Anything to get his mind off the fact Eva's breasts would overflow his hands… that they'd be perfect to bury his face between, inhaling the spicy complexity that was his Eva.

No. Not his Eva.

Just Eva.

Eva dropped her feet and rose. "Uh, what do you think we should do for dinner? Dutch said he'd grill chicken but since he's out…maybe an omelet? Or we could defrost a pizza?"

Jake sat there a second, trying to trample the desire that had sunk its teeth into him. "How about pancakes?"

"Pancakes?" Eva didn't turn around but instead started clearing out the dishwasher. She needed something to do, to keep herself busy.

"I can make my grandmother's recipe. It's a Burnsides classic with a secret ingredient."

"Do we have bacon? 'Cause I can't eat my pancakes without bacon."

"Yeah." He rose and went to the pantry and started gathering all the dry ingredients, including the cinnamon and nutmeg his grammy always used in her pancakes. "So you want to be my sous chef?"

"No."

"Come on, Eva. If you don't want me to kiss you, you have to at least distract me."

"Who said I didn't want you to kiss me?" she said, propping a hand on her hip.

"Um, you did. Remember? And you were right. We can't dabble in attraction."

He set the flour and sugar on the granite counter he and the guys had installed several years ago and turned to get the eggs from the refrigerator. He set everything out and then glanced over at Eva since she'd remained silent on his last point. She stood, hip propped against the kitchen island, watching him with an indescribable expression.

"What?"

She twisted her lips. "Thing is, I want you to kiss me. I want you to do really dirty things to me. Like, bad."

His body ignited. "But…we can't."

"No, we can't, and that almost makes me want it more. It's like setting a fifth of whiskey in front of an alcoholic and telling him not to touch it. I feel like I have the shakes and all I want to do is have one little taste. I mean, is that so wrong? Just a little bit?"

Jake closed his eyes because he couldn't stand the pleading within the depths of her eyes. He opened them and lifted the mixing bowl, his hands literally shaking. "Jesus, Eva. Don't. I don't have the will-power, baby."

"Did I mention the fact that when you call me *baby* it makes me want to slide out of my new Victoria's Secret panties? That it makes me want to lick your stomach and—"

At the sound of the engine pulling in, Eva broke off. Jake glanced over and it looked as if the spell had been broken. Her face flooded with color, and she shook her head as if she couldn't believe the words she'd uttered had made it past her filter. "Oh, my God. What is wrong with me? What did I just do?"

"You didn't do anything. Just words," he said, rifling through the drawer beside him for the measuring cups. "Not that I didn't want to do something, *baby*."

"Yo, what's up?" Dutch asked, bursting into the room. After hanging his hat on the hooks by the door, he bumbled in, knocking his knee against the coffee table, nearly spilling the diet soda Eva had left there.

"Just making dinner," Jake said, giving Eva a nod that said to snap out of it.

"What are we having?" Dutch said, rubbing the belly that hung over his regulation belt.

"Well, as soon as you get the bacon started, we'll have pancakes and bacon," Jake said.

"Why me?" Dutch asked, pointing at Eva. "She's standing right there."

"What, because I'm a woman?"

Dutch rolled his eyes and laughed. "Well, y'all wanted to bring home the bacon and fry it up in a pan."

Eva threw a dish towel at Dutch, who caught it with a hoot of laughter.

Jake didn't like Dutch making those kinds of jokes about Eva, but he knew she didn't like him fighting her battles. She'd said as much a few weeks after she'd started the job. But at least Eva looked back to normal now.

Damn it, he shouldn't have invited the temptation back in, but then again, who was he kidding? It hadn't gone away. His need to taste Eva clung to him like a sweet, exotic perfume he couldn't wash off.

It was only a matter of time.

Unless he could figure out a way to stop the desire pumping through his body. The only alternative he could figure was to start things up with Kate again or leave town. The latter sounded better to him, but he had nowhere to go. Wanting to do Eva wasn't reason enough to vacate his life. Maybe Eva would take care of snipping the attraction they had in half—maybe she'd keep going out with Jamison.

The thought of Eva kissing Jamison made him want to vomit.

Cold goo ran down his wrist, and he looked down to see he'd crushed the egg in his hand and hadn't even noticed.

Dutch tossed him the towel Eva had thrown at him seconds ago and plopped the package of bacon onto the counter. "Hey, at least it's not egg on your face, Beauchamp."

Jake slung the crushed egg into the sink. "Not this time, Dutch. Not this time."

EVA SET THE sock-it-to-me cake on the counter of Clint and Murphy Cochran's kitchen before taking out the disposable plates from the cabinet. No longer living with feminine influence meant the two men existed on frozen dinners, disposable dishes and a housekeeper who came weekly. So Eva dropped by occasionally and brought them something homemade…from PattyAnn's.

"Coffee, Eva?" Clint asked, rolling into the kitchen and arching an eyebrow.

"Sure."

"Can I have coffee, too, Eva?" Charlie asked.

"Absolutely not. It will stunt your growth." She found a knife and started slicing the cake.

"Jake said it would put hair on my chest," Charlie said.

"He would," she said, wishing to hell the subject of Jake hadn't been broached. She'd barely survived the last shift with him, especially when she'd snuck out to get some water to take her birth control pill with and found Jake leaning against the counter clad only in his pajama pants, drinking milk out of the carton. In the light of day, Jake was a man to contend with, but in the low light of the kitchen with his sculpted bare chest in sharp relief, he was exquisite. From the tips of his feet to the strong column of his throat moving as he snuck the milk, he was a study in masculine grace. Eva had backed up, unwilling to create intimacy with him again. Mostly because she wasn't so sure she could have kept her panties on this time. Considering the way Dutch snored, she was certain they wouldn't have had to worry about an audience.

So she'd dry-swallowed her pill, washing it down with a scoop of water from the bathroom faucet. When she came out, Jake was back in bed.

The next day she and Jake had pretended everything was normal, and once she was off her shift, she had plenty to keep her busy with Charlie.

The following day had sped by, and Eva found that being a mother to a near seven-year-old boy was a tough job. It was a struggle to get homework completed, because Charlie was behind in his reading, and the new math program made no sense to her whatsoever. He still had nightmares and wet the bed almost every night, and getting him to eat whole grain bread was akin to asking him to eat dirt. And then there were the socks. Unmatched socks littered her floor. She'd already started a lost sock basket.

"Jake said you went out with Jamison. What's up with that?" Clint asked, scooping coffee into the paper filter.

"Nothing. Just a few dates."

"Hmm," Clint said.

"What?"

"Nothing. I guess I don't see you two together."

"We're not together. We went out two times, and he hasn't been blowing up my phone for a repeat." She slid a plate toward her little brother, who had parked himself at the bar, tapping on her phone, absorbed in some game Wyatt had showed him how to play.

"Yeah, so I guess that means you're dating again? I wondered when you would, you know, after Chase broke it off."

Eva frowned. "Actually, Chase didn't break anything off. We both agreed it wasn't working. You can only feign interest for so long. And dating is a relative term. I live in Magnolia Bend. Not a huge dating pool, as you well know."

Clint pulled out the mugs from the lower shelves. The kitchen had been designed to meet the needs of a disabled person. "Yeah, truer words never spoken. In fact, it's been a while since I had to pretend any kind of interest."

"What about the girl you met online?"

"We're just friends."

"Oh, I thought y'all were more for some reason. Didn't you talk about going to visit her in Montana at some point?"

"Eh." He shrugged, rolling across the kitchen to fetch creamer.

Eva laughed. "I'm guessing that means you're no longer interested?"

"You guess right," he said.

"Can we go now?" Charlie asked, looking up.

"No. We just got here, and you're being rude." Eva gave her brother a sharp look.

"But you said we'd go get the stuff for my party this weekend. Wyatt and his brother can both come. Can we have chocolate chip ice cream with my cake? I want a Ninja Turtle cake, okay?"

"Charlie, I'm visiting with my friend."

"How come all your friends are guys?"

Eva felt her cheeks heat. "I have friends who are girls." Why was she explaining herself to a child? Jeez.

"Your sister's used to being around guys," Clint

said, giving Charlie a smile. The man was still abnormally good-looking, though maybe a bit too lean. "She works with them and has two brothers."

"She never does girly stuff like my mom does."

Eva huffed. "Well, I don't have time. I'm spending all my time doing math problems and cooking mac and cheese. Plus, I don't need pretty fingernails or fancy shoes. I'm a practical sort of gal."

Charlie's eyes widened. "I thought girls liked to look pretty. All the girls I know put glitter on everything and wear bows. I mean, it's sort of sparkly and pretty, I guess. You don't like glitter?"

"No," Eva said, wrinkling her nose.

Clint laughed. "I think your sister looks perfect the way she is. She's wholesome."

"Is that code for fat?" Eva joked, eyeing the slice of cake she'd just plopped on her plate. Maybe she didn't need the extra calories, though she didn't usually worry about slimming down. Firefighters needed bulk, and she spent enough time in the gym that she was solid but not flabby.

"Not even close. You're gorgeous," Clint said.

"And you'll say anything to keep me bringing cake and brownies," she said lightly, but something in Clint's tone and eyes sent a frisson of warning up her spine. It was almost as if his words sounded silky. What the hell was up with that?

She felt a bit like that character from that '90s movie *Something About Mary*. Okay, so she wasn't anything close to looking like Cameron Diaz, but suddenly she had guys circling her. So strange. Guess there weren't all that many single women in Magnolia Bend.

But shouldn't the fact she now had a kid deter some interest? Women always complained that kids were deal-breakers for dudes.

"I'd say anything to keep you stopping by. You're like a breath of fresh air in my life. Besides, I'd never lie to you. You're perfect the way you are, Eva."

Eva smiled. How could she not? A guy says something like that and you have to feel a bit glowy, even if slightly alarmed over the intent behind it. "Thanks, and I'm glad we're friends. It's been a blessing to me, too."

His brow wrinkled at the word *friends*. Or at least she thought it did. Another beep of the alarm.

"You know, I've been thinking how nice it would be to get out of Magnolia Bend for a day. There's a festival in Fort Brantley next weekend. How about we all go? We can take my van and pack a picnic. Charlie, do you like going to festivals?"

"I've never been to one," Charlie said, shoveling cake into his mouth. "But I guess."

"What about it, Eva?" Clint asked, accepting the cake she handed him.

"I don't know. Need to check my calendar."

"We can always do a Sunday afternoon," Clint said.

"I don't want to commit yet," she said, worried that this jaunt might mean more than friendship.

Something in the glint of Clint's eyes and in the way he responded to her remarks had her feeling a bit itchy.

She liked Clint. He had charisma, charm and a killer smile. He also had a commanding way about him, a sort of reliability that projected a sense of safety. Odd for a man who was considered disabled, but still very much present. Thing was she wasn't attracted to Clint...except as a friend.

"Why not?" he asked. Something in his voice sounded hurt, but she didn't want to encourage him, *did she*? God, she hated guilt.

"Well, things have been so unpredictable lately. I have Charlie's birthday this weekend and we're planning to visit his mother soon. Of course, I love a good festival, and Charlie would probably enjoy going, too." Okay, so she couldn't just shoot him down. Besides, an outing wasn't a date. Friends did things together all the time, so she shouldn't misread his intention as something it wasn't. Plus, having a break from the reality of her life right now might be nice. And it would give her another day away from Jake and the infernal desire that had attached itself to her.

"What do you do at a festival?" Charlie asked, looking down at his plate. "Can I have some more of that cake, Eva? It rocked."

Saying something rocked was Charlie's new thing.

"No. You'll ruin your dinner," she said, before

slapping a hand over her mouth. "Oh, God, did I just say that?"

Clint laughed.

For a few seconds they sat in silence, eating cake. Just as Clint rolled to the coffeemaker to pour a cup, his father, Murphy, walked in.

"Mmm, I smell coffee," Murphy said, his rheumy eyes lighting on the coffeepot. Clint's father was a stooped, spare man with few words and a passion for collecting baseball cards. He rarely appeared when Eva stopped by, but Clint professed he ate every crumb of her desserts.

"Who's that?" Charlie asked, pointing his finger at Murphy.

"Don't point. It's rude," Eva said, folding her brother's finger down.

Clint's father narrowed his eyes at Charlie. "Who are you?"

"I'm Charlie."

Murphy raised his eyebrows and did something unexpected—he smiled. Well, at least Eva thought it was a smile. Could have been gas pain.

"Well, then, Charlie, I'm Murphy Cochran. I'm Clint's father, and this is my house."

Clint's face tightened at that declaration. Eva knew it was a sticking point for her friend. Ever since the Cochrans moved from the Victorian house with its narrow halls and steep stairs to the handicap-friendly one-story lake house, Clint had been try-ing to find a way to break out. At first he'd stayed because his mother had wanted to take care of him. Now he stayed because, though he and his father didn't get along, he worried about his father living alone. It was a catch-22.

"Oh," Charlie said, shimmying down from the stool. "Can I go outside?"

"Sure," Eva said, pouring coffee into a mug and passing it to Murphy before pouring herself one. "Don't go near the water."

Charlie slammed out the door.

"Did you hear me?" she called.

The kid gave her a thumbs-up and then clapped his hands so Biscuit, the yellow Lab who lolled in the sun, came running after him.

"Cute kid," Murphy said, looking out at the boy running across the lawn. "Who does he belong to?"

"For the time being, me." Eva slid onto the stool Charlie had abandoned. "He's my half brother, and his mother is in rehab."

Murphy lifted his bushy brows. "That's tough."

She wasn't sure if he meant on her, Charlie or Claren. Maybe all three.

"You're doing good, Eva," Clint said, rolling beside her, brushing her arm with his hand. It was a soft caress that on the surface seemed friendly, but when she looked into Clint's eyes, she wanted to mutter "uh-oh."

"Thanks. I'm doing my best."

Murphy turned the conversation to the upcoming hunting season and then to baseball playoffs.

Before the accident Clint had been a pitcher for the University of Arkansas. There had been talk of his being drafted and playing in the minor leagues. Murphy Cochran had never gotten over the fact that his son had a career erased that night years ago. Bitter, he still stewed over what might have been, taking his anger out on Clint. Clint said Murphy hadn't said five words to Jake since that night.

After another cup of coffee, Eva said her good-byes.

Clint put his hand on her elbow as she turned to step out onto the porch. "Hey, think about the festival. It would be fun to get out of Magnolia Bend for the day."

"I will," she said, placing her hand over his and giving it a squeeze before pulling away.

"Is something wrong?" Clint asked.

"No. Why?"

"Nothing," he said, following her outside.

Charlie ran over, the dog behind him. Both his jeans and the dog's paws were wet.

"Did you go in the water?" Eva asked.

The look on Charlie's face said it all.

"Charlie, I told you to stay away from the lake. You are never to go near water without an adult. Why did you disobey me?"

"Well, Biscuit wanted to fetch the stick, and I didn't know I could throw it that far."

"That explains why Biscuit is wet, not why you're wet."

"Well, she couldn't find the stick. But I knew right where it was. So I helped her."

All the bad things that could have happened flew through her mind—alligators, water moccasins, unstable lake bottoms. Charlie could have been seriously hurt. Why did she assume he'd mind her? "That's not a good enough reason to go against my instructions, my rules. There will be repercussions."

"What's repercussions?"

"You won't be able to watch TV for the next two days," Eva said, taking his arm and tugging him toward her car.

"What? No. I didn't mean to, Eva. I was trying to help Biscuit," Charlie cried, trying to pull away from her.

"Doesn't matter. You put yourself in danger by disobeying me. You're punished."

"No, you can't do that. You're not my mom," he said, yanking his arm from her grasp.

"I'm your guardian, and I'm in charge. You don't mind, you don't get privileges." Eva grabbed his arm again and tugged him toward the car. Out of the corner of her eye she saw Clint's eyes widen.

Yeah, buddy, you want to date this? I don't think so. 'Cause we're a package deal.

"Ow," Charlie screeched. "You're hurting me."

"I'm not hurting you. Get into the car. It's time to go." Eva felt irrational anger rear up inside her. How dare he act like a…brat. She'd spent the past two weeks sacrificing any sort of peace in her life for him.

"You are hurting me and you're mean. I didn't do nothing and you're being a big mean person." Charlie pulled open the back door of her car and climbed inside.

Eva turned to Clint. "I'm sorry you had to witness that. I'm learning kids aren't the most rational of creatures."

Clint lifted his eyebrows. "Yeah, I see. Good luck with that."

"So you want to rescind that invite?" she teased, trying to beat down the irritation she felt at Charlie with some humor.

"No way. I love kids."

Eva arched an eyebrow.

Clint grinned. "Okay, I don't. But I would love to spend time with you."

Again, a warning flag. "Okay, it's your funeral."

"Not yet," he said, giving her a smile and wave as she slid into the driver's seat.

She caught sight of Charlie in the rearview mirror. He stuck out his tongue, crossed his arms and jerked his head in that age-old gesture that meant "you're dead to me."

Great.

"Thanks for the cake," Clint called.

Eva waved and started the car, rolling down the cypress-strewn drive laced in Spanish moss.

"You do understand that all kids get in trouble

for doing what you did." She glanced back at her brother. "Charlie?"

"I'm not talking to you."

"Well, you just did," she said. Inside she still felt shaky. The thought of Charlie floating facedown in the lake haunted her. At that moment she knew this wasn't just about providing care. No, something more was going on inside her. She knew she loved Charlie. He was her brother, and loving him came with the territory. Like having wavy hair and a prominent Italian nose. But suddenly it was so... visceral. She felt an...almost rabid fear of losing him. A bizarre thing she'd never experienced before had sunk its teeth into her.

It wasn't as if she had lived a totally selfish existence, but she'd never really had to put anyone before herself. With Charlie she had to think that way, and more important, she felt that way.

"Can I have some more of that cake tonight?"

Eva would have to actually bake a cake for that to happen. "Only if you help me bake it."

"Well, I ain't watching TV, am I?" he said, his words dry as sand.

Eva smiled. "Guess not."

CHAPTER TWELVE

JAKE WATCHED HIS brother cast his crank bait perfectly, hitting the water along the lily pads with a light splash. So he threw in right beside Matt... mostly because he knew it bugged the shit out of his anal older brother. And that was Jake's job—to be the cockroach tossed into the middle of a sleepover. He kept things stirred up and exciting in their family. One way or another.

"Stop."

Matt was a man of few words. That was why Jake fished with him.

"What?"

His brother just gave him the look.

Matt was the oldest of the Beauchamp children. Solid, reserved and always right. That was Matt's role. He was the rock, totally sensible—and boring, if truth be told.

After a few more casts and Jake missing when a fish struck his bait, they cranked up and headed back toward the boat launch. The sun glowed, turning the scanty clouds a bright persimmon against the lightening horizon. Nothing was prettier than a Louisiana lake at sunset. It was as if God got his swag on, showboating with his paint palette. Made a man almost speechless at times.

"Want to try over there before we load up?" Matt asked, pointing to a small slew where they'd had luck earlier in the summer. He slowed the boat.

"Sure."

Matt motored over, and they cast a few times.

"Thanks for letting the boys come to Charlie's birthday sleepover. I guess the kid's really looking forward to it. And it means a lot to Eva."

Matt grunted.

"She's really got her hands full with him. He's a cute kid, though."

"It's a good thing, what she's doing for him. Lots of relatives wouldn't have stepped up in such a situation, especially if they're single and work odd hours like Eva does."

Jake nodded. "She's good with him. Guess most women are good with kids."

"Most."

"Is Mary Jane okay with the kids missing time with her?"

Matt shrugged.

His brother had been married for twelve years to the woman he'd met at a Kappa Sigma fraternity party. Matt hadn't been in a frat but after having injured his knee and ending his college career, he'd been feeling down. So his best friend had cajoled him out the door and across town to the party where he literally ran into the blonde coed. Mary Jane had actually laughed at the dent he'd put in her Cabrio, and Matt had fallen head over heels for a woman who could laugh at something he considered somewhat serious.

But last year something had changed in their marriage. Mary Jane had left for a job in New Orleans and so far the weekly marriage counseling sessions didn't seem to be working. Or at least not on the surface. Mary Jane still lived in New Orleans. And his brother still moved to the camp when she came to Magnolia Bend to visit the boys each weekend.

"What do you think about Eva?" Jake asked. He blinked that he'd even asked that question of his brother. So stupid.

"What do you mean? Like as a mother?"

"Uh, sure."

Matt reeled his line in then turned to Jake. "Or do you mean as a woman?"

"No. Not like that," Jake said, but he knew his words were hollow.

His brother narrowed gray eyes. "Wait a sec, are you into Eva?"

"Hell, no." Jake threw in beside a hollowed cypress tree.

"Good, because she's totally wrong for you."

Jake nearly dropped his way too expensive rod. "Why would you say that?"

"Because Eva's the kind of girl you don't mess with. She's solid and good. She's not a bimbo."

"And I only date bimbos?"

"Not what I meant. You've dated some decent girls, but they knew the score going in. You weren't interested in financing a mortgage with them or helping them breathe through labor. You were interested in bagging them."

"You make me sound like a caveman."

Matt laughed. "Nah, I don't mean that's bad. You're just not like me."

"You mean living at the camp on weekends?"

Matt hesitated before saying, "Ouch."

Jake immediately felt like horseshit. *No.* Like the fly larvae on horseshit. "Sorry. Uncalled for."

"I get it. You're defensive because you're attracted to her. But I know you, Jake. You're bored. I'd suggest you find someone else to scratch that itch. Eva's too good of a girl for you to break." Matt casted onto the other side of the stump and jiggled the bait a bit. "And make no mistake, you'd break her, Jake."

At that moment a huge bass struck. Matt set the hook, and the big lunker flew up out of the water, thrashing in the waning light of day.

"Get the net," Matt yelled, reeling and working the line.

Jake nearly tripped over the tackle box lying in his path, but he grabbed the net just as the big fish tried to go under the boat. Jake scooped the net in the water and grunted when he lifted. The bass was a monster.

"Woo," Matt crowed, reaching in and detaching the treble hooks from the wide mouth of the fish.

"This one's over five pounds. Damn, he's a monster." Jake hooked his thumb in the mouth of the fish and lifted it. The big boy obligingly flipped his tail back and forth, still fighting against his captor.

Jake took a picture of his older brother smiling… something that rarely happened these days.

"Send it to me," Matt said before lowering the fish to the side of the boat.

"You really think I could hurt Eva?" Jake asked.

Matt looked up. "Yeah. She's had a thing for you as long as I've known her."

Jake felt as if his brother had punched him in the gut. "No, she hasn't."

Lowering the fish into the water, Matt swished it for a few seconds, flushing water through its gills. "It may not have been obvious to you, but I've known it for a while now. She looks at you like you're the lead singer in a boy band. It's that bad."

Eva had a thing for him? He couldn't quite wrap his mind around that. He just couldn't see it. They've been friends forever. Hell, he'd even farted in front of her a few times. Probably scratched his ass and admitted dumb things like how he liked to watch *Pride and Prejudice*. Damn it, he'd done things a dude didn't do in front of a woman who was into him.

"I can't believe it. I mean, she never gave me any signs. I never knew."

"You didn't want to," Matt said, giving the fish a final swirl. "But trust me, you want to let her go."

Matt released the fish, and with a swish of its tail it disappeared beneath the muddy depths.

For a few seconds he and Matt stood there and looked at the water. At the trail of shimmering light the sun left as it sank into the depths. At the rippling surface that hid things that didn't need to be brought into the light of day.

Matt cleared his throat. "Yeah, sometimes you just have to let things go."

Something hot sizzled in the back of Jake's throat at the emptiness of his brother's words. He wasn't talking about Jake as much as he was talking about what he'd been struggling with over the past year.

His brother looked up at him with sad eyes and said, "Ready?"

"Sure," Jake said, his thoughts as jumbled as the line of the reel he'd backlashed and set aside. He'd not had a clue about Eva's interest in him…and he wasn't so sure he could trust his brother's assessment. After all, if Matt could read women, he wouldn't be sleeping alone while his wife was fifty miles down the road, working for some swinging dick with an art degree and a sizable bank account. But truth sat fat and ugly in those words Matt had uttered.

You'd break her.

Eva was emphatically not a woman a man messed with and then set aside.

So was Jake ready for that step in his life?

Commitment?

He'd never wanted to marry and stay in Magnolia Bend like some of his high school buds.

So why are you still here, knucklehead?

He knew the answer to that one—he was a scared pussy, too afraid of leaving the past behind. Because guilt had treble hooks just like his crank bait, and they'd latched on to his soul, preventing him from taking what he wanted.

Sure, his psyche demanded he be true to himself and stop covering his desires with a veneer of good-time Charlie, but that gosh damn guilt tripped him every time. How could he grab hold of life, love and adventure when he'd denied his best friend any chance for the same thing? And he couldn't bring in the fact that their friend Angela had died.

So Jake did the same thing every day. He got up and he was Jake Beauchamp, hardworking fire-fighter, hard-playing Romeo. That was who he was. Didn't have to think or feel. Didn't have to remember the things he'd once wanted or the person he'd once wanted to be.

He climbed from the boat when they reached the camp launch and helped his brother unload. Took a while because Matt was adamant about everything having its place.

As they were leaving, Matt said, "Are you okay?"

"Yeah. I guess."

"Hmm." His brother locked the boathouse and walked toward his truck.

"What did that mean?" Jake asked, following suit.

"Nothing."

"Jesus, Matt. Don't do that. You have something to say, say it."

"You are you, so in this case with Eva, don't be you."

Jake wanted to tell his brother to go screw himself, but he didn't. Because Matt was right. He couldn't take advantage of Eva's feelings and act on the weird emotions twisting inside him. He couldn't risk that. "I won't."

EVA TAPPED DOWN the tent stake and stood, arching her back. "There. Done."

Jake was at the barbecue grill, flipping hot dogs while four little boys tackled each other in the small side yard. The oldest, Will Beauchamp, had organized a complicated, made-up game that was part capture the flag, part football and part wrestling match. Eva didn't understand the rules, but Charlie hadn't stopped smiling since they began playing it.

"Next time I go camping, I'll invite you. You broke my record for tent assembly," Jake said, closing the barbecue lid and grabbing the beer sitting next to him.

Eva crossed the yard, plopped onto the wrought-iron patio chair and took a swig of her water. "Maybe you shouldn't be drinking beer around kids."

"Why not? It's Friday night. I'm an adult. I'm not offering it to them."

"Yeah, well, you're the kind of guy these little

boys look up to. They might think it would make them cool to try it."

Jake gave her a look as if she was a cuckoo bird, but he poured out the half-drunk beer and placed the bottle in the recycling can she'd set outside to collect all the empty water bottles.

"Thanks for coming over to help me," she said.

"That's what friends are for. Besides, I like having you in my debt. Christmas will be here before you know it, and I'll have gifts that will need wrapping."

"Uh, I hate wrapping presents," she groaned. Somehow she'd owed Jake a favor last year, and he'd showed up on Christmas Eve with several shopping bags and a roll of hideous wrapping paper. She'd even wrapped her own gift from him.

"Too bad. Now you owe me. I loaned you the tent and I'm roasting your wieners."

"There's a joke in there somewhere," she quipped.

Jake grinned.

Ever since Jake had moved away from her on the couch at the firehouse last week, things had been easier. Almost back to normal. Almost.

Thing was though Eva had been really good in the past at hiding how much she wanted Jake, once it came out to play in the daylight, that attraction was apparently hard to put back in place. She couldn't help but indulge in watching him, her gaze caressing his physique, her hands itching to touch. It was as if her desire had been encapsulated in a full-body cast and now that the casing had been shattered, it refused to be bound again. Or maybe it was more like her desire was a fertile delta, birthing fantasies of intertwined bodies glistening with sweat. Or maybe it had merely built inside her, festering, begging her to…

Do something.

"Eva!" Feet slapped the patio, jarring her from her musings, and Charlie skidded to a halt in front of her. "Can we blow up water balloons now?"

Water balloons? "We don't have any water balloons."

"Jake brought some." Charlie skipped over to the man who, come to think of it, *had* arrived with a big bag from Target. "Can we do them now, Jake?"

Jake's nephews and another little boy who was in Charlie's class crowded around Jake. "Please!"

"Can you get these hot dogs off for me, Eva?"

"I don't know. Can you wrap your own presents?"

Jake actually hesitated. "I still brought the tent and lit the fire."

Eva laughed. "Okay, go with them. I'll take care of the hot dogs."

"Yay," the boys shouted in unison when Jake jogged over to the bag he'd brought with him. Like puppies they clamored after him, disappearing around the side of the house in the direction of the water hose.

Eva had never hosted a kid's birthday party before. Heck, she'd only hosted one other party in her life— a bridal shower for her college roommate. All other gatherings before then had included Jell-O shots and enough room for a deejay. There had been no matching plates and napkins, balloons or cakes with Teenage Mutant Ninja Turtles on them.

Just as she removed the hot dogs from the grill, a stream of water hit her in the back. "Ahhh!"

She spun, and another blast hit her right in the face.

Jake stood, clad in his PFG shorts and T-shirt, wearing a pair of goggles and holding a soaker gun. "Score!"

Eva shook her hands and darted behind a column just as a blast of water came at her from another direction.

Charlie whooped, followed by the other boys all carrying water guns and holding balloons full of water. "Get her!"

Squeaking, Eva ran in the direction of the house. A balloon hit at her feet, making her slip in her flip-flops. She skidded into the house and slammed the French door just as a stream of water hit it. Twisting the lock, she stuck out her tongue, taunting them.

"Awww, man," Charlie shouted, before turning the gun on Jake.

Jake yelled as the water hit him in the chest, plastering the cotton shirt to his nicely defined muscles. He issued a war cry and then he was off, chasing the boys across the green lawn. Lots of laughter and screaming ensued.

Eva watched for a moment, and as she stood there

an idea uncurled in her head. They'd abandoned the water hose on the side of the yard, so if she sneaked around front to the side gate, she could grab the hose with the power nozzle and soak all of them.

Seconds later she slid stealthily through the gate, kicked off her flip-flops and turned the water to full blast. Grasping the big power nozzle, she whipped the coiled hose behind her and charged out from around the corner. Jake and the boys were in the middle of the small backyard, engrossed in tossing balloons at each other. They weren't prepared for the wild woman barreling toward them. She flipped the switch, and the water shot out in a thick torrent. She went for Jake first.

"Agghhh!" he screeched, grabbing for his super soaker gun. The boys screamed and ran, but Jake stood firm, ducking beneath the blast, looking like a special forces member as he rolled across the grass and came up firing.

Eva felt the water gun blast hit her chest, but she didn't stop aiming her stream at Jake. She planted her feet and let him have it. Until he started toward her, head down, goggles abandoned, scrambling against the force of the water she aimed his way.

Dropping the hose, she ran back toward the side yard. Her bare feet slipped as she rounded the corner, and she careened out of control, landing on her butt in the wet grass. Didn't matter, she was already soaked.

Jake hit the corner hard at a full run and, seeing

her sprawled on the grass, tried to leap over her. His foot caught her knee and he tripped, falling and taking a roll on the grass.

Eva grabbed her sides and laughed.

"Oh, you think that's funny, do you?" he said, reaching out and grabbing her ankle, dragging her toward him. She struggled but there was no contest. Jake was strong and determined…and she was laughing too hard to put up much of a struggle.

"Jake," she squealed when he clutched her elbow and gave her a tug. She toppled onto him, laughing so hard she snorted.

But then her body registered the warmth of Jake. The hardness of his torso against the squishiness of her breasts. Her soft places met his hard places, and the laughter caught in her throat.

Jake looked up at her with his too-blue eyes filled with awareness.

Eva met his gaze, her breath catching as his eyes dropped to her…oh, crap…white T-shirt.

Yeah, she wore a white unpadded sports bra beneath a white T-shirt with a cute turtle on it—her one concession to the turtle theme. She didn't do ninjas. But she would totally do the sexy firefighter lying beneath her. If only she'd let herself.

If only they would both stop fighting it.

Her nipples tightened under his gaze, and she knew he could see through her shirt.

"Nice," he breathed, swallowing hard. "I knew they'd be incredible, but…"

He closed his eyes and clenched his jaw, letting go of her arm.

Eva scooted away, trying like hell to regain control of the stampeding horniness consuming her.

"Eva!" Charlie yelled.

Okay. Yeah. That worked. They were at a seven-year-old's birthday party. Sweet jumping Jehoshaphat. Jake had an erection—if she were any judge of anatomy—and she'd been on the cusp of ripping her clothes off and rolling around in the wet grass with him.

There were four kids just around the corner.

Good gravy.

"Coming," she said, struggling to her feet, leaving Jake lying in the fading day looking so damn good.

"No, you're not," Jake muttered. "Unfortunately."

She almost laughed at the desolation in his tone. But the disappointment welling inside her stifled the neurotic need to lose it over their situation.

They were like teenagers, totally at the mercy of their bodies. The slightest glance of flesh, the whisper of a suggestion, the almost visceral fantasies popping up at the strangest moments—all conspired to fell them…to bring them to the point where they lost all reason and just went at each other like a pair of dogs in heat.

Eva emerged from the side of the house, crossing her arms over her breasts so she didn't give a couple of elementary-school-aged boys a peep show. "What is it, guys?"

"Can we eat now?"

Eva shook her head. "We have to clean up first. Y'all pick up the popped balloons and I'll get y'all some towels. And I have to change real quick."

She slipped into the house, padding back to her room and en suite bathroom. Shucking her jeans, she pulled the T-shirt off and tossed it toward the tub, where it landed with a slap. Then she unhooked her damp sports bra, letting it fall as she reached for a hand towel to dry her hair.

But then the bathroom door opened.

Eva froze as a very wet Jake appeared in her mirror.

Gasping, she clasped her breasts and spun toward him, clad only in her lacy pink panties.

"What are you doing?" she managed.

He shut the door. And then he leaned back against it. He didn't respond, just allowed his gaze to lazily move over her body.

Eva stood there, not knowing whether she should drop her hands and go to him or affect maidenly outrage and order him from her bathroom. Seconds ticked by.

"Do you know how many times I imagined what you look like naked?" he asked, plucking his wet T-shirt from his chest. The fabric sucked against him, making a sound that matched the feeling in her gut.

"No," she managed to say.

"You are my friend, but I'm a man, you know?"

She didn't say anything. Just watched as he moved her way.

"There were times you'd leave the room to go shower and my mind would flash to you standing under the spray. I couldn't stop it, and I told myself that's what guys do. Totally normal." He stopped in front of her and traced the upper curve of her breast. Eva couldn't control the heart thumping in her chest, the breaths shortening as she caught the scent that was Jake's alone.

"And then when I'd go in to shower, I'd smell you. That pomegranate and orange blossom shampoo. Your perfume. Even the strawberry lip balm you kept on the counter. I'd think about your lips... and where you dabbed that perfume." He traced the valley between her breasts. "Here?"

Eva nodded dumbly, wishing she could find the words. But the moment was hushed like a church or some other sacred thing.

"I thought it was normal, but maybe my body knew more than my head. You know?"

She shook her head. "I don't think—"

"Shh," he said, pressing a warm finger against her lips. "Don't say it. Just don't."

Jake tugged her hands away from where they cupped her breasts. She let them fall.

He closed his eyes, expelling a heavy breath.

"Better, way better, than I could have ever imagined."

Eva swallowed as he opened his eyes again, his

gaze hungrily moving over her standing before him. Then he did the single most erotic thing she'd ever experienced. He lowered his head and sucked her right breast into his mouth.

"Oh," she groaned, sagging against the vanity, grabbing hold so her buckling knees didn't send her crashing to the floor.

Jake made low noises in his throat as he grasped her hips and pressed her back toward the mirror with his forehead. All the while he maintained the delicious pressure on her sensitive flesh, alternating nips with gentle suckling.

Eva felt liquid warmth pool in her pelvis.

Like a well-oiled engine, she purred for him.

His hands invaded her panties, sliding around to cup her ass, squeezing as he released her breast, dropping little kisses along her breastbone toward the uber-sensitive column of her throat. Making more low noises in his throat, he captured her lips.

It was heaven—that thrust and parry of his tongue, the way his hands stroked her, turning her warm desire into a raging inferno in mere seconds.

Then he pulled one hand from her ass, hooked it behind her knee and lifted her leg, dropping down to his knees so that his face was level with the juncture between her legs.

"Ah, sweet, sweet Eva," he said, stroking a finger down the crotch of the silky panties holding her damp heat.

She panted, unable to speak as he slid one finger

beneath the lace, teasing, stroking her soft down edging the slickness.

"Just one little taste," he murmured, lifting the fabric and pulling it aside so she was exposed to him.

"Oh," she breathed, her head sinking back onto the cold mirror. He held her leg up with the other hand, and she surrendered to him, letting Jake do whatever he pleased.

She needed him to touch her, to love her, to do what she'd fantasized about in the darkness of her bedroom. She opened her eyes and looked down at him.

"So beautiful. I have to taste you, sweet girl," he said, eyes half-lidded with desire as he leaned forward and—dear Bessie—licked her.

"Ahhh." She tilted her hips as he fastened his mouth on that place that would...

Her body exploded.

Hips convulsed, shaking as she came apart. He held her firm, working her as she experienced the strongest, fastest orgasm of her life.

After what felt like hours, she pressed against his forehead for respite. He looked up at her, his blue eyes dilated, his face portraying the deepest satisfaction.

Eva dropped her leg onto the vanity top with a splat.

She swallowed several times, blinking at him. And then the reality of the situation struck her. "Oh, crap. Charlie!"

Jake actually had the nerve to laugh as he tugged the crotch of her panties back in place. "Not usually the response I get, but—"

Eva pushed him away. She was shocked and confused about what had taken place. And totally freaked about the fact that a bunch of soaked seven- and eight-year-olds galloped about her backyard with no supervision while she straddled Jake's head in the bathroom.

What in the hell had she just done?

Grabbing her bathrobe off the hook, she struggled into it. Her face suffused with color as she registered that Jake still knelt on her bathroom floor, T-shirt still molded to his body, a very impressive erection straining his jeans and a triumphant smile plastered on his face.

Oh, cripes, she was such a whore.

Who did this sort of thing in the middle of their baby brother's birthday party?

A deranged horny woman, obviously.

She pushed past Jake, ducking out in the hall.

It was totally quiet.

Which probably meant the boys were playing with matches, squirting lighter fluid at the grill or choking on the remnants of the burst latex balloons. And what if one of them had a peanut allergy she didn't know about? Or a bee allergy?

Not that she even had bees around. Or peanut butter.

She scurried down the hall and peeked into the backyard.

Then exhaled in relief.

They had gone back to playing the same game they'd been playing before.

Jake set his hands on her shoulders, and she jumped a good foot off the ground.

"Relax," he said.

She turned on him. "Seriously? That's what you say to me after what we just did back there?"

"What do you want me to say?"

Her mouth opened and shut, opened and shut. Like a cartoon. No, like a horrible '80s romantic comedy.

He crooked his head. "Are you okay?"

"No. No, I'm not," she managed to squeak out before stalking back to her bedroom. She shut the door a bit harder than she'd meant to and locked it for good measure.

Jesus.

No, she couldn't bring Jake into her messy life right now.

She sank onto the bed and pressed her fingers into her eyes.

"You're a dumb-ass. You're a dumb-ass," she whispered to herself before opening her eyes and catching her reflection in the mirror above the dresser.

Absolute mess.

The robe clung to her larger than average breasts,

gaping at the chest. Her hair had half dried into something that looked as if a kindergartener had taken shears to it. But her eyes, well, they looked a bit dreamy, and her cheeks were rosy as…roses? Overall, she looked like a woman who'd had a fulfilling encounter with a sex god in the bathroom, followed by a partial meltdown.

She laughed.

Because she really couldn't cry.

"Oh, God," she said, covering her mouth, her eyes going all googly. She'd just let Jake go down on her in the small bathroom with the vintage tile and claw-foot tub. In the middle of a children's birthday party.

Classic.

She didn't have time to overthink it, though, because she had to go put the mustard and ketchup in the cute glass dishes she'd bought for the party. And she needed to get the birthday cake candles out of the bags she set in the laundry room. Oh, and she had left the dump truck–shaped pencil erasers in the passenger seat of her car and still needed to put them in the goody bags.

She hadn't even known that she needed goody bags for each child as a token of thanks for coming to Charlie's party. Thankfully, they'd run into Abigail at the dollar store and she'd imparted her extensive wisdom in the art of kids' parties.

Who knew?

So she didn't have time to think about losing control and doing, well, *that* with Jake.

There were bean bags to toss into clown faces and karaoke songs to sing.

Exactly.

No time to think.

CHAPTER THIRTEEN

JAKE HAD THOUGHT of nothing else for the rest of the day but the image of Eva with her head dropped back against her bathroom mirror, moaning his name. Like a mosquito circling his head, the image wouldn't leave him alone. So he embraced it.

It popped up when he brushed his teeth.

And when he pulled on his pajama pants.

And damn sure when he slid beneath the sheets in the quiet darkness of his room.

He'd promised himself that when he logged into his shift at the station he would put aside the memory of Eva spread before him, sighing with pleasure. Just like laundry he would put it away, compartmentalize neatly...not that he knew what that looked like. Neat freak he wasn't.

But when it came down to it, he sorta failed at tucking the image away anyway.

Because when he got to work, Eva somehow looked more sensuous in her uniform than ever before. Which he knew was crazy because she'd dressed as she'd always dressed—gray polo shirt monogrammed with MBFD tucked into navy uniform pants, dark nonslip-sole shoes on her feet. Her hair lay braided down her back, not a trace of makeup beyond slick lip gloss. But somehow she looked smoking hot.

"You going to eat that last piece of cornbread?" he asked her.

She didn't answer. Just passed him the platter holding one lonely piece of cornbread. Dutch and Hank looked sorry they hadn't thought to ask first.

"Thanks," he said, taking the platter and setting it on the corner of the table.

"What's up with you two?" Hank asked, scraping the last of the beef stew out of the pot.

"Nothing," Eva said, not looking at any of the men. Her spoon had her full attention.

"Well, usually y'all are jabbering up a storm, but for the past few weeks it's been weird. Is it because Wendell is retiring and a spot is up for grabs?"

"Nope," Jake said, shaking his head. "Guess me and Eva have just run outta things to say."

Hank barked a laugh. "About damn time. I was tired of talking about the Eric Church concert or who's gonna kill who on the next *Walking Dead* episode."

Eva stood up, the sound of her chair screeching making them all wince. "I'm going to bed. I've got a headache."

"It's only eight o'clock. Don't you want to watch *Chicago Fire*?" Dutch asked.

"No, I've been getting up early with Charlie and I'm beat. Need some z's."

The other two men looked at Jake with questions

in their eyes. They knew something was wrong between him and Eva, but it wasn't as if Jake could casually say, "Yeah, I went down on her last night in the middle of her half brother's birthday party." Seemed rather inappropriate dinner conversation.

"But it ended in a cliffhanger," Dutch said.

"I have DVR," Eva replied moving down the hall.

The click of her bedroom door sounded louder than normal.

"What did you do?" Hank asked, leaning back with a belch. "She's acting weird."

"It's probably because of her brother," Jake offered, averting his gaze. He didn't want the guys to see the truth in his eyes.

Uh, what that truth was could be a lot of things. Hell, Jake didn't know what way was up when it came to Eva. All he knew was she drove him nuts.

He hadn't planned what had happened in the bathroom yesterday. He'd gone in after her to grab a towel for himself so he could get the wieners inside and set up the hot dog bar for the boys. Her room door had been open a crack, and he could see into the mirror hanging over her bed…which reflected Eva pulling off her shirt.

It was as if his feet moved of their own accord. Before he knew it, he'd walked into her room and rounded the corner of the bathroom. And there she stood, large breasts so…he really didn't have words for them. They were so perfect. Large, round with puffy dark pink nipples. Her stomach was flat, slightly ripped. Her panties delicate against the smooth, rounded hips. She was like an Amazon goddess—lean, muscular and very, very feminine.

He hadn't been able to leave.

Not even if a serial killer with a chain saw had been after him. Nothing could have made him leave.

Except maybe Eva herself.

But he'd seen the desire in her eyes—she wouldn't tell him no. But he didn't ask. No, he took. And it was the sweetest thing he'd done in forever and a day.

Of course, after she'd pulled on clothes and donned her mask of shame, he'd had doubts. After all, he'd promised her he wouldn't kiss her and then he'd tossed that out when the first little bit of temptation came along.

Okay, it was a big temptation.

But still, he'd violated the terms of their agreement in a very big way. He'd finished with the grilling, helped the boys set up the mini-bonfire in the fire pit and then got the hell out of there. He'd spent the rest of the night watching crappy movies, begging himself to not think about how upset Eva had looked after the bathroom incident.

"I'll go talk to her," he said, rising from the table and making his way back to the bunk area. Eva slept in the smallest room, sharing it with Moon, whom she professed was neater than a nun.

He knocked softly. "Eva?"

She opened it before he could knock a second time. "What?"

"Can we talk?"

Staring hard at him, she slowly shook her head. "I'm fine. There's nothing to say."

"Look, they know something's up by the way you're acting. You've hardly said a word all night."

"So? I don't care what they think. I told them I had a headache. Now go watch TV and give me some space."

"No. We've got to address this. Ignoring things isn't working." He pressed his hands to the door frame before glancing back at where Dutch and Hank sat sipping coffee and talking about Hank's son walking on at University of Louisiana Lafayette. "Let me in and let's figure things out. We can't work this way."

She stepped back. "Fine. But I like the idea of ignoring it. I'm horrified you did that—"

"Come on, E, don't make me sound like a sleazebag. Last time I looked, I'm a grown man and you're a grown woman. No need to make what happened in the bathroom sound like a crime," he said, hating the hurt that curled into a ball in his stomach. "Stop making what we have between us bad."

He jerked his head toward the still-open door. Eva closed it. But she didn't look happy about it.

"Look, what happened *happened*," she said. "And it's my fault. I let you do it, and I'm angry at myself for being so weak."

"So here's the deal, Eva—we may not have wanted to feel this way about each other, but pretending it away, wishing it away, is not working. Obviously, the attraction isn't a passing thing for either of us."

Eva crossed her arms over her chest. "I don't want this. I mean, I do, but—"

"We were wrong—wrong to think we can't be more than friends. Time to stop fighting and embrace it."

"Who says you have the power to declare that?" She sat down hard on the bed, her arms moving down to curl about her waist. For a moment she looked like a little girl. She stared at his boots, and he got the feeling her mind whirred with possibility, doubt and maybe...hope.

"No one gave me the power to decide, but you can't say that what we're doing now is working. So why don't we try to see if we're good together before we decide we're bad? We both shot down the idea before really examining it, before trying it on. We might work."

"What?" she said, lifting her gaze.

"Go out with me. On a date." He hadn't intended on suggesting they start dating. He'd only wanted to stop the awkwardness between them. The past few hours had been filled with deafening silence. But taking Eva on a date would do one of two things—it would either prove they should remain friends only or it would break open a new possibility. Either way, taking a few steps on a new path couldn't hurt as long as they didn't get too far down. Of course, they'd sort of already turned a corner in that bathroom.

"You want to take me on a date?" she asked. She sounded confused. As though he'd just asked to borrow her pantyhose.

"To dinner. Or that drive-in movie place that just opened over in Creole Gap."

"You want to go on a date?"

"That's what I said." He tried not to be flippant but her reaction made him defensive. What? He wasn't worth getting her nails done for? Not that Eva ever painted her fingernails.

"I don't know what to say," she said.

"I'm pretty sure it's either yes or no."

A few seconds ticked by before she shifted on the bed and folded her hands over her knee. Like a therapist. Like she was prepared to be logical about the matter. "I know we've had some hiccups in restraining ourselves, and I don't know why suddenly everything's changed, but I don't think we should date."

Something hard and spiteful smacked him. Rejection. "So you'd rather continue meeting in bathrooms for oral sex? Cool, I think it's my turn to receive."

Color flooded her face before she set her jaw. "You're just mad because I didn't collapse at your feet and squeal, 'Oh, Jake, yes, a date would be lovely.'"

"No. I'm mad that you're being stubborn. That you've talked yourself out of giving us a chance."

"For what? A two- or three-month fling before you move on to Tracy at the Cut-n-Curl? For one thing, we work together. When you cut me loose, you'll still see me. And for another, our friendship means more to me than that. I don't want to ruin us, Jake."

"And what if it's not a two- or three-month thing? What if it's more?"

Something flashed in Eva's eyes. The power of the emotion within the depths hit him. Everything Matt had said the day before came spiraling back. *Eva's always had a thing for you.* For her, this wasn't about sex. It was about her heart.

And that made him hesitate.

He'd only thought of the pleasure…of the way she made him feel. Even after talking to Matt, weighing the pros and cons of dating Eva, he'd still managed to convince himself he could handle the fallout when they called it quits. After all, they were adults and friends. It would be like Elaine and Jerry on Seinfeld—two ex-lovers who still hung out. But he'd never contemplated love.

Eva gave an incredulous laugh. "Please, Jake. I've been your friend for over three years. I've watched the parade of women. You're good for two months at the most. I'm not looking for casual, Jake. I never have."

"So you're telling me you thought Chase was forever?" His words were like darts, angry, metallic.

"I wanted to."

Such honesty. One of the things he liked about Eva. When she talked about her personal life, she never covered the ugliness with a pretty latch-hook rug, pretending the damage wasn't there.

"So the answer is no? Because you've already decided you know me. You've decided I'm that kind of guy, huh?"

"I think the answer has to be no," she said, sorrow coating her words, making her voice raspy. "We can't be so selfish as to take what we want without foreseeing the ramifications. The downside is too bumpy."

He felt for the doorknob, her rejection stinging him. He felt under assault—his character assassinated. But it had all been brought on by his choice to live as he'd lived. Jake now reaped what he sowed. Eva thought he was pure heartbreak. "So this is what we're left with? A strained friendship?"

Eva stood, her chin relaying her determination even as her hands trembled. "I want you, Jake. That's something I can't deny, but I couldn't bear it if you weren't in my life. I'll take what we have over what we could lose. I've spent three years pretending. I'll deal."

Jake opened the door, turning back to her. "You're afraid."

Eva nodded.

"That's no way to live, Eva."

"Says the pot to the kettle."

Jake flinched.

She continued. "We do what we do to make life tolerable. My life's not horrible, but I've never had what you have here in Magnolia Bend. You have a big family who loves you, who are always there for you. I've carved a place in this town, and I finally feel like I belong somewhere. If I'm a coward for protecting that, then that's what I am. I won't toss all I am so I can sleep with you for a few weeks. I just can't."

He gave her a curt nod, afraid of the emotion churning inside him. His brother was right. Eva was right. Everyone was right. Jake wasn't the kind of guy a chick dated with the dream of wedding cake and chubby baby feet in her eyes. Though he wanted Eva with a need that had shaken him like a sapling in a hurricane, he respected her feelings.

"Night, Eva."

"Good night, Jake."

He walked out, not bothering to shut the door. Somehow he couldn't. It was too final.

"Hey," she whispered from the doorway.

Jake turned. "Yeah?"

"Tonight was hard after what happened, you know? But it will get better. We're good, okay?"

He glanced back at Dutch and Hank, who were deep in conversation. "Sure."

She shut the door softly, like an apology.

Jake stared at the closed door, knowing they weren't okay and wondering what he could do about it. Maybe nothing. Eva was right. He wasn't a man who could love a woman the way she needed. He was who he'd always been.

Something he'd carried around with him for a long time...something it seemed he would carry awhile longer.

THE NEXT EVENING Eva took Charlie to a special service at First Presbyterian and learned that hard church pews, long choir programs and seven-year-old little boys did not mix.

"Stop," she hissed for the twenty-second time in the past hour as Charlie kicked a steady rhythm on the back of the pew in front of them. Mildred Chandler sent a scowl over her shoulder before straightening her old crow shoulders and issuing a harrumph.

Old hag.

"Did you say something?" Shelby Beauchamp whispered, popping a pacifier into her infant daughter's mouth.

"Uh, no." Eva pressed her lips together, wondering if she was going cuckoo in the third row of the Magnolia Bend First Pres Church. She didn't think she'd uttered the insult out loud, but she was so damn tired she couldn't remember. Sleep had been as elusive as an antelope flying across the Serengeti. If it wasn't Charlie crying out from his wet bed, it was the memory of Jake's face as he walked away from her the night before.

He'd looked so defeated, and something inside her had broken loose. For so long she'd wanted exactly what he'd offered—and what had she done? She'd shoved the chance for something more with Jake away like week-old meatloaf. And why?

Because.

Jake had nailed it—she was scared. Scared all she'd built would topple, scattering ruin around her. She'd worked too hard to build something she was proud of here, and the thought of losing it made her feel sick. And then there was the daddy issue. Her father had been so similar to Jake, passionate about saving people, but unable to stick with any woman. Like so many other women, she'd allowed her heart to chase after a man so similar to the one she'd tried desperately to please. The whole thing was so messed up.

"I'm glad you came tonight," Shelby whispered as Ricky Hebert sang a rich baritone solo about gathering the fruit of the vine.

"Sure."

"I forgot about Charlie when I sent you that email, but it's good you brought him, too. They have cookies and punch after the concert," Shelby said, sliding her eyes to Charlie, who wriggled like a worm in hot ashes.

Her brother froze and whispered, "Cookies?"

Shelby nodded, a smile on her pretty face, as she switched Lindsay Rebecca to her other arm. The baby pulled out her pacifier and screeched. "Daaaaa!"

"Shhh!" Shelby said, plopping the pacifier back

into the child's mouth before turning to Eva, her blue eyes filled with excitement. "Did you hear that? She just said Daddy."

Mildred cast another disapproving glare over her shoulder.

"Sorry, Mrs. Chandler," Shelby whispered, leaning up to the battle-ax's ear. "Linds just said her first word."

The older woman managed a smile and nod before shifting her attention back to the concert where Shelby's husband, John, stood in the back row of the choir. His gaze found Shelby and Lindsay, and his face lit up. John looked the most like Jake, except he was taller, a bit rangier and way more reserved. A steady man, he'd turned the corner on grief with the help of the curvy woman sitting next to Eva. Shelby was akin to sunshine on a dark day, and the town had taken to her like a duck to water. If a person decided not to like her, she'd wear them down with unapologetic humor and cheer.

Finally, the concert ended and Charlie leaped from the bench like flames licked his butt. He nearly knocked Peter Haas down at the end of the row in his quest for cookies, which were being served in the fellowship hall connected to the sanctuary.

"Sorry, Mr. Haas," Eva said, patting the ancient usher on his sharp elbow.

"That's all right. The little fellow must be thirsty," he said with a lift of his caterpillar eyebrows.

"That and lacking in manners. I'm working on

it," Eva said, moving through the light crowd lining the entrance, spying her brother, who already had a glass of punch and was in the process of shoveling cookies onto his plate.

"Hey, slow down, Charlie. You don't need any more than that," she said, curving a hand over his shoulder.

"I'm hungry. I didn't like that spaghetti junk you made."

She sighed and then took the tongs from her brother. "Tough stuff. Now hand me those two cookies and go sit over there next to Will and Wyatt."

Charlie's eyes lit up. "They're here, too? Where?"

Eva pointed out the two boys, sitting at a table noshing on cookies and turned right into Sara Richter, the mother of the little boy who had come to Charlie's birthday party. Her son, Drew, was in Charlie's class, and from what Eva understood he sat with her brother every day at lunch.

"Hi, Sara," Eva said, wrapping the two cookies she'd taken from Charlie's plate into a napkin and tucking them in her purse. She would put them in Charlie's lunch tomorrow. "Thanks for letting Drew come to Charlie's birthday party. The boys had lots of fun."

"Yeah, I needed to talk to you about that. Do you have a minute?"

Dread sank like a stone in her stomach. "Is everything okay?"

"Can we talk in the hall or something?" Sara

asked, her gaze moving frantically back and forth from the podium in the front of the hall toward the exit sign hanging above the double doors leading out into the hallway. *Uncomfortable* seemed to be the word of the evening.

"Sure." Eva gave Charlie a wave and then pointed toward the hall. The child nodded his head and went back to chattering with his newfound friends.

The hall was unlit and quiet. Eva turned as soon as Sara slipped through the door. Sara was tall, spare and had a mole on her left cheek. She worked as a loan officer at the bank and always dressed in neutral colors as if being sedate would make her more approachable. "What's wrong?"

Sara released a deep breath. "Look, I hate to do this with all the stress you've been under. Taking care of a kid when you're not used to it must be a huge adjustment…"

"But…"

"Drew said Charlie threatened to stab him with scissors."

"What?"

"I know, I know. I'm not trying to make a mountain out of a molehill, but I thought you needed to know. I heard that he experienced some trauma at the hands of his mother."

"A little, but his mother never harmed him," Eva said, immediately wondering if in fact Claren had done something to Charlie. She hadn't thought to ask, but the woman *had* been desperate enough to leave him in search of drugs. What other things had she been desperate enough to do? "I can't believe he'd threaten Drew. He likes him."

"It's probably a power play. Charlie lost control of his world, so he wants to control what he can. Drew's a bit shy and impressionable. I can see how he could be easily manipulated. So though I don't think Charlie would hurt Drew, I do think you need to know."

"I am so sorry, Sara."

The woman nodded. "I know. It was really hard for me to come to you, and, hey, I won't say anything to anyone. I talked to Drew about how to handle situations like this. My son won't be ugly to Charlie, but he will remove himself from any situation where he feels uncomfortable. Good luck, Eva." Sara patted her arm and then stepped back into the fellowship hall.

Eva slumped against the wall and stared at a bulletin board announcing church news. There was a colorful pumpkin in one corner and leaves dotting the gingham background, but none of those cheerful, positive flyers and posters made her feel any better.

Charlie had threatened to stab his friend?

She couldn't wrap her mind around Sara's words. For the past few days Charlie had been so good. Mostly. He'd been a typical kid, dropping jelly on the floor and forgetting his signed papers, but he seemed secure, comfortable. As if what she was doing worked.

He had an appointment with Macy Hebert the next

day, so Eva could bring this behavior up with her at the start of his counseling session. But she had to say something to Charlie before he went to school the following morning. She couldn't have something happen, especially after Sara had told her about his behavior. Of course, saying something and doing something were two different things.

Eva pushed off the wall and entered the fellow-ship hall, nearly making it past Jake.

"Eva," he called out.

She turned and pasted on a smile, dreading dealing with Jake, even though part of her wanted to sink in his arms and admit she had been a moron. She wanted someone to hold her, to tell her everything would be okay. But it couldn't be Jake. "What are you doing here? You never come to these things."

"Shelby."

"She sent you an email, too?"

"And threats. She fits right into this family. She's learned how to issue ultimatums with a gracious smile."

"Takes talent," Eva said, craning her head around a group of older ladies discussing the best cranberry salad recipe in search of her brother. He still sat with Matt's boys, happily munching on sugar cookies. He didn't look like a serial killer to her.

Okay, she knew he wouldn't actually hurt Drew. But something was wrong and it was up to her to fix it, which was another good point to add to her list of reasons for not messing around with Jake. She'd taken on an important responsibility in giving her brother a stable environment. Charlie needed her to make wise decisions…to put his needs over her desires.

"So did you like the concert?" Jake said, sounding…not himself.

"It was good," she said, craning her head again. "He hasn't moved."

"Who?"

Jake made a face. "Your brother."

"I know. I'm just keeping an eye on him. That's pretty much my job now." She crossed her arms and tried to look casual, but the information Sara had imparted had her upset. She didn't know how to handle this situation because she knew squat about kids.

"He's just a kid."

"What do you know about kids?" she challenged, lifting her chin. "And besides, neither one of us knows what he's gone through these past months. The counselor at the rehab center said Claren was strung out on a lot of stuff. I don't know what she did or didn't do for Charlie. I should have known, but I didn't. I failed him, and I refuse to do that now, again."

"Bull…uh, feathers. He was not your responsibility."

"He's my brother. I should have checked on him more. I should have known Claren was using again. I didn't help him then, but I'm putting him first now. The kid deserves to have someone put him first."

Jake studied her in the harsh overhead light of the hall, making her tuck a strand of hair behind her ear and moisten her lips. She had forgotten to put on some lip balm, and the first true cool front had passed through town, drying the air out and making her lips chapped.

"I understand," he said, reaching out a hand but then drawing it back. "You're a good person, Eva. I'm proud of you for being so concerned about your brother."

He said it as though he confirmed something in his head. She couldn't guess what that was because while on the surface Jake seemed open, he was definitely closed off. But she could see he'd reached a conclusion. Maybe he saw the reason in her words the night before. Maybe he understood this was bigger than wanting a few rolls in the hay with someone. That the kid was more important than that. That giving Eva security and support was important not just for her, but for Charlie. That he couldn't risk becoming a slave to desire any more than she could remain chained to hers.

Impasse.

"Thank you," she said, craning her head again, spying Charlie scooting away from the table. "I better go. He has school tomorrow."

"Later," Jake said, moving toward the exit, making her wonder if he'd only stayed for her. The idea he'd waited to see her warmed her, made her feel cared for.

Eva made it to Charlie before he could scamper down the hall with Will and Wyatt toward the children's ministry wing.

"Time to go, good-time Charlie."

"Awww, man. Just a little longer. Please."

"Nope. School tomorrow and we have to do some reading tonight so you can take your AR test."

"I don't want to read. It's stupid."

"Charlie," she warned.

"I'm staying," he said, crossing his arms and glaring at her. His chin jutted out and the mulishness in his eyes looked familiar. Monroes weren't known for their bending nature.

"No, you aren't. We're going home now and you're not making a scene." She glanced at the people around her who already cast apprehensive glances toward them.

"Make me," he screamed, ripping himself away from the hand she'd placed on his shoulder. Eva felt the shock of the people around her. Conversations died. People looked at them.

Eva lowered her voice, stooping down to eyeball her brother, whose face had turned red. "Don't do this, Charlie. Please."

"I hate you. You make me do everything," he yelled, darting past her toward the double doors leading to the hall. He ran into an older lady, lurched to the left and then the right, like a football player running toward the end zone.

And then his feet left the ground as an arm swooped in to stop him.

Jake.

Charlie kicked, but Jake merely lifted him off the ground, tossed him over his shoulder and moved back toward Eva. Everyone in the place watched, wide-eyed.

Charlie burst into tears, bellowing for his mother. Jake ignored him and stopped in front of Eva.

He laughed, smacking Charlie on the bottom playfully. "I believe I caught something of yours." His smile encouraged her to lighten the moment.

Eva managed to smile, though the lump in her throat felt suspiciously full of tears. She rolled her eyes. "He's always trying to make a break for it. Who knew being an evil stepsister was so hard?"

A few folks sent relieved glances and went back to talking quietly. Out of the corner of her eyes she saw Fancy set a platter of cookies on the table next to the coffee urn and start toward them.

"Put me down," Charlie moaned, kicking his feet halfheartedly.

"No way. You're so fast, I'm pretty sure Eva should sign you up for football or something. We could call you Touchdown Charlie," Jake said, jerking his head toward the exit. "Allow me to carry your purchase to the car, madam."

Seeing Fancy dodge Mildred, who still looked as sour as a persimmon, Eva nodded and hustled toward the door leading to the parking lot. The waning day with its paintbrush sky met her when she stepped out. Her smile died, and she closed her eyes, breathing out, "Jesus."

"My mother would say to call on him, and in this instance, I think it's a good idea," Jake said, warmth coating his voice, making her relax. This is what the man was good at—making things easier. Making the tragic bearable.

Not that this was tragic…but she was worried about her brother. Obviously, she'd patted herself on the back a bit too early. The kid had issues, ones that scared her.

"Yeah, I probably should hit my knees more."

"I'm gonna leave that one alone," he laughed.

Eva felt the blush hit her cheeks. "Only you."

Which was exactly right. Only Jake.

Wasn't that pretty much her motto in life? Only Jake.

Her knight in a denim button-down walked to her car, sliding Charlie from his shoulders. He held the little boy up under his arms and gave him a slight shake to get his attention. Her brother lifted a rounded, tear-streaked face to Jake.

"You do realize that your sister loves you?" Jake brought the kid closer to him so that their noses nearly met.

Charlie merely screwed up his face and started crying.

"No sense in crying about it now, kiddo. You

didn't act nice to her in there and everyone saw that. What do you have to say to that?"

"I'm…I'm…sor…sorry," Charlie cried, lifting his hands to rub at his eyes.

"That's a good start, Charlie," Jake said, setting the boy down, ruffling his hair. At that moment, Eva saw a spectrum in Jake she'd never seen before. Jake would be a helluva dad. Firm but kind. Funny and yet sensible. Approachable, loving and not too far off his own father.

"Okay," Eva said, grabbing her brother and giving him a hug. "I know things have been hard. I forgive you. We all make mistakes, but we have to do better. Okay?" She looked at Jake, her words carrying double meaning.

Charlie nodded against her neck. She felt a suspicious dampness that was likely tears mixed with snot, but she ignored it and hugged him tight.

How could she want to both throttle and hug someone at the same time?

Jake watched them with a tender expression. "Guess everything's okay now?"

Eva nodded, pulled her keys out of her pocket and unlocked the car. After she got a sniffling Charlie settled, she shut the door and turned back to Jake. "Thank you. That was an awkward situation for me. I actually thought about pulling the fire alarm but it seemed redundant for a firefighter."

Jake chuckled. "Naw, B Shift would have to answer."

"Seriously, though, thank you."

"That's what friends are for, right?" He reached out and tucked a piece of the hair she'd left unbound behind her ear.

Eva swallowed. "That's right. We'll always be friends."

He pressed a gentle kiss on her forehead and stepped away. "See you later, alligator."

"See you soon, you big baboon."

The flash of his teeth in the twilight was like a crumb of bread to a starving prisoner. She wanted more. But she'd make it past this craziness in her life—all of it.

She had to. More than *her* heart was on the line. Charlie's sat right alongside hers, which meant she didn't do what she wanted. She did what she needed.

And even if Charlie wasn't her responsibility, Jake Beauchamp would never be a wise decision.

She had to accept that he was a heartbreaker.

CHAPTER FOURTEEN

JAKE GAVE HIS sister a wave and backed his truck out of the recently repaired driveway of Laurel Woods, his niece beside him in the truck.

"Wait, how much did you say you'd pay me again?" Birdie asked, flipping her hair over her shoulder, looking up from the cell phone permanently glued to her hand.

"Uh, twenty bucks?"

"I get twelve dollars an hour," she said, raising her dark brows.

"You do know I'm a firefighter. We don't get paid much. And don't you have to do service hours or something anyway?"

Birdie made a face. She was a pretty girl who'd gone through a bratty stage last year, wearing black, dressing like a shadow and giving her mother all kinds of fits. But thankfully she'd turned a corner. She'd grown several inches, stopped wearing dark eyeliner and begrudgingly wore a dress every now and then. Still, Birdie had attitude in spades, and nothing got by her. "True. I'll take twelve dollars an hour for the first two hours and then the remainder of the time will be service hours. Deal?"

"Deal," he said as he pulled onto the highway.

Thursday night when he'd taken Clint to Ray-Ray's, he'd learned his friend planned on taking Eva and Charlie to the Peanut Festival in Fort Brantley. Something inside him had rattled around, banging on the steel bars encircling his heart, like some caged beast. And something ugly had propelled him to smile and say "Hey, if you don't mind, I'll tag along."

Clint gave him a death stare, so Jake amended. "I'll bring a date."

Birdie was as good of a date as any, especially since she had her babysitting certification and could take Charlie to jump in the bounce houses and get his face painted.

A few minutes later they pulled up to the Cochran place. Biscuit bounded toward his truck, yipping happily. Birdie bailed out and dropped to her knees for doggy kisses. Abigail really needed to get the kid a dog. He'd never seen someone so crazy about animals as Birdie.

"Birdie!" Charlie crowed from the porch, hustling down toward the dog and thirteen-year-old girl. "Are you coming with us?"

Birdie nodded. "Sure, kid."

"Cool," Charlie said, bypassing Jake and heading straight to the girl.

"What am I? Chopped liver?" Jake muttered, leaving Charlie and Birdie with Biscuit to roll in the few leaves that had fallen from the sweetgum tree sitting beside the lake. Eva and Clint sat on the porch, watching him as he headed their way.

"I didn't know you were coming," Eva said from the large unfinished rocking chair.

"Yeah, I told Clint I'd like to go. I heard there's a guy at the festival who sells knives. Want to pick up a certain brand for my dad's birthday next month. That's okay, huh?"

"Sure."

"You said you were bringing a date," Clint muttered.

"I did. I brought Birdie. Figured Charlie would like hanging out with her."

"How much did you have to pay her?" Clint drawled. His old friend knew Jake's niece well.

"Just twenty-four dollars. And she negotiated service hours."

Clint snorted. "I love that kid."

Eva stood. "Let's get going. I have to get back early because Charlie has homework. He's behind on a few things."

Clint hit the controls on his chair and rolled toward the ramp hidden on the side of the traditional Creole house. His friend looked a bit grumpy about Birdie being Jake's date…what was that about? Did Clint have a thing for Eva?

No, that's crazy. Clint and Eva were friends.

But so were she and Jake…and he'd seen her naked. Well, almost naked.

"Hey, is everything okay with Charlie? Did he see Macy?"

A little nosy maybe, but he'd been there when

Charlie had a meltdown. He'd seen the worry crowd Eva's eyes, seen the sheen of tears following.

"Yeah," she said, grabbing hold of the rough cypress railing, seemingly hesitating. "He's been having some power issues. That's what his therapist calls them. He lost control of his world, so he reacts by trying to exert control on others around him. With his classmates, he expresses it more physically. With me, he manipulates me emotionally. Macy says it's a natural process that almost all kids go through, but with kids who've been traumatized, it can be pronounced. I feel like he's getting good care, and I'm just trying to give him stability and not overreact to his manipulations. Raising a kid is hard. Why don't people know this going into it?"

Jake smiled. "Because no one would have them then."

"Come on, guys," Charlie yelled, running toward Clint and the van he'd started via the remote starter. Clint had a nice van converted to suit his needs as a paraplegic, replete with a lift for his chair and altered controls so he could drive. Birdie rose as Clint ordered Biscuit to the front porch. Oftentimes, Clint took the service dog with him but since Jake and Eva would be with him, the dog wasn't necessary.

Eva and Jake walked down the steps.

"Why did you come?" Eva asked.

Jake didn't look at her. He didn't want her to see his jealousy. "Because I need that gift."

She stopped halfway down the ramp. Turning

back, Jake noted she'd arched one elegant brow. Yes. Elegant. Not that he'd ever noticed before.

"Seriously. I have to get Dad a birthday present."

"We're just friends," she repeated like a mantra.

"Me or Clint?"

"Both."

Jake ignored that and called out, "Shotgun."

"Damn it," Eva shouted after him. "I'm the guest. You're the tagalong. You ride in the back."

Jake smiled all the way to the front seat.

EVA SET HER funnel cake on the table next to Birdie and plopped down. On the stage in front of them, Totally Toad, a Bluegrass revival band, strummed the banjo, making toes tap and hands clap. Eva, however, was focused on digging into the fried, powder-sugared goodness in front of her.

"What's up with you and Uncle Jake?" Birdie asked, taking a slurp of a melted sno-ball.

Eva almost choked, but held it together enough to swallow the confection that suddenly tasted too cloying. "What?"

"He looks at you all the time. Like he wants a bite of you."

"What?"

"I figure you know what I'm talking about. You're weird around him, too—all tiptoey."

"No, I'm not. We're just friends."

"Like my mom was just friends with Leif? Are

you two hanging out, too? 'Cause that's what she called it."

"Called what?"

Birdie merely wiggled her eyebrows.

"Birdie," Eva said, her voice rising. Good heavens.

"What? I'm thirteen. I know about s-e-x."

"Your uncle and I aren't having s-e-x." Eva felt silly spelling it out, but she needed to spell that out. What had happened in her bathroom last weekend wasn't sex. Technically it was foreplay. She thought. "We're friends in the true sense of the word. Maybe you're just seeing me different because of Charlie."

"Why would I do that?" she asked, looking genuinely confused.

"Uh, because I seem more, uh, I don't know..."

Birdie reached over and ripped off a piece of Eva's funnel cake. "You mean like in a motherly way, huh? I guess I can see that. You treat him like my mother treats me. Have you licked your thumb and rubbed something off his face yet?"

Eva shook her head.

"Oh, good. Kids hate that. And it's okay if you do like Uncle Jake. Not a big deal 'cause all the ladies like him. He's that kind, you know?"

"No. I don't."

"A player."

"Oh." Solid observation from a thirteen-year-old. Jake's player status had been part of his persona for so long that apparently everyone understood what his intentions were regarding the fairer sex. Which made her feel doubly good about the decision she'd made to keep her and Jake firmly in friendship mode. Okay, yeah, she still loved him and nurtured that happily-ever-after seed planted long ago at the hands of dog-eared fairy tales. Some things couldn't be helped. She blamed her unrequited optimism regarding her heart squarely on all those dumb books. Her mother and father, however, had set her up for reality.

"Wanna go find the guys?" Eva said, sliding the barely nibbled funnel cake toward Birdie with a hooked eyebrow.

Birdie pulled off a huge hunk, peppering her navy shirt with powdered sugar. "I guess."

They walked through throngs of people standing around beer booths and arts and craft tents as they made their way toward the huge area of inflatables. Out of the corner of her eye, she caught sight of her brother's bright red Spider-Man T-shirt…climbing an enormous rock wall. Her heart lodged in her throat until she realized he was strapped into a harness and Jake stood beneath him, calling out instructions and smiling as her brother maneuvered around the small plastic rocks.

"Cool," Birdie breathed. "I could climb that thing in no time."

"Yeah, I hear you're good at climbing."

Birdie's eyes widened slightly but she ignored Eva's comment in favor of heading toward her uncle.

Eva shouldn't have teased the girl about the time last year she'd climbed a tree to spy on her neigh-

bor who swam laps in his pool…naked. The apology
Birdie had to give led directly to the happy relationship her mother now had with the delicious Leif
Lively. Yeah, Birdie seemed to have an above-average
curiosity about sex and the human body. Maybe she'd
be a doctor…or a porn star. But she damn sure picked
up on things she wasn't supposed to for her age.

Eva watched as her brother passed the halfway
point, his sweet face screwed in concentration,
tongue caught between his teeth as he struggled to
find footholds and heft himself up.

"Good job, Charlie," Eva called up, clapping her
hands.

The child turned his head and gave her a beautiful smile. "I can do it, Eva."

"I know you can, bud." Eva gave him a thumbs-
up, a warmth flooding her heart. The past week
hadn't been easy. After Sara had approached her
about Charlie's threat toward her son, Eva had tentatively tried to open a dialogue with her brother
after they'd read about monster trucks at bed time.

"Charlie, I need to ask you something, okay?"
she'd said.

"'Kay," he'd responded with a yawn. His brown
eyes looked sleepy, and his hair stuck out, reminding her she needed to take him for a haircut.

"I talked to Drew's mom tonight. She had some
concerns."

Charlie didn't say anything at first. Just watched
her with suddenly cautious eyes.

"She told me you said some things to your friend that are hard for me to believe. Stabbing him with scissors?"

"I was just joking," Charlie said, throwing some disgust in his voice.

"I don't think your friend thought that."

"He's just being a baby. I was kidding."

Eva had paused for a moment and tried to think what to say next. "It's never appropriate to threaten someone…even if you're just joking. Drew didn't think you were, and he was upset enough to tell his mother. You made your friend feel uncomfortable. You can't make him do something by threatening him. Understand?"

Charlie had just shrugged.

"You've been a trouper, Charlie, but I know sometimes you get angry about everything that's happened this past month. I know. I felt really mad all the time when Dad and my mom split up. I even slapped a girl in the lunch line at school."

His gaze jerked up to hers. "Why?"

"She called my new jeans lame. I was so proud of them, and she made me feel so embarrassed. Even though she was wrong to do that, I was wrong to hit her."

"Why?"

"Because I allowed my anger to hurt someone. That's never, ever a good thing."

"But she was being a bully. I learned about bullies this week. That's when someone is mean to you.

You're supposed to stand up to them. That's what our teacher says."

"Was Drew bullying you? No. He refused to, what, play what you wanted to play? Give you something you wanted?"

Charlie ducked his head. Guilty.

"You don't control people that way, and you certainly don't use any form of violence against them. I had to learn that the hard way. I went to the principal's office for what I did. Not fun."

"Wow," Charlie breathed, his eyes widening. "You got sent to the principal's office?"

"Yeah." Eva ruffled Charlie's hair. "And this isn't just about Drew and what you said to him. It's also about what happened at the church."

"I was really mad at you," Charlie said, twisting his fingers in the blanket covering his bed. "I wanted to hit you."

"I know, but you can't do that, either. Being a kid is hard. The good thing is that you have people to talk to. And if you don't want to talk to me about something, tell Dr. Hebert. She's good at knowing what a person should do when he feels like you did. I wish I had had her when I was a kid."

"You do?"

"Yeah, someone to listen to what upsets me and then help me figure out what to do? That's gravy."

Charlie gave her a smile. "My tooth's loose. See?"

Nice diversionary tactics. Must be a male thing. "I see. We'll have to put the tooth fairy on standby."

"I want five dollars. That's what Ezra Gerard got for his front tooth."

"So there's a going rate, huh? Well, let's see what she brings when it happens."

For the rest of the week, Eva had tried to focus on her brother and what he needed. After talking to Macy at the counseling center she better understood Charlie's emotional fragility. Macy had suggested she register her brother for fall soccer. Practice had already begun, but since Dutch coached his daughter's team, he was able to get Charlie on his team. So after buying cleats and shin guards at Triumph's Sports store, it had been merely a matter of getting the kid to practice. Charlie had seemed pumped to attend his first practice, but had had a meltdown when he didn't kick a goal.

Up and down, round and round. Child rearing wasn't for wimps.

But watching Charlie's pride at scaling the rock wall gave her a glimpse into why being a parent was so rewarding.

The last few handholds were far apart, but Charlie had nearly reached the top. Eva held her breath as the child reached up as high as he could toward the red buzzer. His fingertips brushed the bright plastic button, and Eva rose on her tiptoes as if she could help him. "Come on, kid," she whispered under her breath.

He stretched, his mouth open, and finally his

fingers pressed. A tinny buzz sounded and then Charlie let go, falling back.

"Ahhhh," Eva screeched, darting toward the base of the rock-climbing wall, her arms uplifted. Adrenaline surged through her before she comprehended he was falling *very* slowly. She felt stupid, dropping her arms.

Clint rolled beside her. "He's strapped in."

"I know. Just a reaction."

Clint smiled gently, taking her hand and giving it a pat. "You're turning into a mother hen, E."

Eva gave an embarrassed smile. "I'm all he has right now. I have to be afraid for him."

Jake flanked her other side, flashing a thumbs-up at Charlie as his little feet hit the ground.

"Woo hoo," Charlie squealed, thrusting his fist into the air. "I did it."

"You totally did," Eva called out.

The guy running the rock wall helped Charlie out of the harness, giving him a high five before he ran to where she stood with Clint and Jake. The kid danced with exuberance— it made Eva's heart smile.

"Can I go get my face painted? Please."

Eva nodded, handed him one of the tickets she'd purchased and watched him zoom off with Birdie, who had finished her sno-ball and had struck the "I'm bored" posture so familiar with teens.

"Jake, do you mind if I have a moment alone with Eva?" Clint asked.

Jake stiffened, casting a puzzled look at Clint. "Uh, sure."

Dread dropped like a fat raindrop into her stomach. She hoped like hell Clint didn't have romance on his mind. She didn't know what was going on. Just that morning Jamison had called to invite her and Charlie out for pizza tonight. She was starting to feel like Mata Hari with all the men circling her... and she couldn't dance to save her life. Oh, the irony of all those times she couldn't get a date.

Jake yelled at Birdie and then jogged to catch up with the kids, who were headed to the face-painting booth.

Clint hit the control on his chair and headed toward a grassy area containing several empty picnic tables. Eva fell into line beside him.

"Is everything okay?" she asked.

"Yeah," he said, maneuvering past a group of women holding up maps and pointing out the various vendors. "I just wanted to talk to you about the race."

"Why? Are you worried you haven't trained hard enough?"

"No. I'm good on that. I'm actually thinking of withdrawing. I feel there are other areas in my life that need some attention."

"Oh, well, I enjoyed training with you."

"I'm not quitting the gym. I've just been thinking about making some decisions in regards to my future. Living with my dad has been miserable these past few years. Mom was a buffer between us and since she died, it's been…tedious. I love him, but he's difficult."

"He's Murphy," she said with a wry smile.

"Indeed," Clint agreed, coming to a halt beside an empty table. "He's been thinking of retiring from the company, and I don't want to run it. Being a tire man was never my plan, so I've been reassessing things, you know."

"I do. Life can throw curveballs. Sometimes they're named Charlie."

Clint smiled and again Eva was reminded how good-looking the man was. "Yeah, exactly. So the reason I'm thinking of pulling out of the race is I received acknowledgment of my acceptance into grad school at LSU. I'll start in January."

"Wow, Clint. That's awesome. Congratulations."

When he smiled, he looked younger. Or maybe it was the spark of determination in his eyes. "Thanks. I'm going to work on my MBA and look for opportunities with companies in New Orleans or somewhere close. I'm determined to make a move in my life. I can't keep doing the books for Dad's company and spinning my wheels here."

"I'm excited for you, Clint." She took his hand and gave it a squeeze. She intended on letting go but he held it fast.

"And I'm hoping you might be open to being part of that moving forward."

Uh-oh. "What do you mean?"

"Well, to be honest, I've grown really attached to having you around. You're pretty much the ray of sunshine in my otherwise gloomy existence."

Oh, shit.

No one had ever called her a ray of sunshine. No, she'd never been sunny, happy and...blinding. She was more mild and overcast. And for him to say she lit up his gloomy existence, well, that was hard to shoot down. She couldn't tell Clint she wasn't interested now—not after his admission. It would be akin to knocking a bird nest from a tree or yanking up a newly budding flower. Cruel as a hard frost.

"Well, thank you." What else could she say, really?

"So I wondered if you might be interested in something more, too?" he asked, looking up at her with an expression that broke her heart. So yearning. So damn, damn yearning. "I'd like to actually take you on a date. No Charlie. Or Jake."

"You've caught me off guard. I've never really thought—"

"I know. Me neither. But it makes sense. We're two young, fairly attractive—" he gave her a smile "—well, at least I am."

She hiccupped a laugh.

"Why shouldn't we see what happens? We're already friends, and they say that's the best place to start in a relationship," he finished.

"Yeah, I've heard the same thing," Eva said, looking out at the families laughing with one another. Well, a few parents were fussing at their kids. Such was the nature of a family. Eva was learning that quickly. "But you can't design love, Clint. Just because it makes sense on paper doesn't mean it's the right thing to do."

"I'm not designing a relationship, Eva. You're such an incredible person."

"No, I'm not. I'm a regular person. There just aren't that many single gals left in this one-horse town."

"I'm not going after the pick of the litter, if that's what you're implying," Clint said. "I find you attractive, and you mean something to me."

Eva pressed her lips together and kept her eyes trained on a small blond boy crying for some cotton candy. She had no words for this situation. She'd suspected Clint might have been moving toward this and now that he admitted having feelings for her, she wasn't prepared. At all.

"I'm not asking you to marry me. Just date me." Clint lightly clapped his hands together as if he were an attorney finishing his closing statement.

Eva swallowed hard, her thoughts running into each other. Should she say yes? Fake stomach cramps? Stall?

Thing was she didn't want to hurt Clint. The man had been through so much—the accident, painful physical therapy, the death of his mother, the coldness of his father. He deserved someone who made him happy, and this was a huge step for him.

But she didn't feel the same way.

"I'm not sure I can do that," she said, sinking onto the picnic table bench, not quite ready to meet his eyes. "You mean a lot to me, but I've never felt the slightest romantic interest. I wish I did. You're a gorgeous guy with such a big heart, but I can't make a puzzle piece fit where it doesn't belong."

"I'm not asking you to feel anything yet. Just give us a chance to see if it's something that could work."

"I don't think we should."

"Why not?"

Because I'm in love with your best friend.

She didn't say that, of course, but she thought it. She felt it. As flawed as Jake was, as selfish, hard-headed and egotistical as Jake was, she loved him.

Her love was an albatross around her neck.

"Because there's nothing there on my side… except for sincere friendship."

There. She'd said it.

"But friendship can change, can't it?"

And that was the question she'd been pondering for weeks. Could it truly change? Sex was one thing. Love quite another. "I don't know, Clint. But right now my life is in flux. I don't know what will happen with Charlie or when Claren will be able to care for him again."

"But you've been dating Jamison."

"Something I'm putting the brakes on. My focus right now is on Charlie."

"So you won't even try?" Clint asked.

Eva shook her head. "I don't think it's a good

idea. You can't plan out these things. That's what you're doing."

"No, I'm not, but if that gives you comfort for turning me down…" He hit a button on his chair and started rolling forward.

"Clint, don't be that way. You hit me with this out of the blue."

The man didn't stop or even acknowledge her words.

"Clint," she said again.

He stopped, his body facing away from her. "I get it. I'm not a whole man and—"

"Oh, my God. I've never treated you that way. Don't you dare accuse me of that. This has nothing to do with your disability. You know it."

He shrugged his shoulders. "You have no other good reason."

"Other than I don't want to? Would you rather me make up feelings? We're friends, and friends don't lie to one another. They also don't put each other in uncomfortable positions. That's what you're doing to me."

"By wanting to love you, Eva?" His voice quivered slightly, making her feel like dog crap. Her belly ached, and her throat felt raspy with unshed tears.

"Oh, God, Clint," Eva said, the tears finally coming. She brushed them from her cheeks, incredulous that their fun Saturday afternoon adventure had turned into this. She'd hurt Clint, a man who'd suffered too much hurt in his life, and that made her feel...well, just horrible. "I'm sorry. So, so sorry. I can't do this right now. It's not the right time."

He didn't respond, just hit the switch on his chair and rolled away, leaving her sitting on the bench surrounded by shrieking kids, laughing parents and the scents of a thousand good things.

Eva pressed her fingers into her eyes and tried to think how to fix this. But she knew there was no good answer. Some things in life had no solution.

Sometimes life just hurt.

CHAPTER FIFTEEN

JAKE WENT TO church that morning. He didn't know why. He just got up, fixed a cup of coffee and sat on the porch of his small garage apartment behind his aunt Opal's house and watched a few cardinals hop around in the waxy camellias surrounding the backyard. At some point he decided he didn't want to go back to bed, watch SportsCenter or mow Aunt Opal's front lawn. He wanted to go sit with his family in their pew and watch his father give a no doubt polished, yet heartfelt message of God's love.

Yeah, he was as shocked as everyone who stared as he ambled down the aisle during the opening hymn. A few people even stopped singing "Rock of Ages." But his mother merely smiled and scooted over so he could sit beside her. The woman never missed a note. His father looked confused…may have even lifted his eyes heavenward…but he didn't fall off his chair behind the pulpit.

The sermon was about the prodigal son.

Jake almost laughed when he heard the topic but managed to suppress it. His brother John, however, did give him a brow wiggle thing that suggested he'd played his part to perfection.

After church he followed his parents like an obedient duckling to their large house, where lunch would be served.

"Jake, can you grab the rolls out of the pantry and pop them in the oven?" Fancy said, tying on an apron and lifting the lid of the slow cooker. "Abigail, put the carrots on. They're on the second shelf of the fridge."

Jake sank into the moment, enjoying slapping a pat of butter on each roll as his siblings rushed around him. Usually, such things threatened to suffocate him, but he needed something at that moment. And that something was the comfort of people who truly loved him.

Unfortunately, Eva had not been in church. Subconsciously, he'd thought she'd be there, and maybe that was the reason he'd worn a button-down shirt and old tie. Eva usually attended church. But not that morning.

Why?

Did it have something to do with the palpable tension that had sat between her and Clint on the way home yesterday? Or maybe the curt goodbye she'd given him? Or the fact Charlie had pitched another fit when she hadn't let him have the money to go on the Ferris wheel for the third time?

Something about the look in her eyes had...made him ache for her in a whole different way.

He didn't like sad Eva. Seeing the pain in her smile, the way she tiptoed around both him and Clint had made him want to fix things for her. But hell, he'd never been able to fix himself, so what could he do but crack jokes the entire way home? Be the same Jake he'd always been. The one everyone expected.

But that morning he'd craved something different. Obviously. He'd ended up here, at his parents' house, the place he'd been both the best and worst of himself.

"So where's Eva?" Abigail asked, pushing him aside to grab a hot pad.

"How should I know?" he said, slamming the drawer when Abigail moved.

"Wow, you're awfully prickly," his sister said.

Fancy looked up from stirring something with fruit in it. "Is everything okay with you, Jake? Have you done something to keep Eva away?"

"Jesus," he breathed, wishing he'd stayed his ass home. "I'm not Eva's keeper."

His mother narrowed her eyes but went back to stirring. Abigail shot him a look he couldn't decipher and thankfully didn't have to, because John and Shelby came into the kitchen. John carried Lindsay Rebecca, who gave everyone a gummy smile. His brother snuck a cherry off the top of the fruit his mother was stirring, earning himself a smack.

"Hey, is Eva coming today?" John asked him.

Jake set the knife on the counter and walked out of the kitchen.

"What the hell is up with you?" John called out.

"Watch your mouth, mister," his mother responded.

Jake looked for his keys. He usually carried them

in his pocket, but his only pair of khaki trousers were a bit too snug and so he'd set them...somewhere. Maybe on the buffet or—

Birdie walked by, dangling them.

"Looking for these?" she drawled.

Jake tried to snatch them, but Birdie pulled them back. "You can have them as soon as I get my check. Make it payable to Bridgette Orgeron. Feel free to add in a tip. I did make Charlie blow his nose once and made him wash his hands after jumping in the bouncy."

"I don't have my checkbook."

"Then cash will work."

"Jeez, Birdie."

"Bridgette."

"Whatever. Can I please have my keys?" The last thing he needed was his smart-mouthed niece, who reminded him a bit too much of his cousin Hilda. Hilda possessed an all-knowing, all-seeing eye. She'd also sent over some clothing catalogs with items she deemed appropriate for him circled. So, no, he didn't feel like dealing with Hilda's mini-me right now.

The girl held out her palm, and he didn't miss the twinkle in her eyes.

"Fine," he growled, unwedging his wallet from his back pocket. He pulled out a twenty. "I'll have to owe you the four."

"Give me that five-dollar bill. A dollar tip will work."

"You're a typical woman. Bleed a man dry."

Birdie laughed. "I'm just learning early."

"Here," Jake said, slapping the five on top of the twenty and grabbing his keys.

"Why are you leaving? You never come to church and Sunday dinner. Why go, you're already here?"

"Because everyone, including you, is being annoying." Jake headed toward the foyer and nearly ran into his father.

"Hey, son. So glad you're here this morning. Meant a lot to see you out there next to your mother." Dan grabbed his shoulders and gave a smile that weakened Jake's resolve.

"Don't bother. He's leaving," Birdie said.

Dan's brow lowered. "What's wrong? I planned that sermon long ago. I hope the subject matter didn't feel directed toward you."

"Nah, unless we're having the fatted calf," Jake tried to joke. He didn't want any sort of cross-examination. He shouldn't have come.

"Well, your mom is cooking a roast, so…" Dan smiled and slapped a hand on his back.

"I think he wants to leave because they're teasing him about Eva," Birdie said, turning and walking out of the room, clutching her money. Little shit.

"Eva?" his father said.

"This isn't about Eva. Still, why is everyone asking me about her? What's going on?"

His father gave him a sheepish smile and jerked

his head toward his study. "Come with me and I'll tell you."

The irritation he felt melted into dread. Going to his father's study for a talk was never a good thing. Those conversations were serious.

His father's study was warm and inviting, though when Jake had been younger he'd never considered it as such. He'd received many a stern lecture while perched on the leather couch sitting against the wood-paneled wall. Bookshelves surrounded a large desk scattered with notes and stacks of different versions of the Bible. Silver picture frames were perched here and there, displaying shining faces of those he loved, including a new one of Abigail, Leif and Birdie taken on the day Leif proposed to Abigail.

"What's up?" Jake said, refusing to sit. He wanted to stand.

"Nothing, but you mentioned Eva."

"Yeah, everyone keeps asking about her. It's weird."

"Well, Charlie might have said a few things."

"Oh." Jake sat. He pretty much knew what Charlie had said...and he pretty much knew that the news of him and Eva kissing had swept through the Beauchamp family like lice through a slumber party. They were probably all scratching their heads, too. "I kissed her."

His father laughed. "We're used to you kissing

pretty girls, Jake. Guess we never thought you'd work your way around to Eva."

"Are you going to deliver the same lecture Matt gave me?"

"What lecture would that be?"

"About how Eva deserves better and yada, yada, yada."

Dan leaned against his desk, folding his hands so they rested against his rounded stomach. "How could Eva ever get better than you?"

"Oh, come on, Dad. I know what everyone says about me."

"And that's what you think you are?" His father shook his head. "I don't know what's going on between you and Eva, but I hope it's something good. Matt may have had different words for you, and I can see him warning you away from her. She's a good person, and no one wants to see her hurt."

A warning lay in his father's words. One thing everyone agreed upon was that Eva wasn't the kind of girl to mess around with. Serious intentions only.

"Do you think I'm…" Jake started and then tapered off. How could he ask his father such a thing? *Do you think I'm good enough for her?*

'Cause that was what he'd been wondering for the past few days…it was the reason he'd tagged along to the festival…the reason he couldn't seem to stay away from her. He wanted her for more than a tangle in his sheets. When she'd implied that he'd only stick around for a few weeks, maybe a month or two, he'd started wondering why he'd never expected more from a woman than a good time. Wasn't as if he'd been raised to avoid commitment. On the contrary, Dan and Fancy were perfect role models for what happily-ever-after looked like. So why had he spent the past ten years or so running from anything that looked like forever? Was he that broken by his past?

"Do I think what?" His father interrupted Jake's thoughts.

"Nothing. I get that Eva's not a girl to be messed with. She's pretty dang special, and I'd never want to be the guy who hurt her."

"I know all that, but we're not talking about hurting Eva. We're talking about you. About your stakes."

"I don't know how to feel, Dad. I never planned on Eva happening to me."

"So are you asking me if Eva could be 'the one'?" his father asked, his eyes growing serious.

"No."

His father sighed.

"Yes," Jake admitted.

"Oh, Jakey. Do you think you don't deserve love? Is that what this is?"

"No." Jake shook his head. And then he felt something collapse inside him. "I don't know. I never wanted anyone like Eva. I mean, not that the girls I've dated haven't been nice. It's just Eva…well, I already love her. You know? She's been one of my best friends for the past few years, and I don't want to lose that."

Exactly the same reason Eva had given when she refused to go on a date with him. He got that. He didn't want to lose her, either, which was why he'd backed off.

"Both Eva and I agree that we'd rather repress these feelings and keep our friendship. It's safer that way, and no one gets hurt." Jake sank back onto the aged leather.

His father cocked his head. "Why, that's quite reasonable, Jake. Hmm."

What did that mean?

Of course he knew. Jake wasn't ever reasonable. He didn't overthink anything. He and Abigail were polar opposites. Or at least they had been. His sister examined every inch of ground between her and her landing point. Jake leaped without looking. "Yeah. Maybe I'm growing up finally." He cracked a self-deprecating smile.

His father tilted his head. "Maybe so, but when it comes to love—or the prospect of love—I'm not sure anyone should ever be reasonable."

"But it's irresponsible to take a chance. I couldn't bear my life if Eva hated me. Thing is, she's just part...of me." Jake sat up, his mind tripping on the words he'd uttered.

Eva was already a part of him. Sorta the same way his mother was part of his father.

She was the person he couldn't wait to tell good news. She was the person who always had a kind word when his world fell apart. She was his sounding board, his confidante, his cheerleader and his conscience.

His father gave him that smile—the one that said, "Yes, I know I'm wise. You're welcome."

"You think I'm in love with Eva?" Jake asked, spreading his hands out to rest on his spread knees.

"I can't answer that, son. And I'm not telling you how to live your life. I'm merely suggesting you stop defining yourself by others' opinions. You're more than what you perceive yourself to be. Honky-tonks, loose women and whiskey have kept you company far too long. Maybe you need to look for something more. And maybe Eva is part of that more."

Jake swallowed the sudden emotion clogging his throat. His father had always believed in him, had always thought he was worthy of more than what he allowed himself.

Why had Jake not believed it?

He'd let himself be swallowed by guilt, paralyzed by cowardice, locked into his life by something he'd not had any control over. Even though he knew he'd created a mold and poured himself into it, he'd never been able to break free. There'd been no motivator, no good reason to want to be a better Jake.

But now?

Now everything had changed. And Eva had been wrong.

Just because he had always messed up every relationship didn't mean he and Eva shouldn't try moving toward love. Didn't they owe it to themselves to test this thing they had? Not just sex...even though he knew it would be smoking hot between them. Couldn't not be. The kisses they'd shared told him all he needed to know about their chemistry. But maybe they needed to let themselves own what they felt.

It was merely a matter of convincing her.

Today. Now.

He didn't want to wait another second.

"I have to go, Dad," Jake said, rising.

"Eva's in New Orleans today. Taking Charlie to visit Claren for the first time since she went into rehab. Might as well enjoy your mama's roast and potatoes. I'm starving, myself." His dad rubbed his belly and smiled. "Plenty of time for romancing pretty little gals later. You, after all, don't need practice."

Jake shelved his disappointment at not being able to go to Eva that second and extended his hand to his dad.

Dan made a face before tugging Jake into a bear hug. Warmth flooded Jake at the comfort of his father's arms. Releasing him, Dan Beauchamp grinned. "You know you take after me, right?"

Jake shook his head.

"I didn't need practice, either."

And that made him laugh.

"Don't laugh. I got your mama on my first try. God is good, son," his father said, wrapping an arm around Jake and steering him toward the kitchen. "All the time."

Eva PULLED INTO the driveway of Dan and Fancy's house and shifted into Park with a sigh.

The day had been exhausting, and the last thing she wanted was to make idle chitchat, but Charlie had left his backpack at the Beauchamps, and he had homework to do.

"Go inside and get your backpack," she said to Charlie, who'd remained quiet as a graveyard the entire drive from New Orleans back to Magnolia Bend. They'd spent the afternoon visiting Claren, and it had been…not exactly excruciating, but very close.

The rehab facility where Charlie's mom was staying had the highest success rate in the area. The doctor and staff were first-rate, treating their patients with utmost respect and compassion. One would think Claren would appreciate the efforts made to help her fight the addiction that had already cost her so much.

But no.

Claren had spent the allotted hour with Charlie raging at the judge, at the medicines that weren't working, at Child Protection Services for giving Eva physical custody and about the fact she couldn't go shopping for Charlie's birthday. Then she'd sorta lost it.

"I suppose he didn't even get a party," Claren had said, her eyes blazing.

Eva didn't want to provoke the roller coaster of emotion that was Claren. "Of course we had a party," she said in a fake chipper voice, patting Charlie, who had remained silent throughout the entire visit. He'd been so excited to see his mother, but as soon as he took one look at her, he'd clammed up, tolerating Claren's hug as if she were a stranger.

"*You* gave a kid's birthday party?" Claren scoffed, pushing back hair seriously in need of a good coloring. Her eyes were ringed in darkness, her pasty skin holding two circles of color in her cheeks. "I would have loved to see that."

"Hey, I can host a birthday party," Eva said, keeping her voice light since the woman looked on edge. "I even got party favors."

Claren looked at Charlie. "Did you have fun, bullfrog?"

Charlie nodded, as if in a trance.

"What's wrong with him?" Claren asked, lifting an accusing gaze to Eva. "What have you done to him?"

"Nothing," Eva said, giving Charlie a comforting pat before rubbing his shoulder. He didn't pull away. Just lowered his eyes to the floor. "He's readjusting. You know. It's a different place, and when he last saw you in court it was sort of traumatic."

"Are you mad at Mommy, Charlie?" Claren asked, pulling her son to her, smoothing back the hair from his forehead. "Mommy is sorry. She'll make it up to you when she gets out of here. We'll go to the carousel and have sno-balls."

Charlie merely nodded, and Claren pushed him away. "You've turned him against me. I can see that."

"No," Eva said, rising from the stiff pleather sofa in the clinic's receiving room. "He's just over-whelmed, Claren. This is all new to him."

"Oh, I can see what's going on. You think you're a better mother than I am. You've made it where he doesn't like me."

"Come on, Claren. You know that's not true."

"Oh, no. Go ahead and play mommy. Try and take him from me. You'll never do it. I'm his mother." She thumped her chest hard as tears leaked from the corners of her eyes. She grabbed Charlie's chin and jerked his head up. "You hear that? I'm your mother."

Charlie started crying and a concerned-looking woman in scrubs bustled over and placed a comfort-ing arm around Claren, talking low in her ear. Claren burst into tears, her hands shaking. Eva pulled Char-lie to her, curving an arm around his small body, wishing like hell they had waited until Claren wasn't so on edge. It had been almost three weeks, and she'd already gone through detox. Eva assumed she'd be back to normal, but the frail, distraught creature in front of her wasn't the strong Claren she knew.

The woman looked up with a kind smile. "I know your mother has enjoyed seeing you, honey. She's missed you something terrible, but she's still get-ting better."

"I'm sorry, Charlie," Claren said, wiping her eyes,

sniffling. "Mama's still not feeling great, baby, but I'm so glad your sister brought you to see me."

Eva nudged Charlie, and the little boy nodded. "Okay, Mommy."

"Come here." Claren gestured, her hands still trembling.

Eva moved Charlie toward his mother. "Go hug your mama, Charlie. We have to get back."

Charlie moved reluctantly to Claren and managed to give her a hug.

"We'll come back next weekend," Eva told the woman whose eyes had refilled with tears. "You take care, Claren. Work on getting better. You have a really good reason."

Claren looked up with watery blue eyes. "I know."

Then the woman helped Claren stand, giving them another patented comforting smile. "Nice to see you folks."

And then Claren and her guardian angel disappeared through double doors, leaving Eva and Charlie alone in the room reserved for guests.

Charlie looked up at Eva and said, "I wanna go back to your house."

And they had left, quick as spit.

Charlie had barely made a peep the entire journey home. At one point he'd nodded off as Eva mentally flipped through all the various craptastic conflicts in her life.

So as she sat in the car in front of the Beauchamp house, she wanted nothing more than to go home, crawl into bed and throw the covers over her head. Everything in life felt too hard at the moment.

She looked at the dashboard clock. Charlie had been gone for almost ten minutes.

"Christ," she breathed, shutting the car off and climbing out.

The sound of boys whooping and hollering met her ears.

"Great," she said to the trees dancing in the wind above her. A leaf swirled into her path, reminding her it was the beginning of October.

Instead of jogging up the front porch stairs and going through the house, she slipped through the side yard to the back corner, where Sunday afternoon football and Wiffle ball games were often held. She nearly ran over Jake's uncle Carlton, who was sneaking a smoke behind an oleander bush.

"Oh, hello," the older man said, hiding his smoke around his back.

"I see the cigarette," she said.

He pulled the still-lit cigarette out and studied it as if he wondered how it had gotten in his hand. "Oh, this."

Eva laughed. "It's okay, Mr. Burnsides. I won't tell."

He cracked a shit-eating grin. "Well, they do say it's good for my glaucoma."

"That's marijuana?"

"Oh, I should try that then," the older man said, stabbing out the bud, tossing it into the depths of the bush and pulling breath spray from his pocket. "I must go help Francesca with the leftovers. She always packs me a nice little doggy bag."

"Have a good evening, Mr. Burnsides," Eva said, suppressing a smile. Uncle Carlton was infamous for being a colorful character in a family filled with colorful characters.

When Eva rounded the corner she saw two good things.

First, Charlie was on the ground, squealing in delight as Jake tickled his ribs in order to steal the football. Seeing Charlie laugh after his earlier stoicism lifted her spirits.

Second, Jake was shirtless.

"Eva," Birdie called out. "Come play with us. You can be on my team. We're the shirts."

Jake, who very obviously was a skin, hopped up with a smile. "Nah, come be on my team."

Eva gave him a flat look. Matt jogged over, shirtless himself, and snagged the football, tossing it to his son. "All girls have to be shirts. This isn't California."

"I need to move to California," Jake joked, walking toward Eva. He grabbed his shirt from a tangle on the outdoor patio table and struggled into it, hiding all that gorgeous male flesh.

Pity.

"Charlie can take my place. I need to talk to Eva for a second."

"Awww," Will cried, "You're the best player we have."

"Have you seen Charlie run? Just give him the ball. Send him John's way," Jake cracked.

John pretended to scratch his nose with his middle finger, making Will, who was old enough to know what it meant, howl.

Dan Beauchamp, however, frowned at his son.

Eva looked up at Jake when he halted in front of her, mopping off his face with his forearm. "Whew, it's hot today."

"I need to get Charlie home and start homework."

He studied her. Eva self-consciously tucked a strand of hair behind her ear. She'd left her hair down today because she hadn't had time to dry it and then braid it. The brown mess tumbled around her shoulders, getting in her way.

"I love your hair down. Smells good," he said, inhaling as he leaned closer.

"Stop."

"No."

Eva swallowed as the desire smacked into her.

Remember me? I ain't going away, sugar. You want him. He wants you. What's the friggin' problem?

Yeah, the need gnawing at her sounded a lot like a Mafia bully—strong and powerful, making insanity sound reasonable.

"What did you want to talk about?" she said, stepping back, trying to erase the sight of a bare-chested, grinning Jake from her mind. "We've said all that needs to be said, right? Or maybe this is about work?"

Jake took her elbow and steered her back toward the front yard. "It definitely has nothing to do with work."

"Wait." She wrenched her arm from his grasp. "I have to get Charlie."

"Hey, Dad?" Jake called back, twisting around. "Keep an eye on Charlie for a few. I'm taking this pretty lady for a ride."

Dan gave Jake a thumbs-up before dropping back to hurl the football across the yard toward Birdie, who flew as if she had the wings of her namesake.

"Jake," she said as he gently took her arm again.

"My truck or your car?"

"What?"

"Seriously, babe. We need to talk. My truck or your car?"

"But—"

"My truck then," he said, sliding his hand down and clasping her hand. Eva allowed herself to be pulled along, wondering what was so damn important. The past few days had been crappy. With shooting down Clint's offer to date, dealing with Claren and facing another reading worksheet with Charlie, Eva was at her limit. She felt weak. She felt as if she wanted to bury her face in Jake's shoulder and let him do whatever he wanted to her.

Which meant going off alone with Jake was not a good idea. But she'd never seen him so insistent. At least not with her.

She climbed into his big red truck, pulled the lap belt across her and stared stonily ahead.

Stay strong, Eva.

Jake started the truck and minutes later, they roared down the highway. He leaned over and turned on the radio. An old Conway Twitty song played. Jake grinned and sang along.

Jake had a good voice—mellow, sexy and rich.

At one point in the chorus, he pointed to her. She sang Loretta Lynn's part. And for a few seconds the world slipped away and there was just Jake, an old favorite song and a pretty fall day.

After driving for ten minutes, Jake pulled off the highway. Seconds later he parked next to an old fence that needed repairing. He shut the truck off.

"Where are we?"

"My thinking place."

Eva snorted. "Since when do you think?"

Jake unclicked his seat belt. "Okay, fine. It's my thinking slash make-out place."

Eva laughed. What else could she do? This was Jake, and he was outlandishly wonderful, deadly sexy and so very, very dear to her. And he had something on his mind. "So…?"

"Get out. I want to show you something."

Eva climbed out and eyed the fence Jake had just

hopped over. It looked like a tetanus shot waiting to happen.

He crooked an eyebrow. "I can help you if you want."

She snorted and backed up. Three steps and an arm lock ensured she cleared the wire fence by a good half foot. Unfortunately, she'd overshot the landing, tumbling forward, skidding on slippery pine needles and crashing onto her bumpus.

She started laughing as Jake shook his head. "Never let a man help you, will you?"

He extended his hand—she brushed her hands off and took it. He jerked her to her feet and right into his arms. "I can let a man—"

His lips covered hers.

"Mmm, Jake," she protested, giving him a light shove. He shook his head and kissed her harder.

And it was wonderful.

So instead of resisting, she lifted her hands and tangled them in his thick hair, twisting her fingers in the softness, opening her mouth so he could do whatever he wanted. His hands curled around her, one hand on her ribs, the other on her waist. He held her tight as if he might never let her go.

Eventually, he tore his mouth from hers, resting his forehead against hers.

"Eva," he groaned. "Oh, my sweet Eva."

Something warmer than desire stole across her heart.

Oh, how she wanted to be his Eva.

He dropped another kiss on her lips before releasing her. "Come on."

She let him take her hand and pull her through the shady depths of the woods. Scrubby brush slapped at her thighs, but Jake held back the larger branches. Eventually they came to a small leaf-strewn hill and just on the other side was Lake Chinquapin.

"Wow, this is pretty," she breathed.

Nearby a cluster of old stones sat. Perfect for sitting on and...thinking.

"Clint's place is right over there, and my dad's camp is way across there, in a small inlet." He pointed toward the opposite shore, where a pier jutted out onto the lake. "Clint and I found this spot when we were kids. Back then they had a small cabin out here and we'd paddle all over this lake. Not sure how these old rocks got here. Maybe Native Americans? We called it Indian Point. I've always loved it. Felt so peaceful, like the wisdom of the old chiefs seeped into me here, helping me out of whatever situation I'd gotten myself into."

Eva dropped his hand and climbed onto the rocks. One jutted over the water. She startled a couple of turtles sunning on a felled tree, and they slipped into the water. "It's...almost mystical. Thanks for bringing me here."

He climbed beside her and lowered himself onto the rock. He patted the concave spot next to him. She sank down and for a few minutes they both stared out at the sun lowering in the sky, its image creating a stripe of golden fire across the dark depths of the lake. A lazy buzzard circled overhead as scampering squirrels prepared for the coming winter, scrapping over acorns in the woods.

"I went to church this morning," he said.

"You did?"

"Mmm-hmm. You weren't there."

"I went to New Orleans. Took Charlie to see Claren."

"My dad told me. He and I had a talk."

Eva swallowed because Jake's voice was low, serious. He hadn't brought her here to watch turtles and buzzards. He had a purpose. And that kiss? What had that been about?

"What did you talk about?" she asked, clearing her throat and wrapping her arms around her knees. The fabric of her casual sundress bunched beneath her fingers.

"You."

"Me?"

Jake turned to her. "Yeah, and I decided something."

She crooked an eyebrow.

"We were wrong."

"About?"

"Dating."

Eva shook her head. "Look, you know I want you. That's pretty obvious, but I think we'd be stupid to sleep together. It never works between friends. Even more important, it never works between coworkers."

"Why not? It's silly to pretend like this thing between us will go away. It won't."

"I'm used to not getting what I want. Problem is, you're not."

He made a face. "What are you so afraid of? That I'll end up being like your dad?"

She felt as if he'd slapped her. On the surface she'd often thought he was similar to her father, but she'd never put it under a microscope. Was that the real reason? She was afraid she'd end up like her mother—broken and looking for another man to fix her, fill the void? Maybe so. Maybe she was afraid of trusting a man who couldn't stay put. But she wasn't going to toss that out there. Sounded irrational. "I'm afraid that once you get tired of me and move on to the next flavor of the month, our friendship would be over."

Jake's face darkened. "Why do you think I'm not capable of staying with one person?"

Eva tried to be matter-of-fact, but it was hard with a teeny voice inside her urging her to consider the impossible. What if Jake could love her? What if she was different? "I've been around for three years, through all of the girls you've *dated*. I'm not saying you making a commitment is impossible, but very improbable. I smell a broken heart."

"For you?"

Eva looked away. "What do you think?"

"Oh," he said, his voice soft. Eva wasn't sure she'd ever heard Jake speak so…reverently. He'd gotten her unstated message—she loved him and he'd break her heart.

"But what if I'm falling in love with you?" he said. "What if you're breaking my heart by not even giving me a shot at yours?"

CHAPTER SIXTEEN

THE DOUBLE TAKE that Eva did was epic Three Stooges. "What? Breaking *your* heart?"

He merely looked at her, trying to convey his seriousness.

"Don't tease me, Jake."

Guess it hadn't worked. "I'm not. I feel different about you than I have any other girl. It's crazy, but I think I am falling in love with you."

If he hadn't been so shocked by his own admission, he might have teased her to lighten the mood. But saying "I think I'm falling in love with you" wasn't something to laugh about. Especially for a guy like him, a guy who'd been allergic to commitment.

Not that this was a commitment. More like a forecast for the big L.

Eva had always been like family. He was devoted to her, loyal, and he knew she would always be there for him. But as those words had tumbled from his mouth, the truth became reality.

This thing he felt was incredibly alive inside him, uncurling and opening itself to possibility. This wasn't about sex—though he was primed and ready

274 SWEET SOUTHERN NIGHTS

if that moment should arrive—but about something scary, strange and wonderful.

Had to be love, right?

Jake looked at her now. At the way the setting sun bathed her bared shoulders in a golden light. At the yearning on her face. At those cinnamon-brown eyes mirroring the shock she no doubt felt at his declaration. And it was as if he truly saw her for the first time. His Eva.

"Wait. Say it again," she said, her gaze meeting his.

"I think I'm falling for you?"

She narrowed her eyes. He knew her thoughts—what kind of ploy to get in her pants was this?

"E, this isn't about sex. I know you think it is. I'm talking about something totally different. I'm talking about love."

"Love?"

"Gotta be. I can't stop thinking about you."

"I'm pretty sure that's not love."

"No, I've never felt this way, like I might shrivel up and die if you dismiss this thing between us as only physical."

She swallowed, twisting the fingers that clasped her knees almost frantically. He could see she was trying to hold her emotions together. "Jake, I told you no, and that's just something you don't hear too often from a woman."

"Bullshit," he said, tugging her arms, making her hands come undone. He took her hand, cradling it, turning it over. Her hands were strong with unpolished, short nails. These weren't the hands of a woman scared of anything. So why was she so afraid to try something more with him? "I'm willing to take the risk. I'm rolling the dice on the chance we could be something more. For once in my life I'm not running from the messy stuff, I'm not hiding from the emotion inside me, but you are. Why are you so scared to trust me? Me?"

She ripped her hand from his. "I trust you, Jake, I do. But not with this. I've wanted you for so long, and I should be jumping into your arms. But I'm scared to let you love me. I've seen girls just like me think they can grab hold of you. They couldn't. So in this I'm being practical."

"Practical sucks, E." Jake spun his legs around so he faced Eva, and then he leaned over, setting one hand on either side of her. She dropped her knees as he leaned in close. When they were almost nose to nose he said, "Tell me you don't love me."

Her eyes welled with sudden tears. "Don't do this to me, Jake. Please."

"No. Tell me. Tell me you don't love me. Tell me to leave you the hell alone."

"Stop."

"Just be Eva. Be honest."

Swallowing hard, she stared into the depths of his gaze. Her pretty eyes shimmered with longing, with something so absolutely sweet his heart tightened. "I want you to leave… Oh, please don't do this, Jake."

"Why? My Eva isn't afraid of anything. She charges in, she doesn't back down. She's not afraid of risk. Not even of a broken heart."

"I'm not invincible, Jake. I cry like any other woman. I'd rather go on wanting you because that's easier than hating you."

"So say it. Tell me you don't love me." He pressed her. He had to. This was it. This was the moment. She either told him to take a hike now, when they were emotionally bare, fantastically vulnerable, or she let him in, giving them a chance at something lasting. If she said she didn't love him, he'd respect her decision. Wouldn't like it, but he'd respect her right to step away from him.

"No. I can't," she said, shaking her head as a lone tear escaped her thick lashes.

He kissed her then. His mouth pressed softly to hers, searching for her answer.

Opening her mouth, she gave in with a little sigh.

Keeping his hands planted on the rock was sheer hell, but he wanted her to meet him halfway, to know that he wasn't seducing her. He was baring himself to her.

After several seconds he lifted his head. "Say it now."

She swallowed. "You know I can't."

He tasted her lips again, pressing gently. Tenderly. "I can't leave you alone, Eva. I'm not treating you like a prize. I'm not a little boy determined to get what I want. I'm a man in strange territory. I can't turn around. I have to see if you and me can be what John and Shelby are, what Abi and Leif are. Hell, what my parents are."

She looked up at him, lifted a hand and traced his hairline. "You're killing me. You know that, right?"

"I'm just being truthful," he whispered against her lips.

"This could get really messy," she said.

Jake answered with a kiss because the idea of hurt seemed too far away. This time he reached for her, hauling her against him. He ravaged her mouth before dropping small kisses across her jawline, seeking the sweet stickiness of her neck.

Groaning against her skin, he savored the smell and taste of this woman who'd enraptured him these past weeks. This woman who wore her braids tight, fussed if he didn't load the dishwasher right and had his back when they charged into a burning house. "You're perfect. So soft. So damn beautiful. Please let me love you. Love me, Eva. Okay? Don't be afraid to love me."

She stilled against him, as though his words had sunk inside her. The moment paused, poignant and surreal. And then she released her breath.

"Okay, Jake. We'll try." Eva dropped her head back so he could better access the delicacy of her collarbone. Jake didn't hesitate, trailing his lips across the length, all the while running his hands over her back. Eva lifted her hands to his shoulders, holding him to her.

A sharp rock jabbed his hand and so he lifted his head. "Let's find a soft patch of grass. Then we'll celebrate being brave by having a good old-fashioned make-out session."

Eva laughed and it shot straight to his heart. The happiness that had played hide-and-seek with him for the past few months slammed into him.

"I like the way you celebrate," she said.

He slithered across the rock to find firm footing. Standing, he extended his hand and then hauled her against him. Hip to hip they stood on the rock. Jake lifted a hand and stroked her jaw. "I can't believe it's you."

"Huh?"

"That you're the one I've been waiting for."

"Am I?" she whispered, looking deep into his eyes as if the truth lay there. "How can you be sure?"

He lifted her hand and pressed it against his chest. "I feel it here. I ache here when I look at you. It's like in the movies. It's crazy."

Eva clasped his shirt and pulled him to her, lifting on her toes. She brushed her lips across his. "It *is* crazy."

Then she kissed him hard, as if sealing a bargain. Reaching behind her, she started tugging. He heard the zip and with a wiggle of her shoulders the material slid down, hanging on her rounded hips. She wore a strapless bra that strained to contain her large breasts.

Oh, how he remembered those sweet breasts. He'd dreamed about them.

Then she twitched her hips and the dress fell to her feet. She wore postage-stamp-sized bikini panties the color of sour apple lollipops.

"Oh, E. You're so beautiful," Jake said, reaching out to stroke the curve of her waist. Her stomach twitched at his touch.

Eva stepped out of the dress. Picking it up, she looked around. "Where's that patch of grass?"

Mouth dry, Jake pointed to a small area beneath a pin oak. It looked like a little piece of Eden...or maybe just a sufficient place to make out with Eva. Either way, he nearly lost it when she turned on her toes and stepped gingerly out of her strappy sandals and onto the still-lush grass.

The sour-apple panties were of the thong variety, and Eva's ass was spectacular.

Jake reached for the hem of his T-shirt and then hesitated. "Just a sec." He ripped his gaze away from her because he couldn't look at her delicious body and say what he was about to say. "Uh, maybe we shouldn't. Not because I don't want to. That's obvious." He brushed a hand down his body, indicating the hardness straining against his shorts.

"What's wrong?" she asked.

"I didn't want this to be about sex. Those words weren't a line tossed out so I could get laid. I meant what I said, and I want to prove it to you." His gaze met hers.

"Oh," she said, wrapping her arms about her waist. "So you don't want to have sex?"

"Oh, I want to have sex. But I want you to know that's not what you and I are about. So I'll stop—and suffer—but I will stop."

Eva unwrapped her arms from her waist and gave him a look straight out of a girlie magazine. Totally come hither. "If I didn't want you, I wouldn't have unzipped my dress. I believe you, so if you want more, come and take it."

Jake was a lot of things, but a stupid-ass wasn't one of them. He grabbed the hem of his shirt and jerked it overhead, dropping it atop her discarded dress. Reaching into his pocket, he pulled out his wallet. He usually kept protection in the inner pocket, and sure enough his fingers hit the telltale plastic condom package.

"Wait," Eva said, snatching his T-shirt and spreading it in the center of the grass. Then she lowered herself on it, extending her legs, crossing them at the ankle. She leaned back on her hands, breasts thrust up. She looked like a War World II pinup girl.

His mouth watered.

"Take off your shorts," she said, her voice smoky, her eyes lit with desire.

He'd seen nothing hotter in his life than Eva, ass on his T-shirt, breasts spilling out of her bra, ordering him around.

Smiling, he tugged down the elastic-banded athletic shorts, wincing when they snagged on his erection. Then he toed off his tennis shoes and socks before standing only in plaid boxers, which were absurdly tented.

Walking to her, he knelt and placed the condom under the T-shirt for fast retrieval.

Eva grabbed his waistband and jerked him to her. "I still have to help Charlie with his reading worksheet, so let's get this going."

"Way to make it romantic." Jake laughed, covering her body with his. Sighing as his naked flesh met hers.

"I'm just being pract—" Eva couldn't finish her sentence because Jake kissed her, rolling onto his back, taking her with him. Her hair fell in a curtain about his face, and he was enveloped in the sweetness of a woman—a woman whose kisses curled his toes as if she was the heroine of a bad romantic comedy. Or a good one.

Either way, she made him jelly beneath her...all but one part. One very important part.

"Mmm," she groaned, her hands stroking his chest, making him even harder, if that were possible. She threw her leg over his, fitting all her soft parts to his.

He reached down and filled one hand with magnificent ass. The other cupped her jaw, angling her head so he could deepen the kiss.

And then her hand hit pay dirt.

"Oh, slow down, sweetheart," he said, removing her hand from his boxers. "I know you're not in that big of a hurry to do homework," he said, kissing his way down her neck.

Eva complied by straddling him and sitting up. She grinned. "I'm sorta a single mother now, so—" she wiggled her hips making him groan "—so let's get busy."

He laughed and grasped her hips. "This is totally reminding me of my high school days 'cause I won't last much longer if you don't stop."

Eva reached around and unhooked her bra, flinging it toward their growing pile of clothes.

Jake sat up, earning a squeal from her, and buried his face between her breasts, dropping kisses while she wrapped her legs around his waist. Her laughter soon died when he tugged one of her nipples with his teeth.

"Oh, Jake." She sighed, her head falling back.

He held her tight while he loved her gorgeous breasts with his mouth, suckling, nipping, nuzzling her into utter bonelessness. She rocked her hips, grinding herself against his erection. The sensation blew his mind.

"I want—" he murmured against her skin "—the first time to be, um, good, but I—"

"No, I can't wait, either," she said, reaching past him, stretching to grab the condom sitting near a clump of dandelions. "Screw going slow. I need you. Right. Now."

Jake rolled her over, lowering her gently to the soft grass beneath them. He took the package from her fingers and then tugged the band of her panties, sliding them down her gorgeous legs until she lay bared beneath him, absolutely made for driving a man out of his mind…absolutely made for him.

"Jake," she insisted, tugging the band of his boxers again. "Come on."

He grinned at her and then shimmied out of his underwear. Eva reached for him but he shook his head, making quick work of donning the protection. Then he wrapped his arms around her, settling between her knees, reveling in the feel of her silky softness beneath his hard angles.

Eva rocked her pelvis, moaning as she closed her eyes. "Now. Please."

Jake caught her chin, forcing her to look at him. "Eva."

"What?" Her eyes popped open even as she still wriggled trying to get him inside her.

"I just needed to look at you as we did this," he said, dropping a quick kiss on her lips as he dipped his own hips and slid inside her.

Those beautiful eyes widened as she stared deep into the depths. Then she closed her eyes, tilted her head back and groaned, "Finally."

And since he felt the same way at that moment, he joined her, lifting his upper body and establishing that age-old rhythm that made everything—bills, homework and global warming—disappear.

There was only Eva and him and freakin' sweet pleasure.

And all Jake could think about, besides climbing to that earth-shattering peak awaiting him, was how had he not known how perfect Eva was for him.

EVA SCREWED HER eyes closed and moved her body in perfect rhythm with Jake. The warm gooey desire she'd felt earlier had simmered into a full rolling boil of heat that consumed her—she felt out of control, fully involved.

She'd envisioned tons of ways Jake could make love to her. In the shower at the station. In her fluffy down bed. In his probably not fluffy but who really cared bed. Against the kitchen counter. On the tailgate of his overzealous truck.

But she'd never imagined she'd actually have sex with the man she'd loved for years…and she damn sure hadn't envisioned it would be on a bed of prickly grass as the sweet Southern night descended around them.

And she'd never known it could be so damn good.

Jake knew where to touch, as evidenced by the way he cupped her breasts, rolling her nipples in delicious torture. And the way he kissed her neck, running up and down the sensitive length, nuzzling her ear, murmuring things like "just like that, baby. Just like that," which only amped her even more.

One of his hands clasped her hips, helping him achieve the perfect depth, knowing the exact spot inside her that needed to be hit. And then he lifted himself from her, emptiness taking the place of his torso, and slid his fingers to where their bodies joined, finding her clit, strumming her, making her arch.

"Mmm, Jake," she groaned, arms dropping onto the grass behind her head. Delicious pressure built, overflowing, shimmering up her body, unleashing.

She broke apart beneath him, fingers clutching grass as she rode the strong orgasm that tossed her so high, high enough to brush her fingers against the sun. Her body pulsated as the small yelp of release escaped her lips.

"Oh, sweet Eva. Just like that," Jake murmured, increasing his tempo.

Eva opened her eyes and watched Jake. He'd anchored her hips with both hands, exquisite torture stretching every muscle in his neck.

Then he pitched forward, his face pressing into the valley between her breasts. Turning his head, he sucked one nipple into the heat of his mouth, and the small respite she'd felt vanished. Almost immediately another hard climax seized her.

Her body trembled as waves of pleasure crashed over her. Jake's hips moved faster, his breathing matching the pace. Then he pulled his torso off her, his mouth falling open, eyes screwed closed. Lifting her hips, he thrust jerkily into her. A quick hard surge and she felt him come.

"Oh, yes…so good…so damn good." He gave a small shiver and then stilled, leaning on an elbow in order to take the brunt of his weight off her.

For a few seconds they lay frozen, the only sound the tangle of their labored breaths.

She hugged him to her, wrapping her arms tight across his back, inhaling his scent, savoring a moment that would never come again—that wonderful sweet first time between lovers.

Jake kissed the spot between her ribs right over her heart and then lifted his head. His russet hair fell rakishly over one bright blue eye. He smiled.

Eva smiled back.

Then for a good ten seconds they merely smiled at one another. Then Jake laughed, making her laugh, too. Words weren't really necessary. Not with the way he looked at her. She knew his thoughts.

Damn, that was good.

Why in the hell have we waited so long?

Could this be what we've both needed...both been waiting for?

He inched up and dropped a kiss on her nose. "I'd say something dorky like I think you complete me or whatever, but that's already been said in, like, a ton of movies. What just happened can't be treated so..."

"Nonchalantly?" she finished.

He caught her lips in a tender kiss, the kind a woman dreams about receiving from the man she loves. "Exactly. This ain't a light thing for me."

"I know."

Jake withdrew and rolled off her, sitting up and dealing with the spent condom with a slight snap of latex. Eva sat up, pulling her knees to her, mimicking the pose she'd assumed on the rocks...minutes ago?

Her world had changed in the blink of an eye.

Tipped sideways by the words of a man she believed in.

"I'd love to snuggle up next to you and count the stars but I have to get back," she said, tracing a line down his naked back. He was so gorgeous, so absolutely beautiful. And he said he was falling for her.

Eva pinched her thigh before looking around for her panties. Jake had tossed them onto her dress, but her shoes were nowhere to be seen.

"I know. Homework. I've never dated a woman who had a kid before."

"Well, technically he's not my kid and was this a date? 'Cause I never do it on the first date."

Jake looked back at her. "Guess I should have followed protocol, huh?"

Eva thought about Jamison and his rules. "Eh, protocol is probably overrated. But a date would be nice. I wouldn't mind some footsie under the table."

"Exclusively," Jake said. "I don't want prissy pants Jamison sniffing around anymore. Or anyone else, for that matter."

Eva sobered when she thought about Clint.

Lord, they were sitting there naked not even a mile from where Clint lived. The pain in Clint's voice wafted through her head, and she felt a sort of shame for having lost her mind over Jake merely a day after she'd shot Clint down, after she'd uttered the words about Charlie and putting him first. What would their friend say about her and Jake dating? Likely no warm fuzzy congrats. Not with the invisible wall of guilt and blame Clint and Jake had danced around for years.

But deliberating all of the hard stuff could come later. No sense in ruining the magic of the evening. She wanted to savor this tenderness, relish the potential for a while longer. Before reality broke in, throwing elbows and knocking cracks into her vision of happily-ever-after with Jake.

Did that mean she doubted a rosy future with Jake? She didn't want to.

But she would never regret what had happened here today. Jake was right. This could be exactly what they'd been waiting for all their lives.

"So you know, I told Jamison that things were too complicated in my life at present to continue dating. He didn't kick up a fuss so I think the flirtation is over," she said.

Jake gave a Cheshire cat smile. "Good. Like you want someone who knows the difference between cashmere and blend to hang around your brother."

"You know what cashmere is?" Eva joked.

"Hilda sent over a dozen men's catalogs a few weeks back. She thinks I need a makeover."

He helped her to her feet and wrapped his arms around her. Rubbing her back, Jake kissed the top of her breast, looked up and said, "I've never been this happy in my entire life."

"Me, too." Eva lifted onto her toes and kissed him, meaning every word of what she'd said. "Now, let's get back before they send the police. I don't want to greet my ex wearing my birthday suit."

Jake glowered. "I never liked Chase. He's—"

Eva pressed a finger over Jake's mouth. "Chill. I never even slept with him. No need to be jealous."

"Like I'm jealous of him," Jake scoffed, releasing her to tug on his clothes. "He probably watches the Hallmark channel and secretly knits baby blankets or something."

"You are so immature," Eva teased.

Jake cocked his head. "Look, I like both Jamison and Chase fine. I just don't like that they put their hands on you."

Eva struggled gracelessly into her dress, tugging it into place with a grunt. "If I were jealous of all the women who put their hands on you, I'd hate half the town. Let's just leave past relationships where they belong. Let's live in the present, including that I presently don't know where I kicked my shoes."

Jake found her shoes and soon they were slipping back through the woods, leaving behind their hidden piece of paradise. Jake held her hand, stopping intermittently to kiss her or cop a feel. Made Eva feel very much like a teenager living in the moment, uncaring of what lay ahead. At that moment, laughing with the man she'd just made love to, life was butterscotch lollipops and warm fuzzy panda bears. Good and delicious.

They reached the truck, still laughing, acting like two kids in Disney World. The sun had dropped beneath the horizon, bronzing the darkness before slipping out of sight. As Eva paused, taking one last look at the rickety fence and the secret spot that lay within the woods, she wondered if she had, indeed, ever been so happy.

To have the man you'd loved for so long take your heart and close his hands around it and say, "This is right," made a gal dream of lace veils and side-by-side rocking chairs. To even nudge a toe toward happily-ever-after with the Magnolia Bend's resident hound dog seemed wishful thinking.

She climbed in the truck and turned to him. "Are you sure we're doing the right thing?"

His answer was another tender kiss. "As I am of anything, E."

CHAPTER SEVENTEEN

THE FLYING ELBOWS and cracks in the rosy veneer of love came at Eva the next morning. Charlie had a high fever, and the toilet had backed up, leading to an expensive plumbing call.

The plumber—Mickey Guillot—she could deal with. He liked coffee, conversation and gave discounts to civil servants like Eva. The high fever and crying from Charlie was something she'd never faced before.

She'd consulted WebMD and then bathed his head with cold washcloths before finally calling Jake's sister, Abigail.

"Did you give him ibuprofen?" Abigail asked.

"No. I thought kids couldn't take that stuff," Eva said, peering down the hall to where Mickey worked in her bathroom.

"That's aspirin. He can have children's ibuprofen or acetaminophen. Do you have any?"

"No," Eva said, wincing as Mickey trudged toward her with a drenched sock in his hand. "I guess I can go to the store at some point...if I can get someone to watch Charlie. Is that a sock?"

Mickey nodded.

Abigail said, "Huh?"

"Hold on a sec," Eva said into the phone.

"No, I'm coming over with the medicine. Be right there," Abigail said, hanging up.

Mickey pressed the foot pedal and dropped the sock into the trash can. "Yep. That's your problem."

"How did it get in the toilet?"

Mickey shrugged. "Kids do the damnedest things."

"Grr," Eva growled, setting her phone on the counter, begging the low throb in her head not to grow any worse. "It's hard to be mad at him when—"

"Eva," Charlie cried out.

"No worries on my account," Mickey said, pulling out his clipboard. "The toilet's working now, and you shouldn't have any more problems."

"Thanks, Mick. Just leave the bill on the counter and let yourself out. I need to check on Charlie."

"This one's on me," Mickey called out as she made her way to the guest bedroom, aka Charlie's room.

She'd left the small lamp on, and it illuminated the little boy blinking plaintively at her. "Eva, I don't feel good."

"I know, sweetie," Eva said, sinking down next to him on the full-size bed, brushing the hair off his sticky, hot forehead. "Birdie's mom is bringing you some medicine that will help you feel better, and then once the doctor's office opens, we'll go see what's going on with you, okay?"

"Okay." He nodded, tears welling in his eyes. "Mom sings to me when I feel icky."

"I'm not a good singer."

"Okay," he said, his lower lip doing that pouting thing that breaks hearts and earns kids things like candy bars at the checkout.

"When I was a little girl, playing on my farm, I jumped into a big haystack and there I broke my arm," she sang in a warbled voice that could only be described as excruciating.

"I know this one. Daddy sang it."

Eva nodded. "He sang it to me, too, when I was little."

"That's 'cause we're brother and sister," Charlie said.

"Exactly."

"Sing some more, 'kay?" Charlie said, closing eyes brightened by fever. His cheeks were flushed, and looking at him made her heart squeeze.

Eva sang the words she knew by heart, all the while wondering how she'd deal with something bad happening to Charlie on her watch. She didn't know how to take care of a kid. Why hadn't she ever babysat or something? Or finished reading those books she'd bought about raising little boys. Not that she was raising him. This was temporary. But she couldn't screw up.

The doorbell sounded, and Eva left Charlie sleeping fitfully.

When she opened the door, Abigail didn't greet her. Leif did.

"Hey, Eva. You remember me? I'm Leif." He held a small bag. He wore some weird-looking karate pants, a rough-hewn linen shirt and his hair was in a ponytail. Even though he had an earthy, hippie vibe, he was so good-looking a person had to look twice. He totally had that Chris Hemsworth thing going. Like Thor on her doorstep…except wearing flip-flops.

"Of course," Eva said, stepping back. She saw Leif quite frequently and didn't know why he acted as if they hadn't attended the same Beauchamp get-togethers.

"Abigail forgot she was baking something and sent me instead. Said you had a little guy not feeling well." Leif held out the bag to her. "Abi sent some over-the-counter stuff, but I have to say, using some natural methods would work as well. I have some honey here—found this over in Mandeville a few months back. That will help the cough. And if he has a headache, you can take this lavender oil—" he handed her a vial "—and this coconut oil, and rub a little on his forehead."

"Oh, thanks," Eva said, taking each container.

"And if that doesn't help, you can use the other stuff," Leif said, pulling out two bottles of over-the-counter medicines. "How's he doing, anyway?"

"He's resting."

"Best thing he can do. Now, do you have any bourbon?"

Eva swallowed. "I'm not giving alcohol to a child, Leif."

Leif laughed, and Eva swore angels sighed and

a rainbow appeared over his head. The man made laughing sexy and reverent at the same time. He could probably get women to pay just to watch him laugh. "No, for you."

"Oh," Eva chuckled, pushing her tangled hair from her face. She probably looked like something a dog had barfed up...or just a tired woman. Not that it would matter to Leif. He was engaged to Abigail, and the glances they exchanged could singe anyone standing nearby. "Well, I probably should lay off the booze with a kid in the house."

"In my experience, having a kid in the house is the best reason to drink," he said with a kind smile. "But seriously, are you okay?"

"Sure. Just dealing with a sick kiddo."

"Jake will probably be by to check on you, but if you need anything, just holler."

Eva made a face. "Why would Jake check on me?"

Leif looked confused. "Aren't y'all...wait, I thought you two were..." He clamped his mouth shut.

"Did Jake say something to you?"

Leif eyed the door. "Uh, I better run. I still have to go to the Short Stop and pick up coffee creamer."

"No, wait. Did Jake tell Abigail he and I are together?"

"No."

"No?"

"I just assumed. I mean, I see the way he looks at you. The same way I look at Abi. Like I can't wait to get her alone. I didn't mean to imply something that wasn't. Sorry about that. I shouldn't have said anything."

Eva smiled, warmth flooding her. So even others could see she meant something to Jake? That was actually comforting.

Last night during the few moments she wasn't bathing Charlie's forehead or sleeping with one ear crooked toward the open bedroom door, she'd wondered if her rendezvous with Jake at the lake had been something she'd dreamed up. Her sane self whispered that Jake falling in love with her couldn't be true...that Jake liked the ladies too much to settle down with just one...that he would move on and leave her way worse off than merely a pathetic woman carrying a torch. He'd leave her broken.

But Leif gave her validation.

"What is it?" he said, his blue eyes growing relieved at her smile.

"Nothing. I just...it's just a good thing you mentioned it."

"Whew." Leif swiped a hand across his broad forehead. "Guess I'll see you around."

"Thanks so much for bringing me these things. Send Abigail my thanks, too."

Leif left her with good thoughts and something that smelled like peppermint? She pulled a soft peppermint from the bag and popped one in her mouth.

"Eva," Charlie called out.

She sighed and went back to her brother. Charlie's

eyes were bright, and when she placed a hand against his forehead, panic hit her.

He was really, really hot.

"Uh, Charlie, I think we need to go to the doctor right now," she said, tugging the covers off him. He lay small and feeble in his Mario Bros. pajamas. Eva helped Charlie sit up, but he seemed to be playing the role of limp dishrag. She scooped him up, shoved her feet in her UGG knockoff slippers and looked for her purse and cell phone.

"I'm cold," Charlie cried, his arms wrapped around her neck, his body so hot she started to sweat beneath her long-sleeved T-shirt.

Eva grabbed a blanket off the sofa, grimacing when she caught sight of the mess in her kitchen. The whole house looked a disaster, but it would have to wait until after Charlie saw a doctor.

The doorbell rang again, and Eva hoped it was Jake. He could drive them to the quick-care facility that she prayed—*please, dear God*—was open.

She opened the door to find the foster care worker standing on her porch.

Crap on a cracker.

"Uh, Mrs. Gunter, uh." Eva blinked, shifting Charlie over to her other arm.

"We had an eight-thirty appointment," Mrs. Gunter said, looking at the watch on her wrist. "You requested an early meeting."

She'd totally forgotten Mrs. Gunter was coming

that morning. Perfect. She looked a mess, the house looked a mess and Charlie was near death.

"I forgot, but even if I hadn't, I can't do the home visit right now. Sorry. Charlie's sick." Eva patted her brother's back. He lay limp against her, dead weight.

The foster care worker's expression turned from annoyance to concern. "What's wrong with him?"

"I don't know," Eva said, trying to hold back the emotion. She wanted to sink down and cry...and at the same time she wanted to tell Melba Gunter to get the hell out of her way because she had something more pressing than discussions of bed-wetting and proper nutrition. "He's got a fever. I think it's high and I'm on my way to the doctor's office."

Melba stepped back. "Come on. I'll drive."

The older black lady closed the door behind Eva and jerked her head toward the dark sedan parked behind Eva's car. "Door's unlocked. Have you given him anything for the fever?"

Eva trotted down the stairs, sweet relief flooding her. She wasn't alone. People who wanted to help were all around her. She could do this thing. She could be the guardian Charlie needed. "No. My friend just brought over some medicine, but then I felt Charlie and knew I needed to take him to a doctor."

"Was it that man who just left? I wondered about him," Melba said, sliding into her car, which had smooth leather seats and smelled like cherry air freshener. The car shone like a new penny.

"He's engaged to my friend," Eva said, making sure Melba understood she wasn't playing footsies while Charlie was in the house. Nope, she did that beside lakes—and had an ant bite to prove it. Eva settled Charlie in the backseat. "I need to get his booster. Be right back."

She jogged over to her car, ripped out the booster and resettled Charlie in the proper restraint. She looked at Melba to see if it netted her a brownie point.

Melba gave nothing away, so Eva slid into the passenger seat and clicked her seat belt into place in the nick of time. Melba shifted into Reverse and shot backward as if they were in a cop movie, chasing a bad guy. Eva grabbed the handle above her head as Melba shifted again, earning a squeal of tires as she headed out of the subdivision. "So where to?"

"Head into town. I'll call Fancy and see what she thinks is best. Fancy is the woman—"

"I know who she is. We've talked before. Let's get Mr. Charlie taken care of, and sweetheart, I'm a by-the-book hardass when it comes to these kids. I don't play. Know what I mean?"

Eva swallowed. "Yes, ma'am."

"But, sugar, what I just saw back there tells me all I need to know."

Eva closed her eyes. "I know. I'm sorry."

"Sorry? For...?"

"For forgetting the appointment. For my house being a wreck and me looking like death warmed over. And then Charlie... I was supposed to help him get over all that happened to him. I was supposed to keep him healthy and well. And he's so sick." Eva sniffed to keep from crying. She didn't want to be weak in front of this capable woman, but she was so tired. Instead of reveling in what had happened between her and Jake yesterday, she'd been deluged by laundry, going over homework and a horrid night of tears, high fever and, yes, wet bedsheets.

"You do know that kids run high fevers often. He has a virus, at worst, the flu. Kids are remarkably resilient. Charlie will be fine, Eva. And I do believe you mistook my meaning. This was not criticism for failing at having your house vacuumed or not wearing lipstick. It was a compliment. You've made Charlie a priority, and a woman who looks like you do—no offense—is worried about the right things in life." Melba reached over and patted her leg. "You're doing fine."

Eva pressed her fingers to her eyes and tried like hell not to cry. Melba's words were exactly what she needed. "Thank you. I wasn't sure I could do this, but I'm hanging in there."

"You're doing good, Eva," a small voice in the backseat said. "You singed me my favorite song."

Melba cocked an eyebrow as she whipped into a turn. "See?"

Eva nodded. "Yeah, but you didn't hear how bad my singing was."

"Sugar, I don't have to."

JAKE HAD TEXTED Eva four times that morning and received diddlely-poop from her.

After yesterday at the lake, his step was lighter, his heart fuller and his back a little sore from a rock he'd rolled onto while making love to Eva. He'd been looking forward to being a bit more front and center in Eva's life, but her failure to respond indicated the opposite.

He wasn't a needy sort of fellow, but her lack of response had dinged his pride. Which was silly. But still.

"Where's Eva?" he asked, tromping into the firehouse, juggling a tin of muffins his mother had made.

Dutch looked up from his position on the couch. Jake's fellow firefighter was deep into another sudoku puzzle. "She ain't comin' in. Moon's switching shifts with her this week."

Irritation filled Jake. "Why?"

"Something to do with the kid."

"Charlie?" Jake asked.

"I guess."

Jake pulled out his cell phone. Still no response to his earlier queries. "I better call."

Dutch ignored him and Moon came in, cracking a fart joke and breaking into the muffin tin. Jake slipped to the back and called Eva.

On the fourth ring she answered, sounding harried. "Hey."

"Hey," he said. "I've been worried."

"Sorry. I meant to call but things have been crazy this morning. Hold on a sec." In the background Jake could hear Eva talking to someone. "I'm going to have to call you back, Jake."

"Wait. Are you okay?"

"Yeah. I'll call you." And then she hung up.

Jake didn't want to feel miffed, because he knew Eva had a good reason. He'd just expected things to be different once he admitted that he thought he was falling in love with her.

Last night when they'd talked over the phone before bed, they'd whispered sweet things to each other. He'd talked about her luscious satin skin, and she'd complimented some of his best moves. They each lay in separate beds several miles apart, but the intimacy and tenderness had been so real. And tonight he'd fantasized about sneaking into her room. Dutch wouldn't hear an explosion in a nitroglycerin plant once his head hit the pillow, so sneaking around and having naughty times would have been a breeze. But that was off the table.

The phone rang.

Eva.

"Hey."

"Sorry I couldn't talk. I was at the pharmacy counter. Charlie has the flu, and I had to get a prescription for some obnoxiously priced medicine. I'm pretty sure I'll be living on bologna this month."

"I won't let you starve," he joked, flopping onto

the old recliner Hank had brought from his house. "Fancy won't let you starve."

"No, she wouldn't. Good thing, because taking care of a kid is expensive…and I've already used four sick days. Thank goodness I'm not on again until Thursday night. Then I'm going back-to-back, taking Moon's Friday shift. I don't know when I'll see you again."

"I can come over tomorrow afternoon when I get off."

"And get the flu?"

"Already had my flu shot." He wanted to tell her he had to see her but Jake was a pro at pretending indifference.

"I miss you, too. I've been thinking about yesterday, about the way your body felt next to mine."

Jake felt his body stir. "Don't go there, babe. I'm stuck here with Farts A Lot and Snores Insanely. I can't get—" he lowered his voice "—horny."

Eva laughed. "Well, the way I look now, you could call me the erection killer. I'm walking ED."

"Never."

"Still, I think you better wait until this medicine is in his system. No need for you to get sick."

Jake said his goodbye and hung up, disappointed he wouldn't see Eva for a few days. But the rightness between them felt so different than anything he'd ever had with another woman.

It shocked him.

For the past few months he'd been restless, hungrier than normal to blow this town and make a new life for himself. Perhaps his discontent hadn't been about Magnolia Bend or his career…maybe it had been about loneliness.

Okay, so picking up a little company for a night or two had never been an issue. Willing women were a dime a dozen around any honky-tonk within a fifty-mile radius. Lonely looked for lonely. But this wasn't about a physical thing. No, what he'd needed was something his brother John had found, something Abigail had found—a purpose for living.

Jake hadn't really had one.

But seeing Eva in a new light, seeing how well she fit him on all levels, made him understand. It was as if he'd been near-sighted and then pulled on a pair of glasses for the first time. All the fuzzy edges dissolved into sharp contrast. So he knew what he had with Eva was right and good. And he damn sure didn't want to wreck it by being demanding or unsupportive.

He'd see if Fancy would whip up her infamous chicken soup for him to drop off, and he'd give Eva whatever she needed, because for the first time maybe ever, someone else was more important than himself.

"Who are you?" he said to his reflection in the mirror hanging over the beat-up dresser beside the twin bed.

Then he laughed. Because at that moment he

was something more than Jake the Magnolia Bend man whore.

He belonged to someone, and that made him feel almost normal.

CHAPTER EIGHTEEN

WHEN JAKE PUSHED through the door at Ray-Ray's, everything looked the same. Should have been comforting to Jake, but instead it felt tired. Same place, different man.

"What's up, Jake?" Ray called from behind the scarred bar. The owner/bartender wiped a mug clean as the perpetually tired Bonnie shuffled past with a tray full of beers for a few rowdy farmhands sitting in the corner playing cards. Jake's brother Matt played darts with the same guys who came every Thursday, and Clint sat in the same spot he'd sat every Thursday since he and Jake had started coming to Ray-Ray's.

Except that this Thursday Clint had driven himself.

"What the hell, dude?" Jake asked, sliding onto a stool at the table.

Clint didn't look up. Instead, he studied the half-filled glass of whiskey as if it was a specimen under his microscope.

"I went to pick you up and your dad said you'd driven yourself. You couldn't text and save me a trip out to the Duck Blind?"

"Thought you liked driving out to the lake," Clint said, not looking at Jake.

An odd feeling awoke in Jake's gut. Clint sounded accusing, but why? The subject of dating Eva would be a hard one to breach since Clint was friends with both of them, and there was this odd jealousy thing happening between them. But Clint would eventually be happy for them. Jake hoped. "I do. I'm pretty fond of the lake."

"I know," Clint said, his tone expressionless. "And so you know, I can damn well drive myself. I'm not some pathetic loser who has to wait on the grand Jake Beauchamp to pick him up."

Jake rocked back at the venom in Clint's voice. "I don't do that."

"Right," Clint said, turning a shoulder toward Jake.

"What the hell is wrong with you?" Jake asked, waving Bonnie away when she headed toward them. Though he could use a drink, he'd rather be clear-headed for the conversation that had been brewing for years.

He didn't need this bullshit with Clint. The last few days had been hard enough not being able to be with Eva, not to mention his job rebuilding a fence for Old Man Turner. And then there was Bobby John, who had approached him about taking some arson investigation classes in order to make a move as the parish investigator.

Bobby John had applied for a position in Shreveport that would pay more and allow him to be near his family—he'd gotten the call that he was hired on Tuesday. The position for St. James parish would need to be filled by the first of the year. But Jake wasn't even sure he wanted to stay with the department anymore, much less switch to that sort of job. But it might be perfect for Eva, especially since the hours were more nine to five. So, yeah, dealing with Clint acting like a bitch over whatever burr stuck in his ass wasn't desirable.

"What the hell is wrong with me?" Clint drawled sarcastically. "More like what the hell isn't wrong with me."

"Come on, Clint. We're so past self-pity," Jake said. "Say what you gotta say."

"Self-pity. Now there's a word," Clint scoffed with a bitter laugh. "I've never gone there. Right? I've been Polly Positive this entire time. But even a man such as me needs to sink down in the crap hole of self-pity every once in a while. Don't take that away from me, friend." Of course, the way Clint said *friend* didn't sound too friendly.

Jake didn't have the energy or the patience to play the game Clint had started. "Say what you need to say."

Clint turned to him then, anger aflame in his dark eyes. "Fine. I want you to leave Eva the hell alone."

"What?"

"Eva. The woman you took to the lake Sunday

and no doubt screwed very well if reputation is to be believed."

"What?"

Clint continued. "Well, I'm making an assumption it was well done. But yes, Eva. That woman. Leave. Her. Alone."

His friend had hit him with a metaphorical wrecking ball, and he lay among the rubble, dazed, confused and, as always, guilty. "How did you—"

"I saw your truck go past my house. Saw Eva next to you. I knew where you were going. You always like to screw at the lake."

"You don't understand. Eva and I are together. She's different."

Clint laughed. Not a ha-ha laugh but a braying laugh of disbelief. "So you're a couple? Yeah. Okay."

"Why can't you be happy for me?" Jake asked, anger starting to chew on his gut.

"Because I hate you."

"Clint."

"Yeah, let's just be honest. Hatred for you has festered inside me for a long time. I got accustomed to it. It was almost comforting. Do I love you? Yeah. Do I hate you for all you've taken from me? Yeah."

Jake had no words. He knew Clint had resented the loss of his legs, had mourned the death of the girl he'd been dating and sometimes allowed jealousy of Jake to break through the surface, but hate? "I'm sorry you feel that way, but you have no right to tell me to stay away from Eva."

"Yeah, I do," Clint said, angling his chair so he faced Jake. His longtime friend's face seemed carved out of unrelenting stone. Something horrible burned inside Clint's eyes, something he'd nurtured for too long. "Because I care about Eva. Because she doesn't deserve you. She deserves more than some man who will use her and discard her. So why don't you, for the first time in your life, take the unselfish route and leave her alone?"

"How can you say those things?"

Clint narrowed his eyes. "Because they're true. Don't you get it, Jake? I wanted Eva. I wanted to marry her and build a life with her. I took it slow, letting her get to know me, being patient, but what good did that do?"

"I didn't know. You never said anything."

"I thought I didn't have to. I mean, you've screwed every available woman in this town. I thought you had the decency to leave the good girls alone. But no. You couldn't help yourself, could you? You just had to take one more thing from me."

Jake slapped a hand on the table, rattling the empty beer bottle that had been left there. It fell over, leaving sudsy foam on the lacquered table. "I didn't take anything from you."

Clint shook his head. "You've taken everything. Don't you get it? You get everything you want. And the thing is, everyone knows you don't really want Eva. You're bored. She's there. You're just messing around and next month, what? She'll be yesterday's news and you'll be on to the next woman. But Eva's different. She's tender and not like those girls who know what they're getting when they follow you out that door." Clint jabbed his finger at the tinted glass door.

"I won't hurt Eva."

"Yeah, you will. You always do. So why not spare her and be noble for once in your life? Leave her alone and let her have a chance at happiness."

"With you?" Jake asked. He'd never felt so slammed, so hurt over the accusations spilling from his best friend's mouth. "You think you can give her what she wants?"

Clint stilled. "I can give her something you can't—commitment and respect. But I may not be the right guy for Eva. I can handle that disappointment. I'm used to life's disappointments. But I do know one thing—you are unequivocally the *wrong* guy for Eva."

Jake gritted his teeth and tried not to unleash his anger on Clint. They were basically the same words Matt had uttered when they went fishing. But still it was hard to hear them from Clint's mouth. "Is this about the accident? Is this some transference of anger stemming from repressed—"

"Don't use some psychobabble you learned in freshman psychology on me. Yeah, I'm angry about the wreck. I'm pissed you came out that night, that you insisted I was too drunk to drive but yet managed to soberly wrap us around a tree. And I get it

was an accident. Just one of those things in life." He
delivered that last line with bitterness.

"No one could have anticipated the deer crossing
our path, could have known the tires were bald on
my truck, could have even understood that moving
me from where I lay would worsen my condition. I
understand all those things. You were trying to do
the right thing and it backfired. So, no, though sometimes I feel envy as I watch you strutting around here,
dancing with some girl and then no doubt giving her
a good time in the back of your truck, and though
I itch to punch your lights out every now and then,
this is not about the accident. This is about Eva and
your track record of being a lowlife with women."

Speaking of punching someone, Jake wanted for
the first time in his life to punch a crippled man.
Clint's words seared him. No, sliced him like a
dull razor. "So I'm what? Destined to be this?"
Jake swiped a hand down his too tight T-shirt and
well-worn jeans designed to show off his ass. Yeah,
months ago he'd designed his wardrobe in order to
get laid. He wasn't proud of it at that moment, but
he knew what he had been.

But Eva had changed him.

Hadn't she?

He certainly had thought so, but with Clint's hard
words bashing him and Matt's earlier admonition
regarding Eva, Jake wondered if the men closest to
him could see what he could not.

Had he been deluding himself? Was being with Eva dishonorable?

"I don't know, Jake, but I do know that if you asked anyone to describe Jake Beauchamp they'd say, 'He's a good guy but a screwup,' and I don't think Eva deserves being a casualty of your messed-up world." And with that last comment, Clint downed his liquor and rolled away, leaving Jake sitting at the table.

Bonnie approached and propped a hand on her hip. "Well, that looked intense. You need a drink, hon?"

Jake shook his head. "I need something stronger than whiskey right now."

"Well, we don't sell that, but if you go up to Hook Road, you can probably score something. Take a gun, though," Bonnie teased, sashaying off with more energy than she'd shown in years.

Jake felt close to tears, the heavy brick of guilt, doubt and disappointment culling a home in his soul. Across the room, he caught sight of Jenny, who gave him a sympathetic look. How many people had heard Clint's accusations? How many now knew that he and Eva had messed around?

Jenny offered him a partial smile and a shrug.

He managed to crook half of his lips into either a grimace or an acknowledging smile. He wasn't sure which.

Matt pulled up a stool and sank onto it. "Well, I told you this would happen."

"That Clint would call me out about Eva?"

"No, that nothing good could come of you pursuing Eva. I didn't hear everything Clint said, and I don't agree with most of it, but he was right about some things."

"So what? Do I just pretend I feel nothing? Ignore her? What do you suggest? Since your own relationship seems peachy keen at the moment."

Matt's mouth turned down, and a coldness descended over his face. "You can learn from my mistakes. Women are complex creatures. You can't pretend to understand them. Just stay behind the line and refuse to cross the field full of land mines."

"Bullshit," Jake scoffed, eyeing the watery whiskey Clint had left behind. From the corner of his eye, he noted his former best friend pushing out the door of Ray-Ray's. He wondered if Clint was okay to drive... and then he remembered the last time he'd begged a tipsy Clint not to climb behind the wheel. None of his business. He wasn't a cop or Clint's keeper.

"That's your response? Bullshit?"

"It's all I got," Jake said, pushing away from the table. He didn't know what to do at that moment. Tell everyone to jump off a cliff...or back off Eva.

He wanted her.

He thought he loved her.

But could he risk her heart?

Not having the answer, he gave his brother a slap on the back. "I gotta get out of here."

"Why?"

"Because I can't think in here. This place is...it's not the place for me right now."

"I get it," Matt said, calling Bonnie over to order another drink. "Think hard about this thing with Eva. She's part of this community, our family, not to mention she's raising a kid. This ain't Kate, a gal who knows the score. This is Eva. Be judicious."

And on those words of wisdom, Jake left Ray-Ray's.

SATURDAY CAME LIKE a ray of sunshine in a sea of darkness. Turned out nursing a child through the flu was no cakewalk. And doing back-to-back shifts at the station wasn't much better. Especially when Jake wasn't there.

That afternoon when she arrived back at her house, paying Birdie for babysitting a suddenly very energetic Charlie for the morning, she set out to give herself a much-needed spa day.

With Charlie napping to old-school Bugs Bunny videos, Eva planned to sink into a bubble bath and read a raunchy erotic novel on her Kindle. She'd been daydreaming about Jake and making love to him for the past few days...well, when she wasn't changing bedding, making chicken noodle soup and spraying everything she owned with Lysol. She would be happy if she never smelled "clean cotton" spray again.

Usually she didn't fuss with painting her nails or waxing her bikini area, but she had promised Jake she'd cook dinner, assuring him the place was de-contaminated, and wanted to feel pretty rather than

like a flu survivor. Last night when she'd texted him
from the station, he'd been a bit terse, but she figured
he'd felt a little ignored by her. They'd essentially
made love, declared a sort of undefined commitment
to one another and then…crickets.

Okay, a sick kid and a job were good reasons for
those crickets, but tonight she'd show Jake exactly
how much she'd missed him. As soon as her nail pol-
ish dried and the steaks finished marinating.

Her phone rang and she saw it was her friend
Jenny.

She let it go to voice mail because the Pink Sensation still hadn't dried. Jenny probably wanted to
go out, forgetting that Eva had Charlie now.

The voice mail dinged.

Eva padded into her bedroom and slipped on a
robe.

"Charlie," she called.

"I'm watching the Road Runner," he called back.

"Are you feeling okay?"

"Yeah, I'm good. I feel like a million bucks. You
can stop asking me that now." He sounded a bit peevish, but it made Eva smile. Getting Charlie through
a scary sickness and 104-degree fever had not only
stretched her mothering abilities but had also challenged her emotions. Guess there was just something about nurturing a kid when he had his defenses
down. She could still feel the way he clung to her,
still ache at his little cries when they'd drawn blood at
the clinic. Luckily, the Tamiflu they'd given him had

helped him get better much faster. The only upside to the whole crazy Monday morning had been Melba Gunter seeing her true parenting skills in action… and ignoring the dirty socks on the living room floor and the empty pizza box in the kitchen. Nails finally dry, Eva padded back into the bathroom, dropped her robe and climbed into her soaker tub full of bubbles.

Leaning back, Eva closed her eyes. She was doing okay. No, better than okay. The man she'd loved for years had told her he was falling for her. A position was up for grabs at the station, which could result in a much-needed raise.

Kids were sorta expensive. And with Charlie finally getting settled in and Claren, who had sent her an apology via email, admitting she needed help and had to stay at the facility a while longer, things were on the upswing. Life was good.

Her phone on the counter buzzed again. Another voice mail.

Maybe she should check it. Maybe something was going on. Water sluiced off her body as she stood and grabbed a towel, drying her hands.

This message was from Jake.

Can't make it tonight. Sorry.

Eva lowered the phone. What the hell kind of message was that?

Disappointment struck hard. Damn it. She wanted to curl up next to him on the couch and watch a movie, like she was his girlfriend. And then once Charlie was asleep, take him to her bed and show him how much she'd missed him. But this was a weird message. No teasing. No flirting. Maybe Jake had already changed his mind.

No. Something had to have come up.

She texted:

Everything okay?

Yeah. Will talk later.

Dripping on the carpet, she stood there naked, wondering if she should text back or let it go.

She did neither. Instead, she called him...the old-fashioned way. It took him a long time before he answered, and when he said hello it sounded empty.

"Hey, what's going on? I thought we had a date with two rib eyes tonight?"

"Yeah, I'm sorry about that, but I have something I have to do. Can't wait."

Eva didn't know what to say to that. Pry? Or...

"Look, Eva," Jake said, clearing his throat, "uh, I think I was a bit premature in saying—"

"Wait. Are you joking?" she interrupted, grabbing a towel and wrapping it around her. She shut the toilet lid and sank down. "You're really doing this? A blow-off before we even start?"

"No, we, ah, it's complicated, E."

"No shit. That's exactly what I told you, but you

said a lot of things Sunday that erased my reservations about sleeping with you." She growled the last part because at that moment she felt like one of those cartoon characters that turned into a blinking dumb-ass. "Did you lie to me?"

"At that moment I sorta felt those things," he said, his voice so dry, so emotionless, so not like the Jake she'd always known. He sounded…bored?

So all along this had been about Jake getting a piece of her dumb ass? How many other girls had he lied to in order to get into their pants? She'd always thought him to be a gigolo, but she'd thought him an honest gigolo. What kind of man used the "L" word to get laid?

She pulled the phone away and looked down at it.

He had to be joking. He couldn't have faked all that. She would have known, wouldn't she? "I can't believe this. I really can't. So me having to take care of my brother, who was running a 104-degree fever by the way, put you off? Is that what you're saying?"

"Um, maybe the distance gave me perspective," he said, clearing his throat again. Like a guilty man. "You suggested going in that direction could ruin things, and the more I thought about it, the more I think you're right."

"Too late. We went that direction. Anytime you snap a condom off after being with someone, you've gone in a direction, Jake. I can't believe you're pulling this shit." She was yelling at him and didn't care. He'd lost his mind. He acted as if he was…lying.

"Wait, are you scared or something? Did someone say something?"

A long silence.

"No. I'm sorry, Eva. I never meant to hurt you."

"So don't. I believed you. I still believe in us. Don't do this."

"But you were right all along," he said, robotically. Like he'd rehearsed it. "We should just be friends."

"You're lying to yourself...and to me. I'm so disappointed in you."

"I'm sor—"

She hung up on him. She couldn't deal with the stabbing pain that had pierced her, blooming inside her like a disease, taking over her body. She tossed the phone onto the counter, clutched her stomach and leaned over, trying not to scream.

He'd dumped her. And, sweet Lord Almighty, he'd barely even picked her up.

"Oh, oh, oh," she said, rocking herself, squeezing her eyes closed as tightly as possible. As if she could will it away. As if—

"Eva?" Charlie said behind the closed bathroom door. "Who are you yelling at?"

Damn. "Uh, no one."

"Your voice sounds funny. Like you're choking on water. You're not drownded, are you?"

"No, honey. Go watch your movie. I'll be out in a minute," she said, pressing a trembling hand over her mouth. Her body shook with unshed tears, and tremendous pressure bloomed in her head, threatening to explode.

Eva pressed her fingers into dry eyes. *Well, there you have it, sister. You did this to yourself.*

And she had. She'd known Jake's MO. Being with him, admitting her feelings, had been a huge risk and she'd crapped out, losing the entire bank. Yeah, Jake was a bastard extraordinaire, but she had known this could happen. But like every little girl in the world, she had believed a man could love her forever.

She blamed it on Cinderella and that Prince Charming crap spoon-fed to her as a child. Happily-ever-after, her ass.

Only one thing to do. Put one foot in front of the other. No time for pints of Ben and Jerry or crying jags or buying new shoes to alleviate the pain of a broken heart. She had Charlie to think of, and that meant pasting on a happy face, ignoring the steaks marinating, and going out for pizza.

She stood up, tossed the towel into the dirty clothes bin and wiped the smudges from under her eyes. She didn't have the luxury of tears at that moment.

Instead, anger grew…and determination…and a hurt that would never go away.

CHAPTER NINETEEN

JAKE WAS DRUNK.

And he'd been drunk pretty much the whole weekend.

Seemed lying to Eva, breaking her heart and being thought of as a no-good rat-bastard made a man crave bourbon.

And scotch.

And Andy Gator beer.

"You know you're too drunk to mow the yard," Matt said from the rocking chair on the porch of the Beauchamp family camp. Matt came here on the weekends, when his wife came back to Magnolia Bend to visit their boys and stayed at the house they'd bought fifteen years ago. Sometimes she took them to New Orleans and her tiny apartment in the Vieux Carre, but most of the time she spared them the exposure to vomit, piss and tourists taking pictures with tired old mules tied to festive carriages. They'd been split up for eight months, and Matt had indicated that though he still loved his wife, he didn't know how to mend what was broken between them.

Which made Jake even more depressed, so he took another swig of beer.

"I'm not too drunk. I've driven that tractor way drunker than this."

"Sure, but the cutting job you did looked like you were hammered. Dad never forgave you for running over that confederate jasmine he'd planted by the boathouse."

Jake gave a bitter laugh.

"So you gonna talk about why you've been the most morose bastard I've encountered in a decade?" Matt asked, sipping his coffee and staring out at the cypress trees draped with lacy Spanish moss. The lake was rough today, and not far from the camp lay the spot where Jake had taken Eva…where he'd said words he had to take back.

He hated himself for that.

"Nah, got nothing to say. Pretty much the way you feel about MJ."

"I'm assuming this is about Eva."

"And I'm assuming you should stay the hell out of my business. You had your say about me and her. I got the message."

For a few minutes the only sound Jake heard was the creak of the rocker on the wooden slants of the porch. A mockingbird flew onto the porch and then immediately took flight again.

"I remember what I said," Matt said with a grunt as he stood, "but also remember the advice came from a man who has no clue about women. Mary Jane was my first love, the first woman I ever slept with. Hell, the only woman I've ever slept with, so my knowledge of the fairer sex is shit. Just consider that."

Matt passed him, snatching the keys to the old John Deere, heading to the metal building that housed all their dad's toys—pirogues, an old Jet Ski and a multitude of tools.

Jake followed him because he was tired of wallowing in his own misery, tired of thinking about what he shoulda, coulda done. He'd done what Clint suggested. He'd unburdened Eva with the heartbreak that was sure to come from loving him. Everyone was right about him. He didn't have the balls or the gumption to go after love.

Love hurt. And life had shown him as much. John's wife had died, Abigail's husband had cheated and Matt's wife had left him.

The flipside to love was pain.

So why would he want to saddle himself with that particular emotion? He already had enough self-loathing rolling inside him. He'd already broken one man years ago and so the solution was quite easy— never feel anything more than casual concern. Well, at least for anyone outside his family. He couldn't fake love for his family—that was as real as the sun every morning and the moon every night. But everyone else? Yeah, if he didn't love and commit to people, he couldn't let them down.

Like he had Clint.

Like he had Angela.

And like he had Eva.

He had so wanted Eva to be his. And when she'd said those things about believing in him...believing in them...he'd almost told her about Clint and his accusations. Her pain had broken his heart. And now he'd have to make his way through life missing the most important piece of himself.

"I can do the weed eating," Jake said to Matt, grabbing the goggles and earplugs off the hook.

"No, you need to go sleep this off. I've been where you are. I've been sick over love. Booze ain't gonna cure it. You've had your bender, you've probably examined what you've done—which I'm assuming is deny yourself Eva—and now it's time to rest, shower and don the mask you'll present to the rest of the world. And that's no piece of cake, bro." Matt sat a hand on his shoulder.

Jake nodded, handing the safety tools over to his older brother. Thank God he had someone to talk to, someone who understood. Not like he could go to Abigail or John. They were so stinkin' in love one could barely tolerate being around them. *So* not the people he needed at this moment.

"Thanks, Matt."

Matt snapped the headphones on his ears and climbed onto the tractor.

Jake headed back to the cabin, knowing that tomorrow he'd have to face Eva. Their shift would be murder, but he had to do it...unless he called one of the other guys and talked about a permanent switch.

God, he'd hate not being on shift with Eva. He'd

grown so accustomed to her face, to the smell of her lotion and the way she ate all the red loops out of her cereal first.

But if he were truly putting her first, as he'd convinced himself he'd done, then he had to finish it. No sense in subjecting her to his presence.

I'm disappointed by you.

Yeah, a woman who said that would likely be glad not to share toothpaste and couch time with him at the station.

Jake pulled his cell phone out of his pocket and dialed Cooper Platt. The younger firefighter had asked about switching shifts with him before because he didn't like one of the guys on his shift. Ernie was a bit of a blowhard, but Jake could deal with the older know-it-all. Coop, Eva and Dutch would do fine together on C shift.

And he could think seriously about another job… or getting out of Magnolia Bend. After the blowup with Clint and with Eva no doubt hating him, he finally had the catalyst to make a change. Well, a different change.

And it started with switching shifts.

For Eva's sake.

EVA WALKED INTO PattyAnn's bakery and spied Jenny in the corner. When Eva had finally got around to checking her messages after an unprecedented crying jag into her pillow that night, she discovered that Jenny had seen or heard something that Eva had to hear about. Jenny had begged to meet her for lunch, and with Charlie over at Abigail's helping Birdie make globe cookies for Columbus Day, she had enough time to slip away.

Of course she looked like crap. After a much-needed cry, the hope of sleep had fled from her like a toddler in a mall, hiding in the circular rack of Never Gonna Be the Same Again, an imaginary store full of tear-streaked tissues, white wine and faded promises. But damn if her pink nails didn't look nice.

"Hey," she said, pulling out the old-fashioned wire chair that was shaped like a heart. Oh, the irony. "What are you eating?"

Jenny spooned another bite of custard into her mouth and moaned. "Egg custard. I swear this stuff has crack in it. I'm getting another one. You want?"

"Nah," Eva said. "Just grab me a coffee. Oh, and hell, an oatmeal cookie. Here's some money."

"Save it," Jenny said with a wave, striding to the counter. No one else was there. Sunday afternoon wasn't a jumping time for a bakery, but Patty Shoemaker opened it from one o'clock to four o'clock each Sunday for cookies and ice cream. She claimed her father used to take her for long drives each Sunday afternoon, finishing it off with an ice cream, so she wanted all kids to have the chance for that memory.

Today she'd have to settle for being the go-to spot for two single gals who needed sugar to deal with heartache.

"Patty says it's on the house for one of Magnolia Bend's bravest." Jenny set the plate in front of her. Eva waved a thank-you to the older woman and then bit into the homemade deliciousness. After pizza last night, waffles for breakfast and now the cookie, surviving Jake would likely net her a few extra pounds.

"So what's up with you?" Eva asked her friend.

"Nothing much. Jamison French asked me out," Jenny said, dipping into the fresh custard. "I hesitated because I thought he was into you."

"We only went out a few times. He's a nice guy but he wasn't for me. I like them rough around the edges."

"I know," Jenny teased, with a quick lift of her lips. "So what should I know about Jamison?"

Eva hoped Jenny hadn't called to pick her brain about Jamison. She was so not in the mood. "He doesn't sweat, his breath smells like cinnamon and he has a set of rules for dating. Didn't even try to kiss me on the first date."

"Reeeeally?" Jenny said with a devilish grin.

"You kissed him?" Eva laughed.

"Oh, I did more than kiss him, but that's a story for another day. A really kinky story. Those prim and proper guys always fool you." Jenny's eyes danced as she dove back into her custard. "But I didn't ask you here to talk about Jamie and his really talented hands. I have a scoop on your Jakey."

"Scoop?" Eva's heart leaped at the thought of any gossip involving her...and Jake. No one should have known about them. They'd been surrounded by only birds, squirrels and silent cypress trees.

"So I was at Ray-Ray's Thursday night and I overheard Jake and Clint getting into it."

"Like a fight?"

Jenny nodded. "Mmm-hmm, and it was over you."

"Me?"

"Clint was cold as ice. Just frosty. And Jake was himself, all smiles when he entered." Jenny jabbed a spoon at her. "I'm not a big gossiper but since this was about you, I felt I should retell it."

"Of course." Eva unconsciously leaned closer. "So…"

"Well, I couldn't hear everything, but the gist is Clint told Jake to stay away from you."

"Stay away from me?"

Jenny nodded eager as a golden retriever with a tennis ball in its mouth. "Yeah, and he was terrible to Jake. Said you were too good for him and that Jake would only hurt you. Said Jake should be unselfish for once in his life. Can you believe?"

Eva swallowed hard and nearly choked on a crumb of cookie. She went into a coughing fit, and Jenny thumped her a little too hard on the back. "Wait, wait, I'm okay."

Patty sat a glass of water down in front of Eva and she gulped it, coughed once more and said, "Are you shitting me, Jenny?"

"I know. Clint sorta looked sexy being all protective like that. I've never seen him be so command-ing. So is he into you, or something?"

Eva ignored that question. "What about Jake? How did he act?" Hope and anger simultaneously grew inside her. She knew something had to have happened. Knew it.

But why would Jake chuck all they'd had because of Clint? Was Jake playing at martyr?

No. He was a moron.

The man had let Clint apply his trademark tool of guilt to hammer the lid on anything Jake felt for Eva. That dumb-ass thought he was saving her from himself.

And Clint?

How dare he presume to know what she deserved or didn't?

So flipping presumptuous of him to meddle in her love life. Of course she'd never told Jake his friend had suggested something more with her. Jake wouldn't have known that Clint's words were moti-vated by jealousy as much as his supposed concern. Like always, Clint had manipulated Jake.

"I gotta go, Jenny," Eva said, pushing back from the table.

"But what about your coffee? You didn't drink it."

Eva stilled, pressing her hands onto the table. "Tell me about Jake afterward."

"Oh, well, he didn't stay. Matt sat down for a few minutes and chatted with him and then Jake, looking like he lost a puppy, got up and left. So is there something going on between you and Jake? Like romantic?"

Eva bit her lip. "Well, to be honest, I had hoped. We'd been flirting with the possibility we were made for each other, but then Saturday night he didn't show up for the dinner we'd planned. He blew me off."

Jenny smiled. "Yeah, I can see you two being right for one another. Jake's that kind of guy, you know. He's looking for something. Oh, sure, he's stomped around this town, hooking up with women, talking a big game, but all that happened to him after that accident has just eaten away at him. People don't see it, but I do. I guess sometimes the same kind of people recognize in others what they know lies in themselves. Jake's been hurting for a long time, but maybe he's been waiting on that door to crack so he could slip inside to you."

Eva felt gobsmacked by Jenny's observation. But as soon as her friend had uttered those thoughts, Eva was certain Jenny had nailed Jake…not in that way…but in his psyche. Jake had been masking his guilt and pain by donning a mask of sunny indifference.

And Clint had erased it as if it was a chalkboard. One swipe of guilt had taken away Jake's chance for happiness.

Eva's chance for happiness.

Eva grabbed Jenny's hand. "Thank you for telling me what happened. I needed to know that."

Jenny squeezed her hand. "I didn't know you felt

that way about Jake. But with that in mind, I think you have some work to do, friend."

"And that's why I don't have time for coffee. I'll see you later, and until I figure this out, don't say anything to anyone, okay?"

Jenny pretended to zip her lips and then she picked up Eva's remaining cookie. "Go get your happy, girl. I'm gonna finish this cookie before I go rock Dr. French's world again. Making a man mewl like a kitten is powerful stuff."

For the first time since yesterday, Eva laughed. Jenny had just given her hope. First, she was going to Clint's to kick his ass seven ways to Sunday. Then, well, she'd have to pick up Charlie. But come Monday when she and Jake reported for their shift, Mr. Beauchamp was going to find out that letting everyone dictate who he is and how he feels was as stupid as jumping off a cliff with no parachute. No matter what, a person shouldn't be defined by what others expect him or her to be. Jake expected to be unreliable because everyone told him he was.

God, men were stupid.

But maybe she was, too.

She could be grasping at straws in thinking that Jake wanted more…but then again she knew Jake. She'd been his friend and the woman who loved him for over three years.

All she had to do now was prove to him that he was worthy of her love.

EVA COULD TELL Clint knew something was up because for the first time in over a year, she'd shown up sans cookies or muffins.

"Eva," he said, reversing his chair and allowing her to come inside the rustic yet contemporary lake house. "What a nice surprise."

"Hey," Eva said, stepping into the large hearth room. Mounted ducks flew over the stone fireplace, and skylights brought in lovely natural light. "Is your father here?"

"No, he's in town picking up some things. What are you doing here? Not your usual day to visit us." He maneuvered so he faced the large floor-to-ceiling wall that overlooked the lake. The water was choppy and though it was far, she could see the clearing where she and Jake had made love. A pair of binoculars sat on a small nearby table, giving her a sickish feeling in her stomach. Had Clint watched them make love?

It was a creepy thought, but how else would he have known about them?

"Good, because I needed to talk to you. Privately," she said.

"Is this about our conversation last weekend? Have you given some thought to my question?"

"No."

He lifted his eyebrows but said nothing.

"This is about you and Jake," she said.

"Me and Jake?" His voice sounded incredulous,

but she could tell he knew what she meant. "What about us?"

"You know what this is about. Don't play dumb. Too many people overheard you in Ray-Ray's. Did you think I wouldn't hear the rumors?"

"I didn't care if you heard the rumors. I meant what I said. Jake has no business messing with you. He's used goods."

"Used goods? Why? Because he's slept around? This isn't the Victorian Age, Clint. Men and women do have sex outside of marriage, quite frequently, in fact. So don't cast that judgment on him. Not even his own father does that."

Bitterness etched Clint's strong jaw. "Oh, I see. It's too late. You're already smitten with the great Jake Beauchamp. Fine. Go ahead and try a go with him. You'll see too soon nothing will come of it."

Eva set her hands on her hips and glared at Clint. "So you think you can manipulate everyone around you, huh? What, you sit up here on your high horse and plan how you can manipulate people using past mistakes against them?"

"You think that's what I do?" Clint's self-righteous smirk disappeared. Target hit.

"Seems like it. You love to lord the fact you were handicapped in that accident over Jake. You've chained him to you with guilt, and the thing is, he loves you."

"No, he doesn't. He feels obligated. Think I don't

know that?" Clint said, his voice sad. Like he wished it wasn't so.

"Maybe he feels obligated, but he shows up. He stayed here and shows up for you every week. If the shoe were on the other foot, would you do the same?"

"But it's not," Clint said softly. "The shoe is on my foot, and I live with that every day. I live with the colostomy bag, with strange nerve pain, with the fact I can't do what Jake does. I can't pick up women, swagger around and sweet-talk everything in a skirt anymore. I live with that shoe on *my* foot every day. So if Jake feels guilty, good. He should."

Eva shook her head. "How can you live like that? How can you hold him in your palm like that and squeeze so hard?"

Clint sat a stone, unmoved.

"But this time you didn't merely manipulate Jake, you manipulated me. You didn't think this would affect me? That I wouldn't hurt because of your selfishness?"

"My selfishness? Because I think Jake will hurt you? Because I think being with him is an exercise in futility? I spoke to him on your behalf."

"I never asked you to. You had no right."

"Maybe not, but sometimes one has to do things for his friends for their own good. Like you do for Charlie."

"Oh, my God. You really believe what you did was right."

Clint shrugged. "Jake will chew you up and spit you out. Make no mistake of that. He can't be happy."

"Because you won't let him. You enjoy using his guilt against him. What does that make you, Clint?" Eva walked over to the man who she'd only thought of in the best of terms until now.

Clint had shown so much good humor and determination in facing his disability. They'd spent many days of the week in the gym working toward his being able to compete in parasports. They'd even planned a trip to Houston for one of the runs. She'd visited him here in this very house, sharing details of her childhood, funny stories from the firehouse. She'd always thought Clint her friend.

But maybe not.

He wanted her for something more than friendship and when he couldn't have her, he made sure that the one person she wanted, the one person she truly loved, wouldn't give her a chance.

Clint was a messed-up dude.

He looked up at her now. "One day you'll thank me."

"Not today. Probably not tomorrow. Likely never." Then she turned and walked out of the room.

"Oh, come on, Eva. Don't leave like this."

She turned around, coming back with long, angry strides.

"Did you watch? Did you spy on me and Jake?"

Clint narrowed his eyes. "And if I did? You pretty

much dropped your sanity when you dropped that dress."

"You did!" She jabbed a finger at him. "Do you know how sick that is?"

"I stopped watching when I saw what was happening. I'm no glutton for punishment or pervert. So, no, I didn't watch you screw my best friend." He pressed a button and rolled toward the ramp that took him to the upper level of the split level.

"You've said your piece. You can see yourself out," he said, before disappearing into the inner recesses of the house.

"You son of a bitch," Eva whispered under her breath, tears pricking her eyes. She walked out for the second time, this time slamming the door because it felt good.

She'd thought he'd admit he'd been wrong to approach Jake about her. She'd hoped he might go to Jake and say he'd been presumptuous, but instead Clint had remained stonily convicted he'd done the right thing.

And that pissed her off.

Because she was a grown-ass woman who didn't need anyone to guard her from anything. It also proved Clint didn't know the first thing about her. She had never needed protecting…especially from her own mistakes.

God, men really, truly were idiots sometimes.

She climbed in her car and called Abigail to tell her she was on her way.

COOPER PLATT WAS more than happy to switch shifts with Jake, and the chief didn't seem to mind, either. So as of ten o'clock Monday morning, Jake was officially a member of A shift. Which meant he didn't have to work on Monday, which meant he had more time to stew over the crappy thing he'd done to Eva. Which blew. Because he really didn't want to sit home reliving their horrible conversation.

Thankfully, Abigail called and asked him for some help. To make ends meet he often took on small repair jobs, relying on the skills his father had taught him as a youngster. As the baby of the family, he hadn't been called on much to lend a hand around the house, until all his siblings had left for college and there was only him to help Dan measure boards and refinish old furniture. Ironically, he found comfort in a hammer and nails, so while many firemen made up for the pittance of a salary by doing lawn service, he hung up a shingle for handyman. Of course he got a couple of calls from lonely ladies who implied their pipes needed cleaning, but for the most part he'd earned a reputation as a guy who could do small projects for a good price.

Abigail had used him a lot in the restoration of her bed-and-breakfast. The main house was beautifully restored, and thus, Abigail had moved on to the small cabins that had once been slave cabins…and more recently had been used as a sort of commune for artists. Abigail had been working to restore the neglected row of cabins so they could be used by guests. She'd been really picky about salvaging all she could from the original structure in order to preserve one of the only plantations with standing slave cabins. The first cabin would not be for guests, but rather a historical tour for visiting classrooms and tourists. Turning something that carried pain into something that could educate meant a lot to Abigail.

So he hopped in his truck and drove out to Laurel Woods, painfully aware he could take a brief hike and reach Eva's house through the woods. The thought made his heart ache but he ignored it. After all, this would be his lot in life for the foreseeable future.

He parked and trudged out to the cabin and found Abigail wearing a pair of rubber boots, some cutoff shorts and an old softball team T-shirt that had seen better days a few years back. Her hair was held back in a bandanna.

"Finally," she huffed, carrying a bucket of worm-eaten boards to a small area where a planer sat. "Look at these and see if any of them can be saved. I'm thinking if we run them through this puppy—" she slapped the machine "—we can salvage them."

"Hello to you, too," he drawled, shrugging out of the long-sleeved button-down shirt he'd thrown on that morning. The first chilly day of the fall had arrived, and for about one hour he had been chilly. In typical Louisiana fashion it was now once again near eighty degrees.

"Oh, sorry. How are you this morning, Jake?"

"Shitty. And you?"

Abigail smiled. "I'm getting married in two months to the man of my dreams, Birdie got an A on her pre-algebra test and I'm booked for the next three weeks."

"So shitty, too, huh?" he drawled.

Abigail rolled eyes that matched their mother's. "I'd ask why you were such a grumpy goose, but I'm afraid of the answer."

Jake shrugged and took the bucket, eyeing the boards inside. "Let me run these through and it will tell us if any of the flooring is worth saving."

"I'll rip out the others," Abigail said, walking back to the dilapidated cabin. "Hey, Margaret Stein told Hilda she thought it was embarrassing that I wanted to capitalize on these cabins. She said it was insensitive to race relations. Do you think that's true?"

Jake looked at the run-down cabins. "I never thought about it."

"I never thought about it, either, but then I did and I kept thinking about how families lived here and even though their lives were horrifying, they mattered. These cabins were the only places they could escape to…maybe I should tear them down and not worry with it."

Jake pursed his lips. "Why don't you restore this one and think about it. Either way, you're turning this one into something that will teach folks about the lives of the people who lived here."

Abigail set her hands on her hips and looked down

the string of four cabins. "Yeah. We'll start with this one."

For the next three hours, Jake worked beside his sister, running the wide boards through the planer and pulling up sections that would have to be replaced. Abigail was a tough taskmaster, which meant Jake earned every bit of the money she'd insist he take. He'd offered to do it free of charge—what are brothers for—but Abigail was as stubborn as she was pretty. He always went home with a check from Laurel Woods.

Finally, Abigail called a halt. "Whew, I think this is enough for today. We'll load these boards and store them in the old garage. Don't want rain to get to them since they turned out so nicely. Guess you never know what is lurking beneath the weathering, huh?" She ran her hand over the ones that had been replaned. They looked incredibly different after the gray weathering was stripped off to reveal the beautiful grain beneath.

"That should be a lesson about people…except for Aunt Opal. I've seen beneath her 'weathering.' She's still as mean as an old tom," Jake said.

Abigail laughed. "Hey, I heard from the checkout girl at Maggio's that you and Clint had a run-in over Eva. Any truth to that?" She cocked an eyebrow and removed the bandanna. Her dark hair with the iconic stripe of silver fell around her face, making her softer.

"Eh, sorta. It's no big deal."

"Maybe not the words you exchanged with Clint, but that it was over Eva? That was news to me."

Jake didn't want to talk about Eva. In fact he'd rather talk about Hitler and the devil than the woman who had tied him into knots. "I don't want to rehash. It's old news."

"Oh?" Abigail said, tucking the bandanna into her back pocket. "Just thought you might want to talk to someone who had perspective into something like this."

He had to take the hook. "Like what?"

"I'm a woman," she said, pointing to herself.

"I know. You have boobs and wiggle when you walk. I figured that out a long time ago."

"Be a smart-ass."

Jake grinned and that felt good. He wasn't totally dead from tossing away the chance he'd been given with Eva. Same old Jake. Smile and crack jokes. "I'm good at that."

"Especially the ass part," Abigail grumbled. "It's just I noticed something different between y'all, and I thought that it was a very good thing. I always thought Eva would be good for you. And you for her. Like balancing the scales."

Jake started stacking the boards on the trailer hooked to the mule his sister had bought to navigate the large property. "Nah, Eva and I are friends. It's better that way."

"Oh, the old friends thing. Been there and tried

that. Doesn't always work when you've knocked boots. Wait, have you and Eva…?"

"None of your business, sis. But Eva has always been my friend. This little blip of what could be was bound to happen. We're two young, decently attractive single people in a two-horse town."

"So why was Clint in your business?" Abigail put her hand on the board he lifted, stilling him. "He doesn't always have your best interests at heart, you know. Clint's not a bad guy. I've always liked him, but he's nursed something for too long."

Jake sighed. Abigail was the person in the family who didn't let go. She would mow you down, sit on you until you cried uncle and arm wrestle you into submission. She pretended to be casual and nonchalant but then before you knew it, you were strapped to a board, a bright light in your face and water dripping a constant beat on your forehead. "I know who Clint is, but his words weren't selfish. He merely reminded me who I am and how that would ultimately hurt Eva."

"Who you are?"

"Look, Matt essentially said the same thing. My track record with relationships ain't great, and I don't want to hurt Eva. Better to nip whatever it is we have going on in the bud," Jake said.

"Okay, first, you're taking advice on your love life from a man who is separated from his wife and one whose only lasting romance was with a woman on the computer. No offense to Matt or Clint, but they don't know shit about women." Abigail crossed her arms and used her green eyes as lasers.

Jake twitched but acknowledged silently she had a point.

"And second, did you even ask Eva if she wanted you to step aside? Seems like calling something quits should be something you decide together. It's rather egotistical of you to think you can call the shots on your own."

And those words jabbed him in the gut. When he had called her Saturday afternoon, it had taken every ounce of strength to blow her off. He'd been like a automaton, never veering from the words he'd practiced the night before. He didn't want to let her see the emotion, the devastation of realizing he was bad news for her. The idea she had a say-so in the situation had never crossed his mind. He'd been trying to protect her, to do what Clint suggested—something selfless for once in his life.

"And finally, this whole image thing. You know that's bullshit."

"What?"

"The idea that people will put you in a box and define you. You know that was one of the reasons I held myself back from Leif? I cared too much about what other people thought of me, of what they expected. After Cal left me and I pretty much embarrassed the hell out of myself, I became overcautious about how people perceived me. I didn't want to be seen as weak or give anyone cause for criticism. And then came Leif, about the polar opposite of propriety. I hid my love for him because I thought it was wrong. I covered my true nature with a veneer of the perfect mother, daughter, sister—"

"I never thought you were the perfect sister," he cracked.

Abigail flipped him off. "You know what I'm saying. You have assumed this role in this town—the rebel bad boy. No one ever knows what Jake will do, right? You've cultivated this thing, but it's designed to deflect any prying into why you stayed here, why you tread water in life."

"I'm not doing that," Jake said, knowing he was a liar as he said it. His sister saw exactly what he'd hidden all these years. He didn't want anyone to look too closely, to see that he was unhappy being Jake Beauchamp. He didn't want people to see the coward he was.

Abigail took a step toward him. "Jake, you can't play at being someone because it's expected. Because if you do, you're living scared."

Bingo.

"I'm not living scared," he said. "And I've already had this talk with Dad. He said what you've said, and it sounds all rah-rah cheerleadery, but that's not reality. Not everything can be tied up in a pretty bow. I lost my innocence long ago."

"Another load of crap," Abigail said, turning and sinking down beside him on the rail of the trailer.

For a few minutes Abigail didn't speak. They both

stared out at the pretty fall day, at the leaves yellowing, the grass giving up, too.

"You weren't ever going to stay here in Magnolia Bend, remember? For that fact, neither was I," she said, her green eyes wistful. "I let Cal take that from me, but you let guilt tie you to this place. Everyone knows that, Jake, especially Clint. That's why it's so easy for him to manipulate you. And so you stayed like a punishment.

"Look, you're an important part of this community. You've saved lives, but you've done your penance for the accident. And thing is, you did nothing wrong that night. Anyone would have done what you did. You tried to help a friend, and what happened was beyond anyone's control. There's no blame. Sometimes in life shit happens. But it's beyond time to let that go. It's beyond time to get up from the altar of self-sacrifice you've been draped across for years."

He didn't say anything. Just looked out at the old slave cabin.

"It's okay to want Eva, Jake. You're not taking anything away from the universe that you're not supposed to have. You deserve to be happy, you deserve to sever the cords you tied yourself up with years ago. I know. I did the same thing and now I'm a different person. No, I'm a better person because I let go of the bullshit."

Abigail wrapped an arm around him and gave him a little squeeze. "Now let's haul this to the garage. I gotta pick up Birdie today because Leif's teaching late."

A half an hour later, Jake drove out of Laurel Woods, Abigail's words gnawing on him. He'd thought he'd done the right thing. Yeah, it hurt. Sort of like cutting off his arm so he might live. But maybe he'd done it for no good reason. Had he allowed himself to be manipulated by Clint, influenced by Matt's own marital struggles?

He didn't know.

Probably.

But the question still sat there like a fat bullfrog—could he and Eva really work?

A week ago, he would have given a fist pump and shouted "hell, yeah." But now, after weighing reality against desire, he didn't know. What if something inside him was busted and he couldn't fix it? Or what if he had been overthinking everything?

He needed to talk to Eva. Not some rehearsed blow-off, but a sincere conversation about his doubts and his feelings.

Time to let go.

Like that song he kept hearing all the little girls singing over and over again last year. Let it go.

CHAPTER TWENTY

EVA HAD NEVER worked with Cooper Platt before and after an evening of listening to him complain about having to watch what she and Dutch liked, complain about the way Dutch ate with his mouth open and then baby talk to his girlfriend for forty-eight point seven minutes straight on his cell phone, she was certain she might strangle him.

When she'd arrived at work and received the news that Jake had switched shifts, she thought she might cry.

"Where's Jake?" she'd asked.

"On a new shift," Hank said, inspecting the engine as he liked to do before his shift. Hank had OCD and thus she always felt prepared for any call that rolled their way. The man was fanatical about everything being perfect on the truck and inside the station.

"What? When did this happen?"

Hank shrugged. "Chief called me yesterday."

"Who's taking his place?"

"Coop."

"Did Jake say why?"

"Nope," Hank said, turning from her. "But last shift you and him were weird and then I heard something from Marilyn Boutte about Jake and Clint fighting over you. That's gonna be a problem, Eva. You know."

"It's not a problem. Jake and I aren't anything." At least not at that moment. But maybe they had a shot and, if so, they'd have to figure things out with the department. Eva wasn't sure they had a fraternization policy. Still, she and Jake were the same rank, so there could be no issue...until Wendell retired and one of them moved up.

Hank eyeballed her. "Jake's Jake. Probably got pissed at Clint for liking you. You know those two have a jealousy thing between them. And you definitely have an admirer." He pointed toward the door leading inside the station.

Eva made a face and then went inside to find a huge bouquet of white roses and a card. They were from Clint and the card simply read *I'm sorry.*

She wanted to smash the vase. How dare he send her flowers? He owed her a face-to-face apology. And he damn sure didn't have the authority to send her flowers...as if he was still vying for her affections.

"Oooh, I don't think any one of us has ever received flowers before," Dutch trilled, clasping his hands and batting his eyes.

"Stuff it, Dutch," Eva growled, ripping up the card and tossing it into the trash can. "I don't want them. Take them to your wife. Maybe your old ass will get laid."

Then she stomped back to her room, shutting the door on Cooper's annoying laughter.

And that had been her introduction to the new and not improved C shift. Needless to say, she went to bed early that night. As she lay there in the lumpy bed in her paneled room at the firehouse, she longed to talk to Jake. But his message had been clear. He was staying away from her.

What kind of move was left to her? Did she confront him? Wait on him to come to his senses? Yeah, that one wasn't a good one.

Or maybe she should just—

The alarm sounded.

"Ah, shit," Eva breathed, struggling out of her T-shirt and reaching for her bra. Tugging on the blue uniform pants she'd abandoned in the corner, she gathered her hair into a knot, stretching the elastic rubber band around it. She really wasn't in the mood for this tonight. She was still catching up on her rest from nursing Charlie through his illness, and she'd slept badly since Jake dumped her. Going out to what was likely a false alarm would prevent her from getting the rest she so badly needed.

She pushed out and joined the guys in the bay. "What's up?"

"Alarm went off at Burlison's Tires. 911 dispatch said visual confirmation of smoke by someone driving by."

"Probably Jimbo drunk again and smoking near the alarm. He got out of line when God handed out brains. We've had two false alarms this year from that moron." Dutch huffed and puffed getting into his coat.

"Let's go," Hank called, ignoring Dutch's comments.

Eva slid into her overalls and bunker coat, pulling the Nomex hood in place. Already she could feel the cloying heat of the oppressive uniform. Then she grabbed her SCBA tank and tucked her helmet under her arm. She slid into her jump seat and then remembered for the first time ever that Jake wouldn't be there beside her.

"Can you give me a hand?" Cooper said, indicating the flap of the Nomex hood that hung out.

"Sure." Eva helped Cooper and then looked over at Dutch, whose bunker coat still had Velcro issues. "You really should fix that."

"I tried. I need to send it off but we don't have an extra one that I can fit into. Moon took it."

Hank hit the lights and sirens and everyone prepared for a possible blaze…even though they'd probably find a drunk Jimbo passed out in the middle of an alarm. Securing their SCBA masks and strapping the air tanks onto their backs, they counted off the seconds. If there was an active fire in the tire store, it could get out of control fast. Tires burned hot and issued a buttload of smoke and chemicals.

Four minutes later they pulled up in front of the store. A column of smoke extended into the night sky.

"Everybody safe," Hank called.

"Everybody safe," they all repeated.

"Now let's get the hoses on this fast. I'm calling another alarm in."

That meant Hatfield station would give mutual aid. Already several volunteer firemen pulled up. And Engine One's sirens could be heard in the background.

"FD2 and FD3 start initial attack. FD...uh, Coop, catch the hydrant for me." Hank stood at the controls, flicking switches and then grabbing his own SCBA and helmet. It would be all hands on deck for this one.

Eva hooked her accountability tag on the cone and went to help Dutch with the hoses. The much-needed snorkel truck pulled up and Moon clambered out. The snorkel could get the water onto the top of the building and do the most work to knock down the blaze that was visible through the windows of the store.

"Okay, let's be careful. This could get hot," Hank said into his mic.

Dutch and Eva lugged the hose toward the front of the building. Several volunteer firefighters had suited up and were ascertaining the perimeter. The fire looked to be the strongest near the closed garage, which was very near where the office was located.

"We need to clear the building. Anyone talk to Jimbo?" Dutch asked.

Eva and Dutch started the initial attack using the Halligan tool to break the glass of the locked front door. Dutch reached through and twisted the lock, swinging the door open. Eva ducked her head inside and said, "We got flames, several columns of tires burning. Lotsa smoke. No visual past twelve feet. No visual on the office."

Eva could hear her own breath. Like Darth Vader. The place was hot, the fire bright, but the smoke was inky dark, preventing them from seeing much. The window that showcased the attached mechanic's bay was dark with smoke, but Eva could see the flames inside. Fear flirted with determination in her gut.

"Let's get that water in to the left, FD3," Hank barked.

"FD2, clear office. Dispatch cannot locate owner."

Eva knew what that meant. Jimbo and his wife were known for their epic battles, and Jimbo often slept on the couch in his office with a fifth of Jim Beam to keep him company. He'd set off the fire alarm two previous times on such an occasion. Chances were good Jimbo was in the office.

Which meant Eva had no time to spare.

She had to get to that office.

"Make me a path, FD3," Eva said into her radio. Faithful to his reputation as a man who could knock down a path, Dutch diverted his stream from the bay area and focused on a path to the office door, which lay beyond the wraparound service desk. The office had all the shades closed on the windows, and when Eva reached the office door, she could feel the tremendous heat surrounding her.

Just as she twisted the doorknob, a wall of fire flared to her right.

Dutch swiveled, fighting the blaze.

Overhead, Eva felt the water pouring down from the snorkel truck. She used the Halligan tool to break the glass as Dutch stepped away to battle the blaze and keep them safe. Reaching through the glass, she unlocked the door to the office and stepped in.

Hazy smoke had filled the messy office but it was obvious the point of origin had been elsewhere. Eva made a quick survey of the office and knew if Jimbo was in the building, he wasn't in there.

"Office clear," she said into her radio.

"FD2, give status on the garage," Hank said.

Eva moved carefully into the smoke-filled space to her left. The water from the pumper trucks poured in, doing their job. "No visible flame inside office. Accessing garage to clear. Looks to be point of origin."

Eva pushed through the door that led into the garage. Smoke boiled out and a blaze erupted with the feed of oxygen. Eva stepped back, shutting the door. She could see nothing and didn't want to feed the fire. "Garage still hot."

Hank's voice chilled her. "FD2, dispatch confirms owner is likely in the building."

"Shit," Eva said, not even bothering to keep that expletive to herself. "I'm opening the garage."

Dutch moved beside her. "FD3 assisting. Right side knocked down. Support taking over."

Eva felt Dutch at her back. She turned and met his gaze. He nodded. He was ready.

Eva opened the door, and Dutch stepped into the threshold using the stream to knock down the immediate flaring as the oxygen once again hit the still-burning tires. It looked like a movie set with the immediate flare.

Working quickly, Eva made her way to the area that held an old metal desk. She got her tires rotated here so she knew where Jimbo and his guys sat when they smoked and shot the bull.

Sure enough, Jimbo lay beneath the desk in an area that thankfully hadn't received much blaze. The smoke, however, was thick, and she needed to get Jimbo out. Eva reached him, noting the door that led out back was only about eight feet away. She couldn't tell if he was breathing or not, but Jimbo looked like a dead man. Her heart thumped in her ears as she jostled him. He didn't respond. He was completely unconscious.

"Visual made. Jimbo's down. Request emergency medical."

"Already on scene. We're sending guys in."

Dutch couldn't leave the blaze. Eva would have to get Jimbo out of there herself. Eva moved her gloved hands down Jimbo's torso. He most likely wore a T-shirt, and though he was a big man and outweighed her by a good one hundred pounds, if he wore a belt she could drag him with the Bowring tool. Her hand met no resistance. He either wore athletic shorts or even boxers. Nothing to attach the Bowring to for leverage.

"Goddamn it," she muttered, reaching for the two-inch-wide webbing strapped to her coat. The length stretched twenty feet and was handy for drag rescues. Eva unrolled the webbing, her breathing sounding more rapid in her ears. She used every fiber of her strength to slide the webbing beneath Jimbo, and then she rocked him the other way so she could wrap it under his arms. Tying a quick overhanded knot, she straddled the man and measured the remaining length to even with her face mask. She made a quick overhand knot then divided the segment between the two knots. Lying across Jimbo, she slid the loop around her face piece and helmet and swam one arm through the opening. Then she rocked back so the webbing was secure around her neck. Once the webbing was in the correct place, she crouched like a tiger, keeping her back straight. She lifted with her legs, shoving one hand beneath the knot sitting atop Jimbo's chest, and then she started walking toward the door.

Jimbo felt like a ton of bricks as she shuffled slowly, knowing that if she tripped or fell, his life was in the balance. Hell, he might already be dead, but she would damn sure get him out the way she'd been taught.

The door was only a few feet away when the roof caved.

Eva felt a beam hit her shoulder, and she fell on top of Jimbo.

"Dutch!" she screamed into her mic.

"Here," he said. "Where are you? I can't see you, Eva." Dutch yelled into the mic, abandoning protocol.

Another shifting occurred and something else fell, some large piece of equipment and it knocked Eva's helmet and mask off.

Acrid smoke enveloped her.

Don't panic. Don't panic.

Her eyes stung and her body ignored the dictates of her mind as she gulped for air, drawing in smoke. It burned like lava.

Coughing, she tried to push the debris off them. Water poured in, splashing into her eyes but clearing out some of the smoke. Still she couldn't breathe. She gulped for air and all she got was smoke.

She felt her body weakening, her vision narrowing. Jimbo lay to her right. She was certain her legs lay on him. She had to find her mask. She needed the oxygen. They could both die if she didn't. Desperately she clawed to find her SCBA mask but she couldn't find it. "Duuu…"

Trying to call Dutch felt futile. Her words wouldn't come and all she could do was gasp for precious air.

But it wasn't there.

She felt herself spiraling into nothingness.

Opening and shutting her mouth, she tried to scream but it was too late. She'd taken in too much smoke. Her lungs burned, her vision blurred. Gulping in more smoke, she succumbed.

And then there was nothing but hot darkness.

JAKE WAS EATING dinner at the Golden Wheel Diner when he heard the sirens. He usually carried his radio with him, even when he wasn't on duty, but tonight he'd left it in his truck. He needed to do some thinking, and the constant chatter on the emergency network was distracting. So he'd left it.

At first he crooked an ear toward the door, assuming it was something small. Maybe a wreck or perhaps someone had set an alarm off. So he stuck to pushing around the dry mashed potatoes on his blue-plate special, but then he heard the other truck…and then another.

Tossing a ten-dollar bill onto the table, he yelled to Art, "Gotta run, man. This should cover it."

Art waved a tired hand his way. "No worries. Go see what the fuss is."

Jake pushed out the glass door and hurried to his truck. Once there, he flipped on his radio. Jimbo had set off the alarm again all right, but this time he'd done a doozie of a job. Three-alarm blaze.

They hadn't had one of those in almost a year. Immediately his heart started pounding.

Eva was on the scene.

Ah, come on, man. Eva is as capable as anyone. Actually, she's more capable than half the department.

But rationalizing how prepared and tough Eva

was did nothing to absolve the chunk of cement that was his gut. He pulled out the siren, popped it on the dashboard and gunned the engine, speeding out of the Golden Wheel, heading to the other side of town where Burlison Tire Center no doubt burned like a bitch.

Three minutes later he pulled up to chaos.

The place blazed bright, and the gray flannel smoke stretched a huge column into the dark sky. Several neighbors stood around, hurriedly dressed, their faces etched in worry. Frannie Burlinson stood clutching her robe in both hands, tears streaking her face as she watched Jake's fellow firefighters work to knock down the fire. Looked to be hottest in the garage space, but the snorkel was doing work, pouring water into the structure.

Jake pushed past Guy Gordon, a captain on B shift. "Jimbo in there?"

"Yeah, Frannie said he got pissed about the Visa bill and told her she could sleep with her goddamn new purse."

Jake eyed the fire. "Where's Eva?"

Guy jabbed a gloved hand toward the garage. "She and Dutch went in to find Jimbo. They started initial assault."

Jake felt that concrete brick in his gut break apart into panic. "Hank sent Eva in after Jimbo? That's—"

"They were on the scene first," Guy said, casting an incredulous look at Jake. "She's doing her job. Saving Jimbo."

He knew that. He still didn't like it. Eva, for all her capabilities, was still...

No. He believed in Eva. He always had.

Jake jogged over to Hank. "What's the status?"

"I don't have time for this, Jake. I'm running the fire right now." Hank turned away, barking commands into his mic. Hank was right. He didn't have time.

Jake hung back, listening to Frannie sob and say things like, "I'm taking the purse back. I'm taking it back."

Something about that broke his heart. The things people do and say to each other, that when it comes down to flames leaping against a deep sky, mean so little. Egos get in the way. Pride gets in the way.

He damn well knew that.

Hank worked a fire like a consummate professional. He remained calm, trusting his men—and woman—to do the job. Jake watched as the flames surrendered to the massive influx of water. The monster was just about contained. Eva would come out. Dutch would come out...carrying a no doubt drunk Jimbo. It would be fine.

But then the garage roof caved in.

Onlookers screamed, firefighters lurched toward the structure. Jake felt as if he might pass out.

Eva was in there.

Eva.

Without thinking he ran toward the building.

"Hey, hey," Hank yelled behind him.

All he could think about was Eva...and how he'd left things. He'd screwed up so badly and he had to get to her. Had to make sure she was safe and understood that he was a dumb-ass extraordinaire. She had to know he loved her and he'd been wrong. Just like Frannie, he had a lot of take-backs.

Just as he got to the crushed opening, someone caught him and pulled him back.

"Are you dog-shit crazy, man?" Moon said, yanking him around. "It's still hot."

"Eva's in there."

"I know. And we will get her out." Moon tossed him aside like a bear tossing a pup. "Stay the hell back."

Jake made another lunge and Moon bowed up. "Don't make me knock you out, Jake. Stop getting in the way."

Helpless to participate on any level, Jake moved back toward the trucks, his eyes never leaving the building. Some of the team had already pulled aside the blackened aluminum door that closed over the bay. It had melted into something that looked like a piece in a museum.

Jake's radio squawked and he heard Dutch. "I'm clear. Eva, I can't see you. Eva!"

The world widened then narrowed and Jake gulped the acrid air, bending over so he didn't pass out.

God, Eva was down.

Down.

It was the worst thing a firefighter could hear. But

to a firefighter who was in love with the one down, it was agony.

"Man down!" Dutch yelled into his mic.

"Goddamn it. Get in there," Hank cried, running toward the structure, helping to pull the charred mess out of the garage.

A flashback of such vivid horror hit Jake. The flashing lights, the smell of hot metal, him stuck beneath the driver's door, hearing Clint yell, "Help me. Oh, God, help me."

Gas, blood, the sound of death.

Jake had tried to move Clint. Made things worse. So he lay like a pathetic coward, waiting for someone else to do what he could not.

But he wasn't that man-child anymore.

He couldn't stand and watch the woman he loved die because he couldn't do what needed to be done.

Jake lunged toward Gary Winter, who stood at Engine One. "Give me your gloves."

"Jake, I don't think—"

"Give me your coat and gloves or I'll beat the shit out of you right here."

Gary's eyes widened and then he shrugged out of his coat and gloves. "Jesus."

"Yeah, call on him," Jake said as he ran toward the building, swerving around to the left side where the back door could possibly be accessed.

Two volunteers were working on loosening the door from the crushed jamb.

"Let me help," Jake said, bracing a tennis shoe

against the frame. All of them pulled, sinews popping, teeth gritting, biceps screaming. The damn thing wouldn't budge.

"Again," Jake yelled.

They all pulled and then suddenly the door flew open and Dutch stood in the opening. The large man had kicked from the inside at the same time Jake and the others had been pulling. Draped over Dutch's shoulder in a traditional fireman's carry was Eva. In Dutch's left hand he held webbing that supported an unconscious Jimbo. For the rest of his life, Jake knew he would remember Dutch's face.

Mask streaked with soot, wet as a drowned kitten, and eyes burning with determination, Dutch walked out of the destroyed building and set Jimbo on the ground. Then he pulled Eva from his shoulder and cradling her, he ran toward the nearest ambulance.

"Eva! Oh, God, Eva," Jake called, running after Dutch.

He passed a team of EMTs—two guys he'd taken classes with—on their way to Jimbo.

Dutch met the EMTs and lay Eva on the stretcher.

Her hair was plastered to her head and her face was almost completely covered with soot. But she was breathing. And coughing.

"She took in a lot of smoke. A big canister fell on her and knocked her air out," Dutch told Manny Ruiz, the EMT clipping the pulse-ox clip on her finger.

Jake was shoved back as Manny's partner, a woman he didn't recognize, covered Eva's mouth and nose with an oxygen mask. Then the woman started her evaluation, prying one of Eva's eyes open to reveal a bloodshot eye.

"Mmm," Eva groaned, her voice raspy as hell. She swatted at the woman.

"We're trying to help you," the EMT said to Eva, holding down her hand.

"Guuuh. Puuh," Eva thrashed, ripping at the mask on her face.

"We're gonna have to restrain her," said the woman, whose tag read Mary.

Jake moved around to Eva's head and leaned down to whisper in her ear. "Relax, E. They're going to help you. Relax, baby."

And she did immediately, lowering her hands. She blinked her eyes, turning her head to look for him.

"I'm right here, baby. Dutch, too." The man stood on the other side of Eva. "You're safe. You did good, Eva," Jake smoothed her hair back, making a shushing sound.

Manny shoved Dutch back and eyeballed Jake. "Let us do our job, guys."

"Check her airway. Look for blistering and edema. She might need to be intubated," Jake said, ignoring Manny. He'd had training in this. Knew the dangerous toxins that had entered Eva's lungs. They had to combat the CO_2 poisoning asap.

Manny turned to Dutch. "Get him out of here. I don't run his show, he don't run mine."

Jake did as Manny said...only because Manny

was the best EMT Jake had ever encountered. Dutch grabbed him by the neck. "Come on. Let them work. You can follow them in."

He didn't want to leave Eva, but he knew that he'd distract Manny and his team if he stayed. And Eva needed to get the best care at that moment.

Dutch looked about as tired as a man could look. When he got to the engine, he sat on the back, taking huge gulps of air. "Shit."

Dutch rarely cussed.

"How bad?" Jake asked, swallowing the ache in his throat. The adrenaline still pumped, making his heart thump and his legs shake.

"Don't know if Jimbo will make it. He was in there a while. Eva should be okay. Her mask got knocked off and I got to her within a minute. She was under part of the collapsed roof. Luckily I could move it. And dang if she hadn't dragged Jimbo to the door using webbing. That Eva, she's something."

A truer statement had never been made.

"She dragged Jimbo to the door? He's more than double her weight."

Dutch managed a laugh. "She used that stair drag we practiced over the summer. Had the dang webbing tied over her and must have crawled to the door using her legs."

Jake shook his head, keeping an eye on the paramedics. The other team had intubated Jimbo and were doing CPR. Frannie stood beside the ambulance, a study in grief. Over at the other unit, Manny and Mary were still working on Eva. They had oxygen on her but the paramedics hadn't intubated. Five seconds after he noted all this, they started loading her in the back of the ambulance.

Behind him the Magnolia Bend Fire Department was moving the fan in to draw out smoke and reveal any hot spots. The snorkel truck had stopped pumping and the units were in the process of clearing the building.

"What about you?" Jake asked Dutch, fishing his keys from his pocket, preparing to follow the ambulance to the hospital in Baton Rouge.

"I'm good."

"You should get checked out."

"Nah. Nothing to check. I did my job."

Jake set a hand on Dutch's shoulder. "You saved Eva and Jimbo. You did more than your job."

Dutch looked up at Jake. "Nah. This is what we do, man. Saving people *is* our job. How many people can say that's in their job description?"

Clasping his friend's shoulder, Jake gave a squeeze. Damn if he didn't want to hug Dutch, but he knew that would embarrass him. Plus, Jeff Wheeler from the paper was headed toward Dutch, no doubt wanting a statement. Jake jerked his head toward the ambulance. "I'm following. I'll call you once I know more about Eva and Jimbo."

Dutch nodded, leaning over to clasp his knees once again, and Jake jogged toward the truck he'd left parked in the funeral home lot. On his way, he passed Chase and Cole, who leaned against their police cruiser. Chase pushed off and met him in the street.

"How is she?" Chase asked, his face etched with worry.

"She's alive and conscious. They're taking her to General.

Chase nodded. "Okay. Let me know if you need anything. She's important to me."

Jake didn't exactly enjoy hearing that out of Chase's mouth, but he understood. Eva, in only three years, had become a big part of their community, and even though she and Chase had called it quits, she was one of them. Friendly firefighter and police officer competition aside, Magnolia Bend's emergency rescue personnel were a team.

Jake ran to his truck, hopping in and firing it, shifting fast to catch up with the ambulance that had already turned the corner toward Main Street. Hitting Bluetooth, Jake dialed his mother.

"Oh, my God, Jake. We heard. How is she?" Fancy cried, not even bothering with hello.

"En route to Baton Rouge General. I didn't see any burns but she took in a lot of smoke. Won't know the damage until they get her to the hospital."

"Oh, my goodness. I can't believe it. We haven't told Charlie yet. I don't even know what to say. That poor child has been through the ringer with his father dying, his mother doing whatever it is she did and now his sister…"

"Don't say anything yet. Let me get there and see what's going on and I'll call you." Jake accelerated up the on-ramp to I-10, heading toward Baton Rouge and the specialized unit that handled burn victims. The ambulance moved fast but the drive time allowed him to rein in the terror at having watched that roof fall, knowing Eva was inside. He'd never felt close to crumpling to the ground the way he had minutes earlier. Jake had never known how much it hurt, waiting to see if someone you loved would come out the other side. In that moment all reason had fled and instinct took over. He had to get to her.

Paired with the terror was the albatross of regret he'd been wearing since Saturday afternoon. He'd lied to her. He'd said they were a mistake…because everyone told him they were.

Who did that? Who let other people tell them how they should feel? What they should do?

Yeah, Jake had almost blown it.

But God willing, as soon as he was allowed to see Eva, he'd make it right. He'd tell her how stupid and insecure he'd been. He'd tell her that he was scared to love her but even more scared not to love her. He'd weep at her feet and beg her forgiveness for letting anyone stand between what they had.

Jake had never loved a woman in his life... outside his family.

But he loved Eva.

And come hell or high water, he'd make her understand that.

THE HOSPITAL EMERGENCY waiting room was full. Tons of teenagers stood around, tapping on their phones. Jake pushed through them and caught a guy wearing scrubs sitting at the triage desk.

"Hey, I just followed that ambulance in. Two burn victims from Magnolia Bend."

The man looked up at him slowly, raising his eyebrows. "And?"

"I need to get back there. That's one of our firefighters."

The man shrugged his shoulders. "I'll go check. You can sit—" he looked around "—somewhere out here. They're all from one of the local high schools. Quarterback got hurt bad in practice."

Jake opened his mouth to tell the man he wasn't about to sit down, but he'd already disappeared into the recesses of whatever lay behind the desk. Jake slapped his hands on the counter and glared at the spot the man had occupied.

Behind him he heard a few girls crying.

A few older guys in coaching shirts stood around looking worried.

Yeah, he probably looked the same way...

except Eva wasn't a star player. She was the woman he loved.

The double doors swooshed open and Clint rolled in, followed by his father, Murphy. *What the hell?*

Clint spied him and maneuvered through the crying girls. "How is she?"

"What are you doing here?" Jake asked.

"Fancy called me."

"Why?"

Clint made a face. "Because Eva's my friend. I care about her. I want to be here for her."

Jake stared at Clint for a few moments. Murphy placed his hand on the back of Clint's chair. United front.

The man in the purple scrubs came back. "They're really busy back there. You're gonna have to wait."

"But I'm her...partner. You can't keep me from going to her. I'm, like, her family."

The man sat down and started typing on the computer. "But the word *like* is the problem. Have a seat and when I know more, I'll come get you."

Clint rolled toward the bucket chairs in a far corner. "Come on, Jake. Nothing you can do now."

But he needed to do something. He couldn't just... wait.

The man at the desk blocked him out, picking up a phone and making a call.

Jake shoved off the counter and followed Clint. He didn't want to be with Clint and Murphy, but there really wasn't another place to sit in the crowded waiting room.

For a few minutes none of the men said anything. Then Murphy stood. "I'm gonna grab some coffee. Either of you want any?"

He and Clint both said no at the same time.

Murphy shrugged and toddled off. Clint and Jake sat there, two friends with so much history, two friends with so much hurt between them.

"Eva came to see me yesterday," Clint said. "God, I can't believe I'm sitting here tonight. How did this happen?"

Jake ignored the flash of hurt that Eva had visited Clint so soon after he'd ended things with her. But why should that hurt him? Clint was Eva's friend, too, and she hadn't known Clint was part of the reason Jake had bowed out of a romantic relationship with her. Or maybe she did. He hadn't a clue at this point.

"She went in after Jimbo. He probably passed out with a cigarette in his mouth. Or he didn't extinguish it properly. The place went up. She was in the middle of getting Jimbo out when the roof collapsed. Dutch said something fell on her and knocked her mask off. Dutch got there fast, but she'd already passed out. She came to but wasn't lucid, though that's common. Carbon dioxide poisoning can make people confused."

"Dad said the chemicals in those tires are dangerous when burned."

"Yeah." Jake nodded, clasping his hands between his knees, assuming the position every worried person assumes in a hospital waiting room. "It's not good, but Eva's strong. She's a fighter. And she didn't get exposed the way Jimbo did."

"Do you love her?" Clint asked.

Jake jerked back, startled at his friend's abruptness. "Why the hell are you bringing that up again?"

"Because she loves you," Clint said, his dark gaze delving into Jake's. "She came over yesterday, mad as a wet hen. Guess people at Ray-Ray's let the word out about our talk. Someone told Eva I said some things."

Jake grunted. So Eva knew what an ass extraordinaire Jake had been…but she also knew he had tried to do right by her, tried to spare her the future hurt. Did that count for something? That he loved her enough to let her go?

"So do you?" Clint asked.

"Huh?"

"Love her. Do you love Eva, Jake?"

Jake pressed his hand into his eyes, as if he could wipe away the throb in his head. But it didn't help because everything in his body surged. His gut churned, his knees still trembled and his heart, well, his heart beat with hope. *Please let her be okay. Please let her forgive him. Please let them have another shot at love.*

Sitting back he said, "I love her."

Clint let loose a labored breath. "I can't believe that, but I can't ignore what you and Eva both want."

Jake straightened. "Why do you get a vote?"

His friend blinked but said nothing.

Jake pressed. "I can understand all you said at Ray-Ray's. Things built up. Both of us needed to air out some things—the accident, the guilt, all the shit we've stacked between us. But Eva wasn't part of us, Clint. You used the leftover guilt I carry around from the accident to keep me from her."

"I wanted her."

"So what? I mean, that's life. We don't always get what we want, right? And she has—"

"I know. That's pretty much what she said to me yesterday. I discounted her…and I underestimated you. Seeing you now, thinking about what I've done to you, I… I was wrong."

Jake didn't say anything. Just stared at a painting on the wall of a Louisiana bayou.

"I'm sorry. For a lot of things. I came tonight not just to check on Eva and be here for her, but to be here for you. Because despite all the shit I threw at you, and despite my jealousy, you are and always have been my friend."

Something inside Jake gave, like someone jerking the plug from a tub of water. The ugliness inside him began to drain. He'd gone for months not knowing why he didn't want to be around Clint. Now he knew. The crap between them had built too high, the pressure too intense. But the simplicity of Clint saying "I'm sorry" had allowed the bad stuff to start draining away.

"Yeah, I've always been your friend," Jake said.

Clint nodded and that was pretty much all that needed to be said. Murphy came back with his coffee and two bottles of water for Jake and Clint. Frannie, flocked with her daughter and sister, bustled in, looking stunned, fear shadowing their faces as they hunkered down in the corner. Then Hank showed up with some of the other guys.

For the next thirty minutes, they all kept a silent vigil, waiting on any news about both Eva and Jimbo.

Finally, the man in scrubs approached them. "Is one of you a Mr. Beauchamp?"

"I am." Jake stood.

"You can come with me," the man said, not bothering to wait on Jake.

"Wait a minute," Hank called, "I'm her captain."

The man turned and gave Hank a withering look. "Well, she didn't ask for you. She asked for him." He jabbed a finger at Jake.

Jake didn't bother offering any explanation. He followed the man, who could seriously use some customer-service training, back through the double doors. The man pointed down a long corridor with patient rooms on either side and said, "She's in eight." Then he turned and left Jake on his own.

A cute nurse in blue scrubs came out of a curtain bay and nearly ran into him. "Oops."

She ran her eyes down the T-shirt he'd bought when he took Birdie to the Justin Bieber concert a couple years ago and his tight jeans. "Bieber? Really?"

Jake managed a smile. "My niece."

"Who you looking for?"

"Firefighter in eight?"

"Down there to the left," she said, giving him a wink. "Only a man with confidence could pull off that shirt."

A man with confidence. Right.

Not something he had a great store of at the moment.

Jake moved quickly down the hall, and then, pausing outside door eight, he knocked.

Nothing.

"Oh, sugar, go on in," a nurse from the large center desk called. "She can't talk anyhow."

Jake fought the fear at the thought of Eva being so bad she couldn't talk and pushed inside the small diagnostic room.

Eva sat up in the bed, an oxygen thing going into her nose, an IV in her arm. Her hair was still damp and plastered to her head, and soot streaked her cheeks. Someone had tried to clean it up but had done a poor job. She wore a white-and-blue dotted hospital gown.

Jake stood there, taking her in, sweet relief flooding him. She was alive. She would be okay.

"Hey," he said with a low voice, creeping inside gingerly, as if he approached a wounded animal.

"You are a dumb-ass," she whispered.

CHAPTER TWENTY-ONE

In FIRE SCHOOL the instructors taught them about how painful it was for a victim to breathe when suffering from smoke inhalation.

Eva now knew firsthand that it was terrible.

Her lungs felt burnt to a crisp and breathing was torture, as if she was underwater. Her throat still had some swelling, so speech was difficult and she could barely whisper anything to her doctors and nurses.

However, calling Jake a dumb-ass was imperative.

'Cause he was one and deserved it.

Jake swallowed and stood like a schoolboy in front of the principal. Except, even haggard with worry and streaked with soot, Jake was the sexiest guilty schoolboy she'd ever seen.

"I know," he said, moving closer.

"You do?" she whispered.

He nodded. "Before I throw myself at your feet and beg for mercy, tell me how you are."

"Good," she said, clutching her throat. "It's hard for me to talk, but the doctors think I was lucky. I'll have to do some breathing treatments. They're about to take me to a hyperbaric chamber. They say it helps reverse the damage. I wanted to see you before they did any more tests."

Jake nabbed a small stool in the corner and sank down beside her. He tentatively took her hand. "I'm sorry."

"You should be."

"I know. I was wrong and I was unfair to you and—"

She pressed a finger to his lips. "You were there at the fire. I heard you."

"Yeah, you think I'd let a fire keep me from my Eva?"

"I failed," she whispered, thinking of the roof collapsing, of Jimbo beneath her...not breathing.

"No, you didn't. You did what you were trained to do, baby. Dutch was there because that's what we do. We're a team. This team didn't fail. We got Jimbo out and we knocked out the fire."

"Is he dead?"

"I don't know. They're working on him. They would have pronounced him at the scene if there was no chance."

Eva brushed the dampness from her eyes with the hand not attached to the IV and tried not to get upset. Steady breathing was needed. "You're right."

Jake smiled then. "You know I like being right."

"Charlie?"

"He's good. With my mom. She wasn't going to say anything to him until I saw how you were doing."

"I'm okay."

'I'll call her. Get her to bring him up here."

"No." She shook her head. Charlie didn't need to see her like this. It would scare him. After all she'd gone through in facing death and staring it in the eye, she kept thinking about what would have happened to Charlie had she succumbed. She was his guardian, and she had a responsibility to him. Protecting him was her job, which meant she had to also protect herself. He needed her.

"He needs to see you're okay. We can't just tell him you were hurt in a fire and not let him see you. Mom will wait until the morning. By then, you'll be cleaned up," he said, wiping her cheek with his thumb, smearing the soot.

Then he tipped forward, burying his face into her side. His broad shoulders shook, and Eva was shocked to realize that Jake was crying. She ran her fingers through his soft hair.

For a good minute he cried, his hands clutching the white sheet covering her legs.

Finally, he looked up, his eyes so blue against the redness. Eva had never seen a man cry, and her heart melted into a pool of sweet, sweet love for Jake.

"I love you, Eva."

So simply stated for such a complex emotion.

"I love you, too," she whispered.

"I want to be enough for you," he said, rising and brushing a kiss against her lips. She felt the dampness on his cheeks against hers. The oxygen tubing up her nose came loose, but Jake caught it and fixed it, carefully smoothing her hair.

"I never asked you to change. I fell in love with you just the way you are," she rasped.

"But I have changed. I think love does that."

Eva thought about Charlie and how much her life had changed over the course of the past month and a half. She was no longer a footloose and fancy-free gal. She had a kid brother, whom she loved, and her life would be different with Jake in it.

Love was hard...no one ever said it was easy. But it was so worth it.

"Yeah, you're right," she whispered. "Love does that."

Jake kissed her once again.

JAKE TUGGED CHARLIE off the elevator. The boy carried a bear dressed like a firefighter, and Jake carried a bouquet of flowers. They'd waited until lunch to visit, giving Eva time to get cleaned up and get some rest. They'd just gotten word that Jimbo's condition was grave but he was hanging in there.

"I don't wanna go in there," Charlie said, looking up at Jake. "This place is scary."

They passed an older man in the hall who was walking with the aid of a walker. He gave Charlie a trembling smile.

"It's where people get well, and hopefully your sister will be able to go home tomorrow."

Charlie blinked up at him with big brown eyes, his hair somewhat messy—Jake probably should have helped him comb it. He ran his fingers through the mop of hair, trying to make it lie down. Charlie jerked away and made an annoyed face.

Jake had tried to spend the night with Eva, but she insisted he go home and be with Charlie. They had continued to run chest X-rays and all sorts of diagnostic tests, so with her in and out and needing what little rest she'd likely get, he complied. He'd stayed at his parents' last night, needing to be around them, needing to be there for Charlie.

"Here's her room," Jake said, knocking lightly on the door. Of course, since she was hoarse, there was no answer. He pushed the door open and stuck his head in. "Eva?"

She had been sleeping, her face toward the window leaking afternoon light into the room. She'd been moved to a proper room last night, thankfully skipping intensive care. She looked wan, but her face was clear of soot, and someone had braided her hair to the side.

"Charlie," she whispered, motioning her brother to her.

The boy grabbed Jake around the leg. "What's comin' out of her nose?"

Eva smiled and pointed. "This is oxygen. I'll let you try it if you want." Her voice was a raspy whisper but sounded better than it had last night.

"Gross," Charlie said, but he let go of Jake's leg and inched closer to his sister. "What's that?"

She pointed to the IV. "This is an IV. It gives me medicine to help fight any infection. My lungs got a little burned, and sometimes nasty germs will attack them. This will stop those little buggers from making me sick."

"Oh," Charlie said, picking up the small elliptical pan on the bed tray. "What's this?"

"That's for when you need to throw up," Eva said, laughing when Charlie immediately dropped the pink pan.

"How are you feeling?" Jake asked, moving into the room, leaning down to drop a kiss on her forehead. She still smelled like the fire, but he could give a damn. She was alive...and laughing at her little brother.

"I'm better. Still hurts to breathe, but they're giving me breathing treatments."

"Uncle Jake said you can come home tomorrow. I gotta show you this picture I colored in art class. Oh, this is for you." He shoved the bear toward her and went to look at the blood pressure machine in the corner.

"Uncle Jake?" Eva asked, arching her brows.

"Yeah, he said one day he'd be my uncle so I could start calling him that," Charlie said.

"Really?" Eva said, sneaking a look at Jake.

He felt himself blush. Last night he'd sobbed like a little girl and now he stood here blushing like a fool. This is what Eva did to him. Made him...strong enough to be himself. "Well, yeah."

Eva smiled. "We'll see about that."

Jake grinned. "Oh, I plan to do my utmost best

to convince you that I need to be Charlie's uncle." He locked and flexed his fingers, giving her a wolf-ish grin.

"I'll look forward to it," she said, giving him the prettiest smile he'd ever seen. "Hank stopped by this morning. He told me you recommended me for the arson investigator's job."

"More money, lighter hours…and you go in *after* the fire," Jake said, moving toward the couch. "I'd never presume to tell you what to do. You're a good firefighter. I merely told the chief that I thought you'd be good at it."

"And you wouldn't?"

"I'm not sure I'm staying with the fire depart-ment," Jake said, clasping his hands and giving Charlie a shake of his head when the kid tried to turn on the machine. "I finally feel like I'm getting a new beginning. I'm thinking about law school."

Eva made a face. "You don't want to be a fire-fighter? That's…that's…well, I'm shocked but not surprised. But—"

"Oh, I'm staying here. You're here."

"I don't have to stay here. I mean, I love Magno-lia Bend but I can move. Wherever you go, I'll go."

"You know that's Biblical, right?"

Eva shook her head. "I wasn't raised by a preacher."

"Some stuff stuck with me, I guess," he joked, ris-ing and taking her hand. "I'm not ever leaving you. Don't you get it, Eva? I finally found my home, and it's with you."

Eva curled her hand around his and pulled him down. He kissed her, tasting her cherry lip balm.

"Ooooh," Charlie crowed in delight. "Y'all are kissin'."

And then someone at the door knocked. In popped Fancy's head. "Yoo-hoo."

"The family's here," Jake said, sighing. No more time with Eva.

"Come on in." Eva smiled and then the entire Beauchamp clan bustled in. Every. Last. One. Of. Them.

And as he watched Eva's face, he knew he could give her no better gift than himself and his family. She belonged like a duck in the water.

Like a pig in mud.

Like a woman made just for him.

As everyone hovered, fussing over her, she caught his eye. He saw so much in those brown eyes.

Pleasure.

Forgiveness.

Hope.

Appreciation.

And love.

And the greatest of these is love. Yep, some stuff stuck.

"I love you," he mouthed. And he meant every single word of it.

* * * * *